The Fortune Café

A tangerine street ROMANCE
A NOVEL IN THREE PARTS

Julie Wright
Melanie Jacobson
Heather B. Moore

Mirror Press

Copyright © 2014 by Mirror Press, LLC
Paperback edition
All rights reserved

No part of this book may be reproduced in any form whatsoever without prior written permission of the publisher, except in the case of brief passages embodied in critical reviews and articles.

This is a work of fiction. The characters, names, incidents, places, and dialogue are products of the authors' imaginations and are not to be construed as real.

Cover Design by Rachael Anderson
Interior Design by Rachael Anderson
Edited by Jennie Stevens and Whitney Olsen

Published by Mirror Press, LLC

Paperback edition released April 2014

ISBN-10: 1941145140
ISBN-13: 978-1-941145-14-2

Welcome to tangerine street

Tangerine Street is a must-see tourist stop with a colorful mix of one-of-a-kind boutiques, unique restaurants, eclectic museums, quaint bookstores, and exclusive bed-and-breakfasts. The Fortune Café, situated in the middle of this charming collection of shops and cafés, is a Chinese restaurant unlike any other because, well, to be honest, the fortunes found in the cookies all come true . . .

Other Works by the Authors

JULIE WRIGHT
The Newport Ladies Book Club Series
My Not-So-Fairy-Tale Life
Eyes Like Mine
Cross My Heart
Loved Like That

MELANIE JACOBSON
Not My Type
Second Chances
Twitterpated
Smart Move
The List

HEATHER B. MOORE
The Aliso Creek Novella series
A Timeless Romance Anthology Series
The Newport Ladies Book Club Series
Heart of the Ocean
Finding Sheba

Part One

Mis-Fortune

One

Emma cringed as she tugged her apron ties tight at her waist and moved to the computer to clock into work.

"You're late," Nate said. He wiped his hands on his apron, though his was not nearly as clean and pressed as Emma's. Nate's apron looked like it had been the victim of an intense food fight, which made Emma wonder what purpose it would serve to wipe his hands on it. Didn't that just make his fingers more dirty than they'd been before? He clicked the clock-in icon on the computer because he'd distracted Emma enough, she'd forgotten what she was doing.

She pulled her hair into a ponytail because no customer wanted long strands of dark brown hair in their meals. "I'm not that late," Emma insisted and then offered a grudging "Thanks" for his help in clocking her in.

"Late enough. He's already asking about you." Nate took out a red handkerchief and wiped his bald head with it. The back kitchen was always a little overwarm due to the ovens and grills.

She tsked. Waitressing for The Fortune Café wasn't exactly a dream job, but it was a *good* job—especially in a touristy town like Seashell Beach where people visited expecting to pay higher prices and leave larger tips. She'd been there for four years, pretty much since she quit school two years into college, and loved her boss. He didn't mind that she sometimes needed weekends off so she could go to comic conventions. He was a fair boss, and funny besides. But he hated the perpetually late.

Nate frowned deeply and put out a wagging finger in exact imitation of their grandfatherly boss. He then spoke in imitation of Cái's accented English. "When one of you is late showing up, the gears of The Fortune Café's clock moan in distress. You tempt fate to pass us over and take away the magic."

Emma smiled. Cái really believed in his magical restaurant. His parents opened The Fortune Café when they arrived in America from Hong Kong when Cái had been a little boy. It had become an immediate success and stayed that way. Emma believed the little business survived the takeover of the new generation only because Cái loved the place as much as his parents had. Years later, the restaurant remained the success his parents had originally created.

Jen, an older waitress, came to the back to pick up an order and laughed at Nate's impersonation. "You pegged Cái right on!" Jen never seemed to say Cái's name right. The name was supposed to sound more like the word *sigh*. Her tongue always looked tangled when she used the boss's name. When she said it, it sounded more like she was saying *say-ee*. Emma tried to tell her to picture him sighing and pronounce his name like a sigh, but she couldn't do it. They'd all given up correcting her. When he was around, she had simply taken to calling him *sir*.

Cái showed up at exactly that moment. Nate hurried to straighten his face before Cái figured out they were messing around. Her boss's gaze fell on Emma immediately. "Did you hear my restaurant cry out in her sadness, Emma?" Cái said, his white hair seeming to float as he shook his head in despair.

She smiled again. "Oh, I heard all right. But I think it's because the door needs to be oiled."

He frowned and lifted a finger to give her a lecture on magic, but she stalled him. "I better get out there. No reason to disturb your restaurant's voodoo by being late and avoiding my work. Someone's already seated in my area."

Cái cracked a smile even as he said, "It is not voodoo. It is my ancestors smiling on me. You open a fortune cookie, Emma, and you will see magic in your own life."

"You *do* know fortune cookies aren't even Chinese, right? But nice try. You keep your magical cookies to yourself." She grinned at him on her way past. She really did adore the old guy. He always treated her like a much loved granddaughter.

He'd been trying to get her to open a fortune cookie since her first day working for him. He said only the first fortune carried the magic, so the first was the most important. She had never opened a cookie. What had begun as a silly game for her had turned into a battle of wills. Cái wanted her to open a cookie, and out of sheer stubbornness, she refused.

She tucked her pen and notepad into her apron pocket and went out to face her customers.

"Hi!" she said with a smile. "Welcome to The Fortune Café where there's magic in the menu. Would you like to hear about our specials?"

The couple seated at table thirteen kept their heads down, studying the menu as if Emma planned on giving them a quiz later.

Usually people looked up immediately when she approached their table, but sometimes, people trusted the menu more than the waitress. She didn't mind waiting, except that the pause stretched into something awkward, and they still hadn't acknowledged her. Maybe they hadn't heard her?

She waited a second longer—long enough to admire the man's dark hair and trim, yet solid, build—before she tried again. "I'm Emma, your waitress. Can I start you off with something to drink?" Someone else had already started them with water and tea, and the wine menu lay untouched on the table's edge meaning they were likely doing fountain drinks.

That was when the man looked up from his menu. Emma glanced at him with a smile that froze as soon as their eyes made contact. "Harrison?" she asked, feeling dumb for blurting out the name she hadn't said since her high school graduation when he'd hugged her and then whispered something she hadn't heard over all the shouts of jubilation. They'd thrown their caps in the air. Everyone was yelling and laughing and hugging. Harrison's whisper had been lost to the celebration. When she asked him to repeat himself, he almost did, but her boyfriend at the time had tackled her from behind, and when she looked up to see Harrison, he was gone, lost in the sea of students. She hadn't seen or heard from him since.

Such was the way of high school.

The way his blue eyes softened at seeing her now did something to make her breath catch in her throat. "Emma Armstrong!" he said. He stood, knocking his long legs against the table, making the water in the glasses swirl and spill over the sides to the tablecloth. He didn't seem to notice the disturbance or that his napkin fell to the floor as he folded her into the hug that took her back those seven years to graduation night. They'd sat together at that final event of high school. Of course they sat together. His last name was Archer, and hers was Armstrong. They'd been seated next to each other in every class they happened to have together for nearly their whole high school careers. There had been a few teachers who didn't do assigned seating, but even then, they had ended up next to each other, habit and insecurity proving stronger than a desire to meet new people.

As he hugged her now, she realized he smelled the same—spice and soap. It felt like opening a scrapbook and being pulled into all the memories hidden inside. She didn't know what cologne he wore, only that she couldn't stop herself from breathing in the memory of him and feeling an immediate sense of security in his arms. It startled her to realize that she hadn't felt so safe since her dad died.

The other person at the table cleared her throat.

Harrison pulled away abruptly as if he'd forgotten something. "Right. Emma . . ." He waved a hand toward the woman who was his date. "You remember Andrea, right?"

Andrea appeared startled at the notion of having to remember Emma. Not that Emma was offended or anything. Emma didn't remember her either. But she smiled anyway. A big smile hopefully would equate to a big tip. "Nice to see you, Andrea."

Emma prided herself in being a well-practiced truth teller. When her mom asked if Emma liked a new dress, Emma would smile and say, "It's fun for you!" Which was the equivalent of, "Wow? That dress belongs in a landfill instead of on a person." Not that she could, or *would*, say something like that to her mom.

She had a lifetime of firsthand experience growing up with a mother who always spoke her mind—even when that mind was filled with poisoned darts. Emma believed the old saying that the truth hurt. But she also believed it didn't have to. Her mother's bad example taught her that the truth could be told without the barbs. She didn't have to admit that Andrea wasn't memorable. She could simply tell her it was nice to see her. True. No poisoned darts.

Andrea squared her shoulders and scrunched her nose

in a way that was probably supposed to be adorable, but came off as her squinting in too bright of light. "I'm sorry. I don't remember you at *all*."

Emma tried not to be bothered by Andrea's lack of tact and held her pen and pad a little higher. "Can I start you two off with some drinks while you look over the menu?"

Harrison seemed to have not heard the question as he took his seat again, oblivious to the fact that his napkin still lay under the table. "Wow. Emma! Look at you. You look great!"

This was probably *not* the thing he was supposed to say to a girl while he was on a date with another girl. She really hoped Harrison would be paying for dinner, because if Andrea was paying, he'd just lost Emma any kind of tip at all. "Thanks, Harrison. You both look great too." She found that as she said it, she totally meant it. He'd been a nice enough looking teenager but as a man? Harrison's dark hair, blue eyes, and intense smile were incredibly attractive. Mind-numbingly gorgeous. Totally and completely heart stopping. "Drinks?" she said again, trying to remember that, though they were friends in high school, he was there on a date with someone else. She wasn't supposed to be ogling the customers.

"I'll have Perrier," Andrea said over Harrison's, "I haven't seen you since school. What have you been doing with yourself?"

Andrea had gone from mildly annoyed to the kind of furious that made Emma take a step away from the table. "Perrier's a great choice," Emma said. "What would you like to drink, Harrison?" She really hoped a direct question would pull him out of his trip down memory lane.

"Dr. Pepper would be great."

Emma tsked. "Mr. Pibb okay?"

He grinned. "Sure. I don't mind slumming it with the good doctor's less educated, less spicy younger brother."

She smiled at her order pad. That was the best comeback she'd heard since coming to work for The Fortune Café. Most people grumbled over the inconvenience of an alternate. "Good choice. And really, from what I hear, Mr. Pibb has a much better social life than his doctor brother. He doesn't have any kind of reputation to uphold. Makes fun so much easier."

Harrison laughed.

Andrea scowled.

Emma took that as her cue to let them review the menu on their own. "I'll be back in a minute with your drinks. If you have any questions about the menu, feel free to ask." She tucked her order pad in her pocket and hurried to the back room to fill the order. She hadn't actually written the drink order down. She didn't need to because she always remembered what people ordered. In all her years, she never delivered an order wrong. She usually scrawled pictures of her comic characters on her pad because it made people feel good to see her writing something. She'd long since traded out her order pad for a small pocket sketch book.

Sometimes, like today, she drew caricatures of the customers at her tables. She usually resisted this temptation because someone might see the pad and complain. She didn't want to offend Cái's customers. But Andrea with her snaky, oily attitude kind of called for a picture. Emma had drawn a picture of Harrison wrapped inside the coils of a snake with long eyelashes. It was easy to give the snake features that made it look like Andrea. Andrea's big eyes, her puffed out cheeks, her dark red hair that likely wasn't natural but which would make an excellent color for snake scales later on if Emma decided to ink this picture.

Nate peeked over her shoulder. "What're you working on?"

"Nothing," she said too fast as she flipped the top of her pad so the pages were safely hidden.

"Nothing huh? Picking on the customers again?"

"More like customers picking on me." Emma sighed and tucked the tall red glass under the Mr. Pibb nozzle. "That's a woman who could really use one of Cái's magical fortune cookies. Maybe she'll get one that says she has a sparkling personality, and she'll poof into a nice person."

"That bad?" Nate asked.

"Maybe." Emma shrugged it off. She'd definitely had worse. And the chances were good that Harrison was paying, so Andrea's venom wouldn't matter to her. She'd been saving money to finance the launch of her web comic into a real, tangible book. She had a good following on the internet. She'd been producing free content for the last three years—longer if she counted the various other comic ideas. But the one that kept people coming back was *Dragon's Lair*. She created the *Dragon's Lair* comics after going to work for The Fortune Café. She had a magical Chinese dragon named Sigh who spoke true fortunes with varying results of hilarity, irony, and depth. Emma found you could put a lot into four panes of pictures and a few words. The restaurant served as her personal muse.

She truly hoped if she put in the money necessary to publish her serial comic in a full color book, those faithful followers who checked every day for their fix of *Dragon's Lair* would pony up the money and buy the physical form. She didn't want to go into debt for her venture just in case it failed. Better for her to fail with money that belonged to her than with money she owed to someone else. Presales had been astonishing. She'd made the final payment to the printer already, and the books were on their way to her—which meant she would have no living space at all until she moved through inventory.

Emma didn't think it would be a problem—not with the booth already scheduled at the LA Comic Con. She planned to succeed fabulously.

She topped off Harrison's drink when the foam went down, grabbed the Perrier out of the cooler, and headed back out. She hoped, in that amount of time, Harrison remembered he was on a date.

He didn't.

"It's been hard to keep up with everyone here at home since I moved away from Seashell Beach," Harrison said after she placed the drinks in front of their respective owners.

"You moved?" She had to respond. To ignore him would be rude.

"Yeah, Boston. Went to design school and just kind of . . . stayed."

"But you're home now," Andrea interjected. "That's the important thing." She put her hand over his and gave it a little pat of ownership in case Emma was somehow misreading their relationship.

"Well, I'm glad," Emma said, not misreading anything. She hoped for his sake he didn't marry this girl because insecure women made terrible companions. She knew this from experience. Her dad had lived his whole life with the insecurities of her mom. It hadn't made anyone in her family very happy. "We ready to order dinner yet, or do you two need another few minutes?"

"We'll need a few minutes," Andrea said, as Harrison said, "Tell me what you recommend from the menu."

So she stayed. She kind of had to when he asked a direct question about the menu. But Andrea didn't like it, not at all. Emma peered over her sketchpad and smiled. She really loved the restaurant. Loved the food. Loved that Cái cared enough to serve the very best from his kitchen. The place really was magical, and in spite of what Cái said, it had nothing to do with the fortune cookies. "I love the xiao long bao, which is a sort of soup dumpling. Or there's the shumai, which is also a dumpling sans the soup."

"What's in these dumplings? I'm vegan, since animals shouldn't be a commodity, so . . ." Andrea blinked her eyelashes and sat up straighter as if she'd just announced she was the president. Emma looked at the leather boot on Andrea's impatiently tapping foot and the buttery leather clutch sitting on the table near Andrea's plate. Nothing said committed-to-the-cause better than a vegan wearing leather.

"The dumplings come made to order. You can put whatever you like in them. Most people do shrimp or pork, but you can have them stuffed with tofu or spring garlic if you like. For your entrée, the ants-climbing-trees is wonderful if you like it hot, which I love it hot, so . . ." Emma blushed a little at the possible ways *that* could have been taken. She likely wouldn't have considered her word choice at all except that Harrison's lips curved up in amusement whereas Andrea's curved down along with the narrowing of her eyes. "I mean, anyway, there's all the usuals: broccoli beef, beef in oyster sauce, lemongrass chicken, and the dry garlic spareribs are proof that mankind is inspired. Pretty much I like everything. If we go over all my favorites, I'll just be standing here reciting the entire menu to you."

Harrison closed his menu. "I'll have the dry garlic spareribs. I could use a little inspiration about now. And we'll have the shumai as an appetizer. Can we do half of them with pork and half with whatever she'd like?" He pointed at his date in the same way a car owner would point at a rock chip in his windshield as he went in to get it repaired. The point said, "Can someone fix this annoyance, please?" What was Harrison doing on a date with this girl?

"Sure thing!" Emma said brightly as she doodled the snake wearing a snakeskin boot with the word Prada on the label. She added the caption, "Animals shouldn't be commodities."

Andrea frowned at her menu and said nothing at all. Harrison waited. Emma waited. When it became apparent that Andrea had no intention of ordering yet, Harrison took the opportunity to chat some more. "You still into art?"

Emma's pencil jerked over the paper accidentally putting a line through the snake's middle. "What?" She tucked the sketchbook into her pocket. Had he seen it?

"You were always drawing in school. When we had to trade papers to correct them, yours always had sketches of dragons on them."

She had to give him credit. He had a superb memory. How had he remembered her dragons after all this time? She smiled. "And yours always had funky shapes and swirls. Looks like you were made for design school."

He seemed pleased in their shared recollection. Before he could respond, Andrea shoved her menu at Emma. "I'll just have the lo mein."

Emma nodded, and backed away to place the orders at the computer.

"Aren't you going to write my order down?" Andrea asked.

"Right. Sorry. Of course." Emma pulled out her sketchbook and added a forked tongue to the serpent's mouth. "That wraps this up. Your meal will be out shortly." She escaped to the kitchen.

When the appetizers were ready, she made Nate put on a clean apron and deliver it to the table. And she brought a Mr. Pibb refill out with one of her other table's appetizers so she had an excuse to make a quick getaway from the table while still doing her job.

She delivered the meals but hurried as she eyed the next table over where they still needed to place an order. She worked hard to stay out of Harrison's lingering gaze. She didn't blame Andrea for being mad. She'd have been mad too if her date spent the evening checking out the hired help.

But as much as she tried to avoid Harrison staring at her, she found herself unable to keep from staring at him. As a matter of habit, she always kept watch over her tables so that she knew when they needed refills or new silverware or if they were waiting for the check or looking around for an extra soy sauce bottle. She tried to watch over all her tables, but for whatever reason, she couldn't keep her eyes from wandering back to where Harrison sat and watching him only.

Had he looked like that in high school?

She didn't think so.

Because she was sure she would have remembered that confident posture, the way his muscles flexed under his long-sleeved, black pullover as he leaned back in his chair and stretched out his legs, the way his dark hair looked like he'd fallen out of bed and raked his fingers through it before leaving to start his day in that messy-but-perfect style, the way his eyes focused intently when he was giving something his full attention—which he finally did after a short while, giving full attention to his date.

She grunted at that and then felt guilty for being unhappy that he was doing the right thing in paying attention to the girl with whom he'd gone to dinner. "Gah!" she said as she dragged a hand down her face. "What am I doing?"

"Taking them the check," Cái said from behind her, nearly scaring her enough to fall through the swinging door.

"Cái!" She harrumphed and snatched the plate with the check and fortune cookies from his hand. "You scared me!"

"Something interesting happening at table thirteen?"

"No, I'm just making sure they have everything they need." A crummy excuse for gawking, but she clung to it regardless. Harrison laughed at something Andrea had said. Emma frowned. So the unmemorable-Andrea-from-high-school could be funny. So what? What did it matter to her?

Emma then wondered what sorts of things made Harrison laugh. Did he laugh all those years ago when they had to sit together through English and biology and the dozens of other classes? She didn't remember much laughing, but . . . back then, she hadn't had much to laugh about.

"Are you going to take them their check?" Cái asked, tapping the plate now in Emma's hand. "I hand-picked those cookies just for this occasion. Something special for tonight." He beamed, his old man wrinkles folding up on his face in a way that made Emma smile.

She hoped Andrea's fortune said something about stepping barefoot on a Lego. Then she grunted at herself again and forced the mean thought from her head as she pushed through the swinging door and out onto the restaurant floor.

She placed the plate of cookies with the check near Harrison's hand and was glad to see that he was not holding Andrea's hand. "I'll be your cashier, so when you're ready, just leave this on the edge, and I'll come pick it up for you." She turned to drop off drinks to table twelve and to check on table nine. As she exchanged polite banter with the couple at table nine, noise came from behind her.

Not good noise, but angry noise. And it was growing in volume.

"What do you mean you're sure that your fortune has nothing to do with me?"

Andrea.

And she was *furious* over something.

Harrison whispered and made a placating sort of gesture, but instead of being appeased, Andrea shoved her chair back as she flew to her feet. "I have been waiting for seven years, Harrison! *Seven!*" At the final word, she picked up one of the uneaten tofu dumplings and hurled it at Harrison's head. He dodged the aim and gave a look of bewilderment at the fact that his date *really* did just launch food at him. His shock left him unable to duck the second volley. That dumpling caught him square in the face.

Emma had wanted to call "look out!" or something but

was so awed by the fact that a grown woman was flinging tofu dumplings in a public place that she could only gawk along with the rest of the customers.

"I helped your mom plan her thirtieth wedding anniversary party, just so you'd come home and finally commit to *us*!" Another dumpling soared through the air; he managed to dodge that one. Emma winced with the sound of the splat against the ground and wondered if Andrea had eaten *any* of her dumplings.

She finally ran out of dumplings and moved on to her main course.

"There isn't any *us*." Harrison's voice sounded panicky and perhaps a little bit afraid of this manic-lo-mein-lobbing female.

"Do you realize I've picked out *bridal dresses* and *children's names* with your mother? Do you realize that you continually sabotage all the work we've put into this relationship?"

Lo mein hung from his ear. He held up his hands in a surrender motion, but picked up his plate and faced it toward her like a shield. "Look, I'm sorry. I didn't realize . . . Andrea. I appreciate that you're friends with my mom. But c'mon! You think all dogs should be euthanized."

Emma's eyes widened at that. What kind of person didn't like dogs?

"I was joking when I said that!" Andrea shouted.

Harrison looked wild with desperation to make Andrea see something that was very clear to him. "I, look, let's—" He hurried to shield his face from the new barrage of noodles.

A voice was at Emma's right whispering, "You've gotta stop this!" It was Jen, and she was right. They were misbehaving while at Emma's table. That made them her responsibility. And they really couldn't continue. Andrea had nearly run out of things to throw, and Emma didn't want her resorting to the plates on neighboring tables.

Emma approached the table as if she was on safari and hunting a crazed lioness. She wished she hadn't left her serving tray on the stand at table nine. She could have used the protection its flat surface would have provided. Cái exited the kitchen behind her to see what all the commotion was about at the same time Harrison's eyes met Emma's.

Andrea turned her gaze on Emma too. Emma blinked in surprise at the loathing in the woman's eyes. She was clearly off her meds. Emma's mouth fell open in horror as Andrea snatched up the plate with the cookies and the bill and heaved it with as much force as her fury would allow.

Except she had bad aim, and the plate headed straight at Cái.

Emma leaped in front of Cái and tried to block the projectile. The plate caught her flat against the arm she'd flung out to shield her face, and as she made a fist against the shock of pain, she heard the oddest thing.

A crunching sound.

The kind she knew from years of cookies broken open at tables.

She had caught one of the cookies. And it had broken on impact inside her hand.

Two

Andrea made a squeak of surprise at her actions. Her eyes were as big as the plate she'd thrown. She seemed as shocked as everyone else. She vacated the building at a dead run.

"What was that?" Emma whispered. And then she made a low "Ow!" noise and tried to shake the pain from her arm.

Pandemonium followed. Customers were everywhere talking all at once. Emma met Harrison's gaze and felt as though he had locked her in place. She could barely get a breath in with him staring at her like that.

Someone righted Harrison's chair for him, and a few guys patted him on the back while a few women looked at him as if he was a puppy at the animal shelter that they personally needed to save from The Lunatic Woman who wanted all dogs euthanized. He must have found his napkin on the floor because he now used it to mop up his face.

Much to Harrison's dismay, several of the customers had dialed 911 during the attack of the victuals. The chatter made it clear that few people had never seen anything like it, and most people agreed that they still couldn't believe they'd witnessed such a spectacle. Emma couldn't believe it either.

"Your girlfriend is um . . . *passionate*," she said as she made her way to Harrison through the porcelain chips of the broken plate and slimy remnants of what had once been perfectly good dumplings.

Well . . . not *perfectly* good. They were made with tofu after all.

"She's not my girlfriend," Harrison said.

"At least not anymore!" one of the other customers called out. The other people at his table laughed. Harrison did too. Emma smirked, glad to see a guy who could take a joke, even during public humiliation. Most people had gone back to their meals, gorging themselves on tasty food and good gossip. Emma and the staff would have to wait for the police to arrive and somehow repair this disaster.

"Did you see that?" Cái demanded of everyone. "That crazy woman threw a plate at my head. My plate! At my head! In my restaurant!" Emma tried to console him that the plate had been meant for *her* head, not his, but he wouldn't be comforted by anything, at least not until his little wrinkles lifted into a look of curiosity. "Emma. What is in your hand?"

She looked down at the cracked cookie still in her grasp. "I caught it." She felt a little self-satisfied over that. It was a good catch. Though her forearm didn't feel nearly so lucky. The bruising from the plate's impact already glowed purple beneath her skin.

"You opened a cookie!" Cái clapped his hands and actually had the nerve to look pleased. *Pleased*. And after she'd saved him from a plate to the head!

"I did *not* open a cookie. I caught it. Not even close to the same thing." She'd spent too many years sticking to her guns on the point of not opening a cookie. And this certainly couldn't be counted.

"But it broke open in *your* hand." He wagged a finger at her. "I told you these cookies were special. It is only right that you should get one." Yep. The little guy had smug written all over him. She rolled her eyes and made a *psh* sound, deciding it would be better to pay attention to the customers than to the restaurant owner who believed in magic cookies. She turned back to Harrison.

"You know I could've boxed that all up to go if you really wanted food that could travel," she said as he tried to wipe off the dumpling splatter stuck in the corner of his eye.

He smiled, in spite of the fact he likely didn't feel very smiley. "I'm really sorry about all this." He'd apologized to everyone several times already, but he didn't appear to have any intentions of stopping. She felt sorry for him in every way.

He bent down to pick up the fallout from the floor, but Emma stopped him by laying a hand on his arm. "You're making this harder than it has to be. I have a good broom, a good dustpan, and an excellent mop. Your date didn't do anything worse than many of the toddlers that have been through here. We know how to handle it. You, on the other hand, should go rinse your eyes out. Who knows what kind of damage tofu does to tear ducts."

He glanced down at where her hand still rested on his arm. She snatched her hand back and stammered, "The bathroom is just past the hostess counter."

"Are you going to read it?" he asked.

"Read what?"

"The fortune you're still holding." He nodded to her other hand, the one not guilty of being overly familiar with customers, the one still clutching a cookie.

"That's what I was going to ask!" Cái huffed. He watched her closely in case she decided to hide her cookie among the debris on the floor to be swept up later. In truth, she probably would have done exactly that if she hadn't had such a curious and *intent* audience.

"Fine, Cái. But I still say it doesn't count since it *broke*. Broken does not mean opened." She separated the two halves connected by the paper and pulled the paper from the half cookie while she popped the other half in her mouth. She deserved to eat it if she was going to be burdened with the message inside. She read it. "Huh. Totally unlikely," she said and popped the other half of the cookie in her mouth.

"What does it say?" Cái asked.

"Sorry, Cái, it was a voodoo-wasted sort of moment. Bummer to disappoint you. She scrunched the little paper up in her hands and stuffed it in her pocket.

"But what does it say?" Cái demanded to know.

"Aw, c'mon. Put him out of his misery," Harrison said, as if he had anything to do with it.

"What? And ruin the possibility of it all? Wouldn't telling about it make it null and void?" She was just messing with him. She didn't believe in any of it.

"You're talking about wishes!" Cái said. "Completely different side of the divining spectrum."

"Divining—" She blew out a long breath. "Cái, I totally love you, but I think you're one fake Chinese cookie away from the nutter house, you know that?"

"Just read it to me." He practically begged. "I had a good feeling about them when I put the cookies on the plate. I knew these were special. It is fate that you became the owner of this fortune and not the Lunatic Woman. You have to tell me."

She would have probably given in if the police hadn't shown up at that moment. Pandemonium erupted again. Lots of people stepped forward, wanting their five seconds of glory by recounting the tale. Harrison refused to press charges. Cái refused to press charges, using the same argument Emma had used when Harrison tried to clean up the food by hand: any restaurant that dealt with entitled toddlers knew how to handle displaced meals.

The real victim in the assault had been Emma. There was no hiding the swelling mass of purple on her arm.

Much to the dismay of every would-be witness within the walls of The Fortune Café, she also declined the opportunity to seek justice by pressing charges. To be honest, she simply didn't have time. She still had to ink an entire storyline *and* get shipping envelopes ready to go for when the orders came in. As it was, she would be spending every spare moment for the better part of a week signing books and shipping them off.

All she wanted at the moment was to clean the mess up, finish serving her tables, and go home to the real work.

The police finally gave up trying to coerce her to press charges and left. The customers trickled out, realizing the excitement really was over.

Harrison refused to leave. He insisted on making "restitution," as he called it. As if he were some teenage delinquent put on community service for bad behavior. He swept the mess while Emma finished caring for her tables. He mopped the floors as she handled the checks for each one. He wiped down all the tables—even the ones not in her area. The three busboys, Jeff, James, and Rob acted as though they'd discovered the TARDIS was a real time machine. Nate, the sous chef, declared Harrison to be the patron saint of the restaurant and told him they'd make a bobblehead in his honor, and Cái smiled as if very pleased with how well the evening had gone in spite of the fact that he had a bruised waitress and a shattered plate. Soon, the only people in The Fortune Café were the staff and Harrison.

"Can I take you home?" Harrison asked when the closed sign had been flipped, and everyone but Cái and Emma had left. She'd wanted to take off, too, but felt weird leaving when Harrison seemed so intent on staying.

"I have my bike."

He nodded. "Oh. Okay. So how about I walk you while you walk your bike. I'd offer to put the bike in my car, but I'm in the two door."

The two door?

"Or we could leave the bike here, and I can just drive you home."

She cocked an eyebrow at him. "I kind of need it to get back, and I have this rule about not taking rides from strangers." She wasn't so sure why the idea of him going home with her filled her with such terrifying excitement.

He put his hands over his heart and gave a pained expression. "I'm wounded! How can you call me a stranger after all those years of cheating off my papers?"

"I never cheated."

"Huh. Yeah, that must've been me cheating off you then."

She gave him a playful shove. "You didn't cheat either. You were always top of the class. You graduated with a 3.8 or something."

He grinned. "You know my grade point average, yet you call me a stranger?"

What she didn't want to admit was that she used her time commuting to process through lines of dialogue and story in her head so that she hit the ground running as soon as she walked in the door at home. What would he think if he knew she was still doodling dragons after all these years? Especially when he'd become a grown-up and had a grown-up business. Most people didn't understand her love of her web comic—especially when she worked so hard to meet deadlines for something she gave away for *free*. It was bad enough he'd seen her in her "waitress" world. She couldn't let him see her in her nerdy comic book world too.

"How will you get back to your car if you walk me home?" There. That was a good excuse for him to part ways with her.

"I'll walk back to my car."

"You're making this really complicated," she said.

He leaned against the door frame. "No. *You're* making this really complicated. Just say yes."

She never said yes to people. Couldn't. Her life didn't have room for extra people crowding their way in. Not anymore. But as she stared into his eyes, she thought about graduation day, throwing her cap into the air, and Harrison's warm breath against her ear as he whispered something she never heard. "Okay. Sure," she said, not quite believing the words had come from her mouth.

Cái escorted them out and locked up behind them. Then he grinned at her through the window and waved with a fortune cookie in his hand. The little punk still looked smug. She'd have to let him know she was immune to his trickery.

Harrison waited while she unlocked her bike from the telephone pole and kicked back the stand. She usually rode on the bike trail that followed along the boardwalk and turned her bike toward the beach. They followed along her usual route with the bike rolling along between them.

The sound of waves breaking against the sand and fizzing back out into the ocean filled the silent spaces between them. Awkward. "So," she began, "you're in town for your parents' thirtieth wedding anniversary?"

He seemed surprised. "How'd you know?"

"Your date sort of shouted it. I think everyone on Tangerine Street knows. She yelled loud enough to shatter the windows in most of Seashell Beach."

He winced. "I am so sorry—"

"No. No more apologies. And who knows? Her outburst might be good for business. People might keep coming back to the café if they think food fights are part of the evening entertainment. Seriously though, you can't help the actions of another person."

"I can. Sort of. I should have picked a better place for that conversation."

Emma laughed. "That wasn't a conversation. That was a death match. If you'd been in private, no one would've ever found your body."

Harrison laughed too, and Emma sighed with a bit of personal satisfaction. She'd made Harrison laugh. Take *that*, Lunatic-Andrea.

"So what happened?" she asked, feeling only kind of guilty for prying. She really did want to know, and seeing Harrison again after so long, she couldn't help but be curious about him. How was it possible that she sat next to him for all those years and never saw him the way she saw him at this moment? They'd always been friends, sure. But now his presence intrigued her. She felt hot and cold all at once. She was either violently attracted to him or coming down with the flu. She felt a pang of missed opportunity, but then . . . wasn't her life just a long series of missed opportunities? *Stop feeling sorry for yourself.*

Harrison had taken a long pause to try to figure out how to answer her question. Finally he said, "What happened . . . what happened was I opened my fortune cookie, and she insisted on me reading it out loud."

"A fortune did all that?" Emma asked. "Cái must be right. There really is a force to be reckoned within those cookies."

Harrison laughed again. *Point two for me*, Emma thought, then chided herself. It wasn't a contest. How could it be a contest when the other girl wasn't even around anymore?

"So what did your fortune say?" she asked, more out of habit than anything since she used people's fortunes in her web comic all the time. The difference here was that she found herself genuinely wanting to know what kind of fortune incited Andrea into a rage.

"Oh, I see how it is. You won't tell anyone what your

fortune says, but you expect everyone to tell you?"

Emma had actually forgotten she received a fortune. It wasn't like it really belonged to her since she hadn't willfully opened it. "Fine. I'll tell you mine if you tell me yours," she said.

Smells from other restaurants floated out onto the boardwalk from open doors. A low hum of conversations from other people out walking and joggers pounding past filled the air.

He stopped under a light post and pulled his hand out of the pocket of his jeans. Good quality jeans. Likely name brand, not that she knew offhand any currents trends or brands worth knowing about. That part of her life had ended just after high school when she'd fled the walls of her home and got her own apartment. She no longer felt the need to keep up with anything. That had been her mother's thing, not hers.

He peeked at her from above the strip of white paper. He cleared his throat. "Tonight," he began in a deep, mysterious voice, "you are reunited with your soul mate."

He gave her a meaningful look, and for a moment Emma thought he was telling her that *she* was his soul mate. But he'd received the fortune while with a date, so of course he wasn't meaning that. Seriously? A good-looking man walks her home and she starts reading signals into everything? Emma forced herself to laugh at his theatrics. "Well, Cái must be wrong after all. There is no way that girl is your soul mate." She didn't know why she felt the need to point that out to Harrison. He was a big boy. He could handle himself. And maybe Lunatic-Andrea was what he really wanted in his life.

He tilted his head as if needing to view her differently in order to understand her. A small smile played out over his full lips. She hated that she'd noticed his mouth at all—full or otherwise.

She edged out of the light so they could keep walking.

He finally said, "Wait a minute. What about yours?"

She kept walking, but he snagged her hand to stop her. "You promised."

"You know what I don't understand," she said instead of answering his question. "Why did that make Andrea, who I don't remember at all from school, incidentally, rampage through the restaurant?" She tried not to let herself shiver over the fact that he still had her hand.

He let go, ran his hand down the back of his head, and took a deep breath. "She thought it was about her."

Emma cast a sideways glance at him. "That doesn't sound good."

"Nope. Not good at all. She flat out proposed."

Emma cringed. "Ouch! She proposed? Not to sound like a poor excuse for a feminist, but shouldn't you be the one popping the question?"

"Somehow my opinion was left out of the equation entirely."

Emma hid her smile at the forlorn tone of his voice. "So can I take it that your response to her response was a no?"

He reached over and flipped his thumb over the switch that rang the bell on her bike. "Ding, ding, ding!" He called out. "We have a winner!"

She laughed and popped her front tire over the curb to turn them off the boardwalk and across the street away from the beach. She felt slightly sheepish over being a twenty-five-year-old woman who had a bell on her bicycle. After all, Harrison had just proved that bells on bikes were useful items.

"The thing is," Harrison continued, "my sister and Andrea are really good friends. They always have been. And that friendship expanded to include my mom. My whole family loves her. They've been scheming plans for my wedding since, well . . . forever."

"Seven years," Emma said.

He flinched. "You heard that too, huh?"

Emma waved her arm to encompass the road they walked on. "Like I said, all of Seashell Beach heard it."

"To be fair, I've never seen her do anything like that before in my life."

"A first does not make it a last," Emma said, then cringed. It wasn't any of her business, and it made her look catty to insult this girl she didn't know.

He smiled. "She's really not crazy. I just burst her bubble is all."

Emma blanched at the word crazy. She wasn't really in a position to be judgmental about crazy, even if she had taken liberties in calling Andrea a lunatic. She mentally repented and vowed not to call Andrea anything derogatory again. The vow seemed easy enough to make; after all, what were the chances of her ever seeing Andrea in the future?

"She really thought that there was still a chance between us," Harrison continued. "And I don't know . . . maybe I thought there was too until—" He blinked as if waking up from a dream and shook his head.

"Until what?"

"Nothing." He shook his head again. "It's nothing. Hey, you said you'd read me your fortune."

"Right. The dreaded fortune . . ." She fished around in her pocket, nearly toppling the bike while she wasn't paying attention to the cracks in the sidewalk. She stopped under the nearest light post, cleared her throat, and tried to read in the same mysterious sort of voice Harrison used. She ended up sounding like a chain smoker. "Look around. Love is trying to catch you." She waggled her eyebrows and stuffed the strip of white paper back in her pocket since no trash cans were nearby.

"And you dreaded that why?" he asked after a few ticks of silence.

"My catching a cookie doesn't mean anything is trying to catch me. I'm kind of a recluse. Not a lot of love to be found in the eremite lifestyle." They stopped to wait for another traffic light. Her apartment hadn't ever felt so far away before. The bike certainly shortened the trip. Walking made it seem like they were heading to another continent.

She worried they'd run out of things to talk about with the many blocks away from the beach still left to travel, but they didn't. She felt surprised by all there was to reminisce over. She was even more surprised at how easily she learned new things about him. She learned he loved dogs in spite of his ex-date wanting them all euthanized. He sheepishly admitted that he'd been exaggerating when he'd made the crack about the dogs to Andrea, but Emma had the sneaking suspicion that he hadn't been exaggerating at all. Vegan wearing leather. That was the only fact she needed to cement her judgment of Andrea. She gave herself permission to keep her opinion of Andrea. Having an opinion on the woman was not the same thing as making derogatory remarks about her.

Emma learned while walking with Harrison that his parents were well-off people who were having a fancy sort of anniversary party—the kind her mother would have referred to as an "event" and would have loved to attend if she was still out and allowed to do social things, which she *wasn't* if Emma had anything to say about it. Though in truth, Emma had little to say in anything regarding her mother.

Emma learned that Andrea had gone to the same design school he had, but that he had stayed back east instead of coming home after he broke up with the girl because he didn't know how to face his family when he knew they all planned on an engagement. This meant that he hadn't just been casually dating with Andrea.

She tried not to let that bug her. But it did. Like a big black beetle crawling up her arm sort of bugged her. She mentally froze the picture of the beetle on an arm and decided she'd need to work the image into one of the comics.

She learned he opened his own design business and that he did quite well for himself. She loved his entrepreneurial spirit. That same spirit was what drove her to work all hours of the night to get the web comic into print. If she sold through this first shipment of books, she'd be able to cover her bills for the next five years. She would be her own boss and live life on her own terms.

"So did Andrea want to work for your design company?" Was it wrong to ask questions about the ex-girlfriend so soon after a hard breakup? She considered the breakup hard since the plate that had hit her arm had certainly been hard. *Beetle crawling up a bruised arm . . . That was the image.*

"Not really . . . more like wanted to *run* my business for me."

"Ah. Gotcha. I know exactly what you mean."

"And why is that?" he asked.

She considered for a moment before giving a half truth. "My mom is like that. Running other people's lives. Growing up was sometimes . . . stifling. My dad took the brunt of her full force though. He sheltered me from a lot. He was a great guy."

"Was?"

Her chest constricted. *Was.* Lucky Dad. He'd had a heart attack during dinner one night. He was now forever beyond the reach of her mother's grasping, clinging hands. But his freedom meant Emma no longer had the luxury of sheltering under his shade.

She took a shuddering breath and glanced up at the changing traffic light along with the white walk signal. "Yeah, well, he died last year." She pushed her bike out into the street ahead of him, not knowing why she told him about her controlling mother or dead father. She hadn't seen this guy for seven years and she was stripping down to her soul for him? *Amateur.*

He quickened his step to catch up with her. His fingers briefly brushed the hand she used to hold her bike up by the handlebars. "I'm sorry to hear that."

The touch felt intimate. She hadn't realized how raw her soul still must have been for that brush to ache as much as it did.

"It's okay. He's in a better place." She didn't add that even if there was no life after death, he was still in a better place. Any place was better than life with a constant diet of crippling criticisms.

"How's your mom handling it?"

Speaking of the insane. "It's hard to tell with her."

"I remember you having trouble with her in the past."

She blinked and drew a sharp breath. He'd known? How had he known? Her tongue tangled trying to find an answer when he stopped her from trying. "I'm sorry. Am I getting too personal?"

She nodded.

He nodded too. "Sorry," he said again. "Change of subject. Did you do any college after we graduated?"

Her chest constricted with the questions she hated, so she decided to get it all over with in one fell swoop. She'd learned long ago that it was easiest to disappoint people all at once rather than in little bites. "I moved into my own place right after graduation, went to two years of community college before the debt to income ratio became ridiculously unbalanced. I dropped out to work for a while and had a few horrible jobs, then went to work for the café and liked it. It kind of fit me and my lifestyle. So now I'm a waitress and still living in a one bedroom apartment, and I'm content, so please don't try to give me any advice on how to make my life more fulfilling or how college would be easy to finish if I decided to go back or anything."

He didn't respond immediately, so she sneaked a peek at him. He was frowning. "Why would you think I'd be giving advice on life fulfillment?"

"Everybody else does." Well, not *everybody*—her dad never did. But her mom . . . Emma sucked in a lungful of air, feeling stupid for allowing the bitterness to creep into her voice.

He stopped walking. "Hey. Do I look like everybody else?"

She stopped too, and gave him her full attention, taking in the way the streetlight haloed his head. He certainly *didn't*. But she wasn't sure she wanted to think of how he looked. "No, you don't," she said honestly.

He stared hard at her. "Are you okay?" he asked.

"I'm good." She moved forward again, grateful that movement made it harder for him to look at her that way. She hadn't dated anyone since her dad died. She'd forgotten how intense a simple look could be. She'd forgotten how her heart could pump blood so fast through her veins that it left her dizzy. She'd forgotten how to feel.

"This is me!" she said too brightly when they finally reached the steps to her apartment. "Thanks for walking me home. The last time anyone walked me home was when my dad—" She stopped, horrified to be caught trailing down that particular memory lane.

He smiled though, like he understood. "What do you do with your bike?" he asked, and she felt immense gratitude with him changing the subject.

"I take it upstairs with me. It's not like this is a bad neighborhood or anything, but I'd be devastated if someone stole my ride." She did an inward eye roll. "I mean, I *do* own a car," she spit out in an attempt to appear less needy and pathetic. "I just don't like driving when we have such mild weather. I like the thinking time and exercise of riding my bike."

He took the bike from her and picked it up. "Upstairs then?"

Emma's face warmed, and she held out her hands to try to stop him. "Harrison, no, really, I can take it up. I do it every day. Sometimes several times a day."

"But today you have someone else to do it for you. C'mon. Let me carry it. I could never show my face to my mom again if I didn't help."

"Are we talking about the same mom who is probably listening to your girlfriend sob about you right now?"

He laughed as if that image didn't bother him as much as it bothered her. "Yeah, that one. And she isn't my girlfriend."

He started walking up the stairs in spite of the fact that she hadn't confirmed his direction. With little other choice—unless she planned on wrestling the bike away from him—she followed him up.

At the top of the stairs, he set the bike against the wall and waited. She pulled out her keys and wondered if she should open the door and just go inside, or if she should tell him good-bye first and wait for him to leave before she opened it. The trouble that sprang from being a recluse was not knowing what to do in social situations where everyone else on the planet felt perfectly comfortable.

"Do you know what time it is?" he asked out of nowhere.

She pulled out her phone to check the time, but he held out his hand. "Mind if I see?"

She handed her phone off and felt confused as he tapped the screen. She jumped when his phone rang from inside his pocket. He checked his phone while handing hers back to her. "Oh look!" he said. "You sent me a text. Must mean you want me to have your phone number."

She laughed. "Well played, Harrison. Do you do that to all the girls?"

"Honestly, that was a first. But worth it, I think." He watched her with a curiosity that made her shift uncomfortably. But she was glad that he appeared to be a little nervous too. "I'm in town for two weeks," he said. "My parents' anniversary party isn't until the weekend after this one. I don't know why I took so much time off. I just . . . guess I wanted to be home for a bit."

She nodded, not sure why he was telling her any of this.

"So I wondered if maybe you had plans tomorrow night."

"Oh. Oh!" She blinked, startled at the implications of this question. "I work tomorrow night."

"What about the next night—or the night after that?" He quickly added the last part when he saw that she was about to decline.

"I'm kind of booked solid this whole week," she said. The LA Comic Con was that weekend. She had a lot of preparation left to do before Friday, and then she had the entire weekend, which she hoped would be a flurry of selling books and growing her fan base.

"Oh." He looked down, obviously disappointed. "You're dating someone then? In a relationship?"

"Relationship? Me?" She barked out a laugh. "No. I don't really have time for—" She broke off her typical commentary on people being time-takers and her not having room in her life, because for the first time in forever, she wanted to *make* room. "Maybe you can come to the café tomorrow night. I can take my dinner break, and we can eat together."

He brightened. "Sounds like a great idea."

She grinned. "I'll treat you for dinner. Since your previous experience was so . . . you know I can't come up with a word that doesn't sound like I'm making fun of you, so we'll just say your previous dining experience was simply *so*."

He laughed.

She liked it a lot when he laughed.

"What time?" he asked.

"Five." Emma scrunched her nose. "Is an early dinner okay?"

"Seeing you again is okay."

Her heart pounded so hard she worried he might hear it. She honestly never remembered any guy making her feel wobbly-kneed and cloudy-headed. She couldn't stop staring at his lips. Why couldn't she stop staring at his lips?

She forced her eyes back to his but found he was staring at her lips too. She swallowed hard and jangled her keys to break the tension between them; not that the tension was unpleasant, but it was so *full*.

"I'll see you tomorrow," she said and jangled her keys again.

He leaned in, his breath warm and minty, and settled a slow, lingering kiss on her cheek near her ear. "Yes, you will," he whispered.

She closed her eyes and soaked the burn from his lips touching her skin until it filled her completely. When she opened her eyes again, he'd already gone. She didn't remember hearing his footsteps descending the stairs. She didn't remember feeling him leave. All she felt was the flare of possibility igniting in her core.

Three

Harrison couldn't believe he'd dared. He'd kissed her—granted it was only a cheek and he'd kissed dozens, if not hundreds, of cheeks before. The design business was cordial like that. A kiss on the cheek meant friendliness and social comfort.

But he hadn't meant anything like simple friendliness in that contact. And it had been hard to keep from straying over to her mouth where she kept biting on that lower lip in a way that made him near crazy. He raked his fingers through his hair as he walked back to his car.

Emma Armstrong. After all these years.

The guarded look was still there, the one that had held him at bay during all of his high school years, the one that said, "Back off—I bite." But he wasn't an insecure sixteen-year-old any longer, and the fortifications she'd so carefully built around herself didn't intimidate him.

Emma's reserved nature was totally unlike the challenge he had yet to tackle once he arrived back at his parents' house. Harrison considered avoiding the home scene by booking a hotel, yet staying anywhere but under her roof would irreparably hurt his mom's feelings.

He had to go home to deal with the mess that came from dating girls who'd managed to buddy up with his whole family while he wasn't looking.

He reached his car, drove to his parents' place, and thought back to high school, to that first day when Emma had shown up in his life. He hadn't hit his growth spurt and pretty much everyone towered over him. He'd felt like his parents had sent him to a special school for giants.

Biology. He'd walked into class late with his class schedule nearly turned to pulp in his sweaty hand, and the teacher had directed him to sit in between a pretty girl and some guy suffering from gigantism. As they went through the class syllabus, the frog dissection unit became a hot topic of conversation. When one of the other girls mentioned being horrified over having to touch a frog, the giant next to him had laughed and in an abnormally low voice said, "Don't worry, we won't use real frogs. This kid they put next to me is small enough; we can use him instead."

It wasn't a huge deal—not looking back on it—but at the time when he felt so small physically, he had been devastated to be made to feel emotionally small.

That was when he really noticed the pretty girl, because she turned to the giant and said, "Sadly, we won't be able to use you for the unit where we study the brain since you're obviously lacking in that area." The pretty girl, who he later learned was named Emma, gave a half smile and with it, the gift of self-respect back to Harrison.

The other girl had laughed at Emma's joke, and the giant grew sullen and thankfully left Harrison alone after that. He'd only survived high school because she'd kept him from becoming a target right there at the beginning.

He'd pretty much worshipped her in silence ever since.

Emma Armstrong.

He'd gotten to know her without ever asking her a question through the personal essays and poems they'd traded for correction and peer review during the four years' worth of English classes. He remembered the personal essays about Emma's mom being painful to read.

He truly believed he'd never see her again. But he smiled at the fate and fortune that led him back to her. His smile didn't drop until he walked into the front foyer of his parents' house and his dad gave him a look over the top of his old man reading glasses. "Your mother wants to talk to you, and your girlfriend just left."

"She's not my girlfriend," Harrison said for the hundredth time that night.

His dad gave a pained expression that was echoed in the big entry hall mirror. "I'm not getting involved. I'm only delivering the message."

"Coward," Harrison said to his dad.

His dad nodded with exaggerated movements. "Cowards live longer. And that, my son, is your life lesson for the day. Be Switzerland to your mom and live to tell the tale."

"Harrison? Are you home?" His mother called from the general direction of her studio. He'd inherited his design savvy from his mother's artistic nature. People paid a lot of money for her paintings. What set her apart from the other painters was the social commentary found in every single work. The world loved her satire fused in oil and canvas.

"Yep," he answered.

"Come here so we can talk."

"Be neutral! Remember Switzerland!" his dad whispered.

He glared at his dad while moving to do as his mom asked.

He leaned into the doorframe of his mom's studio where he breathed the familiar scent of turpentine and linseed oils.

If he actually crossed over the threshold, he would be forcing himself into a position of child-being-scolded. As a self-made man, he really felt no inclination for regression.

"Andrea was here." His mother started in before even turning to look at him.

"I'm sure she was."

"And crying," she said.

"Not surprising."

His mother finally turned to face him, her bun pulled back tight enough to make her look severe, her painting smock a smattering of raw colors. "Andrea was *crying*? And all you have to say for yourself is that it isn't surprising?"

"Did she tell you what *she* did to me?"

His mom narrowed her eyes at him and pointed one of her painting knives at him. "Blame shifting?" She tsked. "She said you provoked her."

"Telling someone you don't want to marry them isn't a good enough reason to throw a temper tantrum in a restaurant."

His mom frowned. "You really don't want to marry her? Why not?"

"She assaulted a waitress."

She considered this new information before shaking her head as if the idea was absurd. "She did not."

"She did. Threw a plate at her."

His mom smirked. "Same waitress you flirted with?"

Harrison laughed, but his face heated. "That would be the one."

"She said it was some old flame from high school. Is she right?"

Harrison squinted at his mom, trying to decide how best to answer. "Flame is definitely the right word."

"So when are you going to bring home this new-old flame to meet us?"

Harrison relaxed and decided his mom wasn't actually

on Andrea's side enough to merit him getting scolded too much, which meant it was safe to enter the studio. He gave his mom a hug, not even caring that she had her painting smock on, and he'd likely ruin his clothes. He felt a lot of gratitude in her taking his side instead of Andrea's.

She released him and turned back to her work. "Honestly, Harrison, I really do like Andrea, and she practically planned my entire anniversary party. Can you do me a favor and keep the peace until after the party?"

"I'm not going to agree to marry her to keep the peace," he said.

"And what will we tell Kristin?"

"Why is who I date or marry any of my sister's business?" He fiddled with an old palette knife abandoned on the work table.

"Andrea is Kristin's friend."

He grunted and flipped the knife over. "So why doesn't Kristin marry her?"

"Don't be sassy. Now hand me that knife before you flip it into the paints. Tell me about this other girl."

He told her everything he could remember about Emma, and she listened while she worked. Talking to his mom in her studio reminded him of all those years growing up when he got home from school and went straight to her studio to tell her about his day. A lot of life found its way to getting resolved in that studio.

She finally sighed, patted his cheek with a multicolored hand, and said, "Seven years is a long time to be away from anyone. Be careful. People change. You don't really know this girl at all. You only know your memory of her. And if you decide you like her the way she is now enough to have me meet her, I'll make my judgment then. If I don't like her, we'll just lock you in a tower until you agree to marry Andrea. The Rapunzel story isn't just for girls, you know."

"May I remind you that I'm only twenty-six? It's not like

I'm rushing into anything," he said. She laughed and then kicked him out of her studio so she could get real work done.

He went to his old room that his parents had turned into a very nice guest room, propped himself up on the half-dozen decorative pillows, and opened his laptop. Emma had been awfully evasive during their walk home. He hoped she had some sort of online presence where he could spy on her at his leisure.

He grinned when her name pulled up dozens of websites. Not only did she have a web presence, but she maintained prominent visibility.

"Still doodling dragons, Emma?" he said out loud to his laptop screen. He clicked around her site to get the feel of the layout. He stopped when he arrived at the preorder page for the first book released in the *Dragon's Lair* Universe. "And turned it into a business," he murmured. "Good girl." She had an impressive fan base. Every new installment of *Dragon's Lair* reached thousands of viewers. Every blog post incited hundreds of comments.

She earned her fans' loyalties, he decided after reading through a few months' worth of comic strips. Emma was funny, smart, and satirical in a way that made the reader feel in on the joke. He laughed out loud at many story lines and got emotional with several others.

His mom had warned him that people changed over the course of seven years. And she was right. Emma had changed, but as far as he could see, she'd only changed for the better. He stayed up late into the night, reading her blog posts, her comics, and doing the entirely creepy, stalker thing by figuring out her posted schedule of events.

He reasoned that she wouldn't have put it online if she didn't want people to know her whereabouts. She'd meant it when she said she was booked for the week. Unfortunately, Harrison only had two weeks before he had to head back. Two weeks to get Emma Armstrong's attention.

He closed his laptop and squirmed down under the comforter. He needed some sleep because his sister would be showing up in the morning for some planning meeting or whatever. Kristin would likely have Andrea in tow to try to fix what they would undoubtedly see as something Harrison broke. He needed to be well-rested to face them, and well-rested for his dinner plans as well. He'd get to see Emma again in less than twenty-four hours.

He tucked an arm under his head and stared at the dark ceiling, pictured Emma's face, and smiled. He wasn't one to believe in anything prophesied on a white strip of paper inside a cookie. But he'd felt the jolt when his eyes landed on that fortune and then another jolt when he'd looked up to see Emma just across the room.

The girl he'd experienced unrequited love for back in high school stood before him. She remained beautiful. She remained kind. "Tonight, you are reunited with your soul mate," he whispered out loud to the dark. He grinned to himself, feeling like life had finally thrown him a bone.

He'd let her slip away due to the fear and insecurity of youth. But he had no intentions of losing track of his soul mate ever again.

Four

"Did you take your medicine?" Emma tried not to growl out the question as she wedged the phone between her shoulder and her ear and searched her desk for her hands-free headset. With all the work on her comic, she'd let everything else—like organization, regular meals, and health code ordinances—fall to the wayside. This meant she'd likely locate her headset only *after* it became outdated technology. She gave up, straightened, and sucked in several deep breaths before responding to her mother's excuse for not taking her medication.

"Mom! The doctor prescribed them to keep you from becoming sad. If you took them like you were supposed to rather than throwing away the prescription *I* paid for, then you *wouldn't* feel sad right now."

She covered her eyes with the heels of her palms, drummed her fingers on her forehead, and listened to the rantings and rumblings of how some lady had stolen the grocery cart her mom had wanted when she'd gone to the store and how she ended up not buying anything at all because it hurt her feelings so desperately that anyone could be so rude and how she followed the woman around the store intending to give her a talking to when they left the store.

Emma's head snapped up as she palmed her phone. "Wait. What? You stalked a customer through the store? Mom, you can't do that. You *cannot* do that to people! You could get arrested."

Her mom couldn't understand how following someone might equate to being arrested.

She finally did let out the growl she'd been trying to hold back. "Because it's creepy, Mom! You scare people! Okay, you know what? Never mind. Let's move on. Tell me what happened." She needed to find out the important information—like if her mother really had been arrested.

With her eyes closed, Emma bit into her lower lip so hard it actually caused pain as she shook her head and listened to the rest of her mom's exploits through the grocery store. The trip had ended up with a fruit display being displaced and rolling all over. Her mother was too distraught to remember which kind of fruits and spent a good three minutes fretting because she couldn't come up with the name.

By the end of the story, Emma discovered that the police hadn't been called, but store security had. "What does it mean," her mom asked, "when the security guy says he *invites* me to never return to his store? Am I invited or not?" She sniffled out the question with a pathetic burble noise.

"He doesn't want you to come back," she told her mom, which only elicited wails and protests. "Look, you're going to be fine. Please take your medicine. I'll stop by tonight after work, but right now I have to go to work or I'll be late."

She shouldn't have mentioned work. Emma knew what came next: snorts of mockery about how waitressing wasn't really a job along with jabs at how scribbling pictures online was an embarrassment to the family.

I can't do it, Dad, Emma thought. *I can't do this.*

While medicated, her mom was fine, great even . . . sometimes. But Emma knew what embarrassment to the family looked like, and it had nothing to do with *Dragon's Lair*. When her mom stubbornly chose to hide her medicine, or throw it away, or dump it all into the toilet, she became this cruel, frightening *thing*.

Emma never understood the creature that emerged in her mother.

Other kids battled monsters under the bed or in their closets. But Emma's monster didn't live in a closet or under any bed where it would be convenient to forget it—easy to live a life separate from it. Her demon lived inside her mother's mind. It went to parent-teacher conferences, to school plays, and on trips to Disneyland where it clawed free and rampaged in ways that made Emma feel hollowed out emotionally. She thought about Harrison and all the daydreams she'd been having of him since he'd left her porch. He was so interesting and funny. She thought about her mother's demon unleashing itself in front of Harrison's beautiful face, his eyes widening in shock at things her mother might do, and her heart slammed her ribs in protest against the two of them ever meeting.

Her dad had handled the cracks in their lives—mostly. He took care of everything, straightened up everything, smoothed out ruffled feathers, and wrote checks and made apologies when necessary. Emma thought she could pick up where he left off when he'd died.

But she hadn't known. She hadn't known how the marrow from every aspect of her life could be sucked dry by her mother's instability. Of course, things weren't just harder because her dad was no longer there to take care of it, but they were harder because he was no longer *there*. And her mom didn't know how to handle the endless hopelessness created by his absence. Not living with her mom, Emma couldn't enforce regular medicine habits. As a solution, the psychiatrist had recommended Emma move in with her mom in her old childhood home.

She didn't—*couldn't*—do that. She couldn't live under the same roof with the comments made of slivers and broken glass, not again—not unless she planned on going insane too. Emma fired that psychiatrist, deciding that he might be just drumming up business. If he made her crazy too, he'd have another client.

Her older brother and sister were no help at all. They didn't get it. How could they? Blake and Rosalee were over a decade older than Emma. They remembered their mother as caustic and biting, but they'd already moved out by the time she became a menace to society and entirely unstable. They lived in different states—too far away to be useful—a thing which Emma felt certain they had done by design.

Emma, unfortunately, was only a phone call and fifteen minutes away in light traffic. And because, out of her siblings, she was the one unmarried, childless, and unsuccessful career-wise, she was the place her mother focused all that negative energy. Made for super fun weekends when her mom would declare herself suicidal and camp in Emma's apartment so Emma could watch her.

"Why don't you call Rosalee?" Emma suggested, staring at the clock and willing the second hand to stop sweeping over the face.

"And how is Rosie going to help me all the way from Seattle?" her mom demanded to know.

"I told you I'll come by tonight—as soon as I'm off work."

"If you loved me or cared about me at all, you'd come now," her mom said.

With her mom, love was a tool for manipulation. "I'll make it so I get off early. Put in one of your movies and wait for me. I'll be there soon." She hung up before her mom could protest. She hated it, but the hasty-hang-up was a necessary evil. If she allowed her mom to linger through teary or angry good-byes, the phone call would never end.

Though Emma was already running late, she had to text Harrison to let him know she couldn't have dinner with him after all. If she didn't take a lunch break, she could leave work earlier. She hated breaking off the beginnings of something that felt like it had potential and hated that she had to do it over text, but what other options existed? And wasn't it better? She again imagined one of her mom's explosive tantrums happening in front of Harrison again.

Yes. It was better to never let anything start than to have him bear the mortification of her mom. She hit send on her phone hard enough she could've put her finger through the glass, grabbed her keys since she'd need the car to get to her mom's, and kicked the door shut before thumping down the stairs to the carport. If she hit the lights right, Cái's restaurant wouldn't cry out in despair or whatever it was bewitched restaurants did. She made it with thirty-eight seconds to spare. Cái's restaurant was safe.

"So," Cái said as she clocked in and tied the apron around her waist. "Feeling *fortun*ate?"

"That's a terrible pun, even from you." She moved to where the kitchen connected to the dining area. The kitchen's humid heat stifled and chafed today in a way she found she couldn't handle.

Cái followed her. "Okay, fine. I leave the jokes to you and your dragons, but I think you owe me an apology." His wrinkles folded into a wide smile.

"I am not apologizing for the crazy lady." She wasn't sure if she meant Harrison's date or her mother, but either way, she wasn't apologizing.

"Who cares for crazy lady? You owe me an apology for spending four years making fun of my restaurant's divine calling."

"An apology would indicate some remorse and some intention to stop making fun of your voodoo. And you think I'm stopping why again?"

He snapped his fingers in her face. "Your fortune! It's come true."

She glanced at Nate, who shrugged and then mopped a handkerchief over his forehead. So she wasn't the only one who felt like the kitchen was too hot to handle. "You don't even know my fortune, what do you—"

"*Look around. Love is trying to catch you.*" He grinned, knowing he'd surprised her.

Who told Cái what her fortune had said? Emma frowned; how could anyone have told when Harrison was the only other one who knew?

"You knowing what it said proves nothing," she scoffed, still a little unsettled because he had insider information on the contents of her cookie. "It's not like it came true."

"Really? I think you should have another look around," Cái said and pointed out toward the dining area to where the windows overlooked the ocean.

Standing outside the restaurant and appearing a little nervous was Harrison. His blue long-sleeved pullover accented his build in a way that made her take in a sharp breath. His fingers gripped a small bouquet of . . . what *was* he holding?

And more important than what was he holding, what was he doing there? "Why is he here?" She actually whispered the question out loud.

"I would think that's obvious," Nate said when it became evident the only answer Cái planned on giving was a cocky grin. "He's trying to catch you."

"He is not!" she whispered. "Is he?"

Nate laughed. Cái beamed. Jen rounded the corner to try to enter the kitchen but stopped when she saw her pathway blocked. "What are we looking at?" she asked.

"We're watching love catch our Emma." Cái's voice sounded reverent, confident, and self-satisfied all at the same time.

"We're apparently watching magic," Nate tried to clarify.

Cái pursed his lips and wagged a finger at Nate. "Ah! But love is always magic!" he insisted before giving Emma a shove toward the dining area at the same time that Harrison opened the door.

A wave pounding the sand outside felt like a punctuation mark to Emma's increased heart rate. She stumbled forward and heard Jen make a noise of approval about Harrison's shoulders. Emma stepped forward before Ali, the hostess, could gather menus and lead him off to a table. She took his arm and swung him out of Ali's path.

"What are you doing here?" she asked, hoping he didn't repeat the words from her fortune that were now on constant repeat inside her own skull.

"You tried to ditch out on our date."

Wait a minute. He was calling it a date? Not a get-together, or hanging out? Why did that make her legs feel all wobbly and her feet feel all tingly? She gave her head a slight shake to stay focused and said, "I wasn't ditching. Something came up. Something unavoidable. I—"

"These are for you."

He handed off the bouquet, which she could see was a bouquet of... "Pencils?"

"Sketching pencils. I didn't know what brand or anything, so I bought a bunch of everything in the art store." He shrugged and smiled, looking hopeful and sweet and perfect. She had to work hard to not stare at his lips.

"You bought me sketch pencils? I don't think any..." She took a few deep breaths. Was this for real? Was Cái's magic cookie really right? She looked up at him, feeling a heat in his eyes as soon as their gazes locked. "Thank you, Harrison. I can safely say that no one has ever bought me anything like this. I'm impressed enough that you remembered I sketched on the sides of my school assignments."

He gave a noncommittal kind of shrug. "Actually, I cheated a little. I Googled you."

She felt her smile freeze in place. He'd gone online? He knew about the comic? *And he still showed up to see her?* "Wow. I don't think anyone's ever said that to me before. Googled me, huh. I'm not going to lie, it's a little . . . unsettling." Granted, she'd have done the same if she wasn't caught between work, her mom, her book launch, and Comic Con.

"Your web comic is really clever, funny enough I laughed out loud several times and made my mom's poodle bark at me from the hallway. Your work is impressive."

The words were water in a drought. Had anyone she knew personally aside from her few friends at the restaurant ever said anything positive about *Dragon's Lair*? And he called it her *work*, not her hobby, not idle doodling, nor a waste of time. "Thank you, Harrison," she said. He couldn't know how much exactly she was thanking him for—not just for the pencils, but for the validation.

"Sorry to interrupt you," Jen said as she shot a meaningful look toward the corner table of the dining area, "but table nine has been seated."

The spell was broken. She had a job to do. But she couldn't let Harrison leave, not yet. She leaned in to whisper, not because she needed to but because she wanted an excuse to breathe him in. "Wait a few minutes at table thirteen, I'll be over in a minute, and we can talk more then."

He leaned in to whisper back, "Where's table thirteen?"

For a thrilling moment she hoped his lean was as on purpose as hers. "Where you were seated last night."

"Ah. That explains it. Table *thirteen*, demonic date

possessions. It all makes sense now."

She laughed and gave him a gentle nudge in the direction of his table.

She pocketed the pencils with her sketch book and hurried to table nine, reciting nearly the entire menu before the couple let her leave to fetch their drinks. Once she had their order placed and drinks on their table, she went back to table thirteen, thinking how much better he looked at that table when there wasn't an angry woman sitting across from him.

"I only have a few minutes but wanted to apologize again for our plans tonight."

He gave her an inquisitive look. "So why no lunch break? Don't you legally have to take a break?"

"I have to leave work early tonight. If I don't take a break, I can get out of here sooner. My mom, um, needs my help."

A worried expression crossed his features. "Is she sick?"

Emma knew what he meant. He wanted to know if her mom had a cold, or the bird flu, or cancer. He wasn't asking if her mom was *mentally* sick, and Emma didn't want to tell him, especially after he made several remarks about how Andrea's outburst the night before proved he was right about backing off. He didn't want a woman with any irrational tendencies.

Emma couldn't confess that she was genetically tainted by irrational tendencies, or at least tainted by association. Because even though she'd been the one to cancel their date, she found herself interested, interested in his making a business out of his creativity, interested in his smile, interested in his smile being aimed her direction, interested in a man who thought to bring her pencils because he recognized it would be a meaningful gift. He knew she'd had problems with her mom, but he couldn't know the depth and breadth because what if that made him *not* interested? "She *is* sick," she said. "I can't leave her alone when she's like this. I'm so sorry."

He looked more relieved than he did disappointed. Had he believed that she was ditching him for less respectable reasons?

"Is there anything I can do to help?"

Send me to a day spa, she thought. But instead she said, "Not really. It's just something I need to handle."

"I bet it stresses you out a little though, right?"

You have no idea. "Why would you say that?" Did he think she was some heartless cavewoman who didn't like helping her sick mom? And okay, that was sort of true, but also sort of not true. She really did love her mom. But with her brother and sister abandoning her to the task, she felt like she'd been given a dull sword to battle her demons.

She inwardly grunted at herself. She was not a heroine in her web comic. She didn't own swords, and her demons were not long-fanged creatures with ten heads. They just felt like they were.

"You have your Comic Con in LA this weekend. It's a lot to do when you're caring for a sick parent as well."

She almost asked how he knew that, but then remembered that he'd stalked her online, giving him access to her entire schedule for the next week. "It is a lot to do," she agreed.

"Want some help?" He repeated his previous question.

"Help?"

He grinned. "Yeah. Help. You know, that thing when you don't have to do everything all by yourself because other people lend a hand and make it easier. Synonymous with assistance, comfort, relief, support."

She had the crazy desire to reach across the table, grab him by his shirt, and kiss his face off in the overwhelming gratitude she felt that he would even offer assistance. It was an offer she could never take, but the very suggestion of kindness warmed her soul. "Why?" she asked.

He raised his eyebrows in question of her question.

"Why do you want to help me?" she clarified.

"Payback," he said, "for all the times you've helped me."

She shook her head, confused. "But I haven't—"

He lowered his voice. "Yes, you have. I always had a friend to sit next to as long as you were in my classes."

"Assigned seating does not count as *help*," she hedged.

"It counts because it wasn't always assigned. And you never moved away—even when you had a choice. You always talked to me before class started. You always loaned me pencils because I never remembered mine." He lifted one shoulder at the same time a corner of his mouth lifted in a rueful smile. "I figured I owed you a pencil or twenty since I'm pretty sure you never got some of those pencils back."

She laughed and looked back toward the dining room she'd been ignoring, hoping he didn't see the blush that surely crawled all over her face. "I have to get back to work. Thank you so much for those pencils. And for everything. Thanks for the offer. If I need help with anything, I'll call you, since some sneaky guy put your number in my phone."

He drummed his fingers on the table top. "Gotta watch out for those sneaky guys."

"Especially when they're good-looking."

Her face heated up from merely warm to sun surface temperatures when she realized she said that part out loud. But the look on his face, the one of approval, and the leap of excitement in his eyes were reward enough to make her not regret it so much as simply feel embarrassed by it.

"I'll call you maybe," she said. "If I need anything. Thanks for coming in to check on me. See you later?"

"You absolutely will," he said.

She rushed to the back kitchen to fetch table nine's food and get it delivered to them. She'd been talking long enough that the orders had to be ready. On her way back to deliver the food, she halted mid-step, startled to find Harrison still sat at table thirteen. Hadn't they just said good-bye? Why was he still sitting there?

As she maneuvered her tray over to table nine, she shot another look back at him and her toe caught the edge of a chair. The stumble off-balanced her with the tray in her hands, and it tilted and crashed to the ground. That was when she realized that not only had she dumped an entire order on the ground, she'd nearly dumped it on an actual customer. "Oh my gosh, I'm so sorry," Emma said, horrified that she'd been too sidetracked by looking at Harrison to focus on her job. "I've never done that before. It's lucky you moved right then, or you'd have sweet and sour sauce all over you right now."

The younger woman shrugged off her near calamity as if it was nothing. Emma ran back to let Nate know they needed table nine's orders remade, then rushed to table nine to apologize for the misfortune, promising the couple free dessert to make up for the inconvenience. Only then could she focus on the mess.

Except that Harrison was already there cleaning. "What are you doing?" she asked.

"This is that helping thing we talked about a minute ago. I'm getting the feeling you don't let people assist you enough, or you wouldn't have to have me continually defining it for you."

Cái peeked around the corner and saw Harrison kneeling on his tiled floor cleaning up Emma's mishap. He grinned at Harrison. "You know if you want to work here, I can get you an application."

Harrison laughed as he scooped up sweet and sour glazed chicken and dumped it into the bin Emma had retrieved for him. "Well, I do know where all your cleaning supplies are located. Do employees get any kind of perks?"

Cái wagged a finger at Harrison. "You already had your

fortune. What greater perk could you need?"

Emma groaned as she dumped the last bits of broken dishes into the garbage can. "Cái thinks his restaurant is magic."

"Really? Why?"

"Here, the fortunes *really* come true." Emma nodded as if sharing a great secret instead of a great bunch of baloney. She lowered her voice to a stage whisper. "We have magic cookies." She nodded again and winked at Cái, who for once didn't seem to be taking the bait.

He only grinned at her. "Yes, Emma. Yes, we do. Don't you agree, Harrison?"

Harrison gave Emma a look she couldn't read, but he didn't answer. He straightened and made a grab for the mop, but Emma pulled it from his reach. "Don't tell me you're buying into Cái's creepy cookie theory."

"I'm just glad to be here." He then said, "Except actually . . ." He pulled his phone from his pocket and scowled. "Hey, I gotta go run some errands and keep my world turning for a little while longer."

She nodded her agreement, and he turned away, his face unreadable as he peered at the screen of his phone and hurried out of the restaurant. Maybe she'd freaked him out when she told him that Cái believed in magic cookies?

She glanced around the kitchen area and swallowed her disappointment. Harrison had left, and his leaving felt abrupt enough to be called an escape. She considered asking Cái for a refund on her cookie fortune but felt too disheartened.

Better to get back to her job and focus so she didn't drop any more trays. She serviced the table where the young woman she'd nearly spilled the tray on sat. The young woman sat with two older couples and a guy who looked annoyed to be there. It had to be a meet-the-new-in-laws get-together. And Emma was the *lucky* waitress who served them.

She felt sorry for the girl and, as she went back to the

kitchen to place the orders, decided that the one good thing about being perpetually single was that she'd never have to do the awkward in-law meeting.

Except looking at the bright side of her singleness thrummed something raw and painful deep in her stomach. She'd had a boyfriend in high school, but none since.

When her dad died and the world fell on her shoulders, there hadn't been time for men. Besides, who wanted to date the girl with the neurotic mom? The couple of dates she had been on had been interrupted with phone calls demanding immediate attention as her mom wailed her distress loud enough that the guy had heard every word. Those guys never called back.

She didn't want Harrison to be like those men. She didn't want him to think she wasn't worth the trouble. Because no matter what she'd said to Cái, she really liked the idea of Harrison chasing her. But maybe it was better if Harrison didn't chase her, because there was no way she could allow herself to get caught. She couldn't pull anyone else into the emotional black hole of her mother's life.

She was glad she'd canceled the dinner plan, glad she'd told him how busy her life would be, and glad that he'd checked for himself to find that she'd been honest about that. He was only in town for two weeks. He could spend that time with his family and go back east, and she could continue being resigned to living her life as the reclusive girl with the crazy mom.

Because she didn't want him falling through the chasm of her mother's depression. That was a fall she had to take alone.

Five

Harrison glanced at his phone again to see the address his sister had forwarded him. She wanted him to meet her at the seaside reception center where she'd planned to hold their parents' thirtieth wedding anniversary party. He'd managed to avoid her since the restaurant fiasco. He wasn't up to her instigating a face-to-face confrontation with Andrea. But the anniversary party was important. He couldn't put it off any longer. He pulled into the parking space next to his sister's sedan and then entered the marbled building to find her.

She stood at a fountain that burbled in the center of the main room. She stared at a large menu in her hands. It appeared that Andrea wasn't with her. "Hey, Kris!" he called.

"Harrison!" she called back, but hers was not a friendly greeting. It was a definite growl. "You're in trouble."

"Usually am." He gave her a hug even though she stood rigid and glaring at him. He refused to let go until she gave in and hugged him back—even though she did it with a swat from the menu to his shoulder.

"I can't believe you humiliated Andrea in front of an entire restaurant." She took another swipe at him. "And then you never called her to apologize."

She raised her hand to smack him with the menu again, but he caught her hand.

"Called to apologize? I can't believe you're taking her side. You're unbelievable. I'm the blood relative here, and I'm the one who was assaulted and humiliated. *She threw her meal at me.*"

"She actually did tell me that." Kristin's voice softened a little. "How's the waitress?"

Harrison let go of Kristin's hand and narrowed his eyes. "She didn't press charges. Andrea's lucky."

Kristin finally had the decency to look abashed. "It was bad enough she could've pressed charges?"

"Andrea threw a plate at the owner, but it hit Emma instead. Property was damaged, Emma's arm looks like a car ran over it, and a huge mess was made."

"She did say she had no idea what came over her. Your rejection threw her pretty hard. She really does love you, Harrison." Kristin lifted her eyebrows. "I have no idea why."

"And it isn't that I don't care about her—although I confess I'm far less inclined to care about her after her little outburst—but we're not good together. You know? Not like you and David. Not like Mom and Dad. Some people make sense. Others . . . don't. Andrea and I don't make sense together. You can respect that, right? No more trying to force us back together?"

"She's my friend. I hate to see her heartbroken."

"I'm your brother. Doesn't my heart count?"

Kristin blew out a breath of annoyance and put her arm around him for a squeeze, though he flinched because he thought maybe she planned on swatting him with the menu again. "I guess so. But please tell me you'll still bring her to

Mom and Dad's party. Things will be so awkward if she has to come alone."

"Kris . . . what if I want to bring someone else?"

"The waitress?"

"I can't believe Andrea even brought that up to you guys. Don't say it like that. Emma isn't just the waitress. I've known her since high school. She saved me from getting beat up every day. She's . . . always been interesting to me."

"You are such a wimp. A girl had to save you from getting beat up?"

He leaned over to the fountain and flipped his hand so water sprayed out at his sister. She let out a squeal and moved to retaliate except one of the employees of the center ducked his head outside of his office to see what was going on. Kristin straightened up.

"It's just a night. You don't have to be there as Andrea's date, but she *is* going to be there. I can't not invite her just because you get all lovesick over a waitress. And it'll be insanely awkward if you bring a different girl. Maybe go stag? I just want the night to go well for Mom and Dad, okay?"

"I'll think about it, but I promise nothing." With that declaration, he and his sister got down to business.

She toured him through the location, showing him where the food would be set up, where the DJ would be able to hook up his equipment, and how the dining tables would be arranged around the dance floor. She handed him the menu and rattled off all the details of the food, expecting Harrison to pay attention. He had a hard time focusing, because he kept thinking about Emma.

He had really wanted to take her to his parents' party. Maybe he could talk to Andrea and work out something that wouldn't be awkward, but he doubted it. The way she'd flipped out on him was unreal, a complete mental break.

He followed his sister around the gardens with the outside fountain while she droned on and on about fairy twinkle lights. He hadn't even known fairy twinkle lights were a thing. He made all the appropriate expected comments about how fairy twinkle lights would be great and of course a vegan option made sense for those guests with particular food needs, even though he knew the only guest his sister worried about was Andrea.

Harrison appreciated the work his sister had put into the event because he knew it really did mean a lot to his parents. He also appreciated that his sister had insisted she needed help in planning and had strong-armed him into taking two whole weeks off for the party.

He might not have met up with Emma otherwise.

He owed his sister big time for that one. And he planned on using the two weeks to the fullest. He smiled thinking about the way Emma had blushed when her boss had teased her over the fortune she'd received. And though Harrison didn't put any stock in the silliness of clairvoyance, the fortunes he and Emma had received were totally dead accurate. He'd been brave once and actually said the words "I love you" to Emma on their graduation day, but he hadn't been brave enough to say them loud enough. He had loved her all those years ago. Loved the quiet way she helped other people—the quiet way she helped *him*. Loved the doodles on her papers, and had loved reading the papers themselves. As soon as he saw her again at the restaurant, he knew he'd been reunited with his soul mate. And he had every intention of chasing her down. So what if he had to give up one night to the anniversary party?

He still had eleven other days and nights before his flight took off. He planned to use them to maximum capacity, which meant he needed to hurry his sister along with her little tour so he could call Emma and see if she needed any help with her mom. He could offer to bring over some soup, or whatever. He sighed as Kristin pointed out the various places they could use for family photos.

He was ready to chase Emma in earnest.

Six

Emma's shift ended, allowing her to thankfully clock out and flee Cái's curious looks and overbearing remarks. He wanted to see her happily settled. He wanted to believe that somehow his restaurant would be the reason behind her happiness. The fact that he followed her around the kitchen saying, "A man doesn't marry a girl's mother. He marries the girl!" proved he didn't, and wouldn't, understand.

She probably shouldn't have told her boss about how she couldn't allow Harrison to chase her, even if her fortune was supposed to be true, because her mother required too much energy, and she just didn't have time for it.

Cái lectured like he was preparing her for a master's degree in romance, so slipping behind the wheel of her car and driving away toward her mother's house was a huge relief. An interesting change. Emma never imagined she'd be glad to be going to her mom's house for anything.

Driving time was good for her. She liked to process life, and driving allowed her time to do just that. Except . . . she couldn't think about *Dragon's Lair*. No witty dialogue came to her; no interesting four-paneled plot presented itself. She only thought of Harrison and wondered what he might be doing at that exact moment.

Her phone rang. She took a deep breath and with traffic being bumper to bumper and her hands-free headset still being lost, she didn't bother glancing at the screen before answering. She knew it was her mother. The miracle was that her mom waited so long to start calling. The calls would come every minute on the minute if Emma didn't pick up immediately.

"I'm on my way," Emma said into the phone, not bothering to hide her exasperation.

"Really? That's a wonderful surprise for me, but I thought you were going to your mom's house," a man's voice said.

Puzzled, she moved the phone away so she could see who'd called. Harrison's name glowing up at her from the screen startled her so much she nearly dropped the phone. "Harrison?" she said, confirming what her eyes saw, but her mind couldn't make itself believe.

"Why do you sound like me calling is the most unlikely thing to ever happen?" he asked. "I stole your number fair and square, which means I'm within my rights to use it." His teasing tone made her stomach flip.

How could just hearing his voice make her feel all melty? She wasn't even sure she could get air to move past her vocal cords. She tried though. A barely perceptible squeak came out.

"You there?" His voice was warm and rich.

"I'm here," she said.

"So I've been thinking that maybe when you're done at your mom's, we could get some dessert or go for another walk or something. I don't mind if it's late. Or maybe I could go to your mom's house and help with stuff there. I'm great at doing dishes."

She smiled in spite of herself and pulled onto her mom's street. "Doing dishes or breaking dishes?" she asked.

"Hey, the broken dishes were the fault of the other person. Remember?"

Emma hadn't actually meant Andrea when she made the broken dishes comment and felt her face grow warm that he thought she had. "Sorry, I was actually referencing my brother. When we were younger, he sometimes broke dishes or threw them away to get out of having to clean them."

She heard the smile in Harrison's voice as he said, "That worked? Man, I wish I'd been more clever as a kid. It never occurred to me to find alternate methods."

Emma smiled. "Yeah, that's my brother all right, always looking for a way out of responsibility."

"But not you," Harrison said, the admiration in his words almost tangible.

"How do you know *not me*? You haven't seen me in a long time." She turned into her mom's driveway.

"Because you're going to take care of a sick mom."

"That's different from dishes."

"No, not different at all. Responsibility is responsibility. Sure, there are different levels. Some responsibilities weigh more, but at the end of the day, the guy who gets it done is the guy you can label responsible."

She turned the key to kill the engine. "Did you just call me a guy?" she asked to deflect her discomfort in his compliment.

He laughed. "Not a chance. Do you want me to come over and keep you company? Play checkers with your mom? I don't mind driving."

"No really, I'm okay. I got this." As she exited the car and glanced up at her childhood home, she knew she meant it.

Harrison was right about the weight of responsibility. Caring for her mother had the equivalent weight of a mountain. But in the last year she'd come to understand its weight. She knew how to shift it around on her shoulders to make carrying it bearable.

She walked up the front steps, knowing she should tell Harrison good-bye before entering the house. Her mom's loud voice carried well enough that he'd be able to hear anything she might say. Emma opened her mouth to tell Harrison that she'd call him when she finished up at her mother's. He wanted to go out, no matter how late, and in spite of her earlier resolution to stay away from him, she really wanted to see him again. But as she began the sentence, she frowned and really looked at her mom's house.

All the windows were open, the curtains moving against the faint breeze. Open windows felt wrong. Her mom grew excessively more paranoid every day. She never left windows open. But more than that strangeness was that not one light glowed from behind them.

"Mom?" Emma whispered.

She'd forgotten Harrison in that brief moment of assessment, but his voice coming through the phone reminded her of his presence. "Is everything okay?"

"I don't know," Emma answered. "It looks like no one's home."

"Maybe she felt better and went to the store or something."

Emma shook her head, though he couldn't see the movement. "No. She doesn't have a car any longer." A car accident. Her mom had insisted it wasn't her fault, but Emma never found out the particulars. Sometimes, with her mom, it was better not to know.

"Okay, Harrison, I'm going to ask you to do something weird."

"Okay . . . what?" He must have understood that something wasn't right because he dropped the playful tone.

"I need you to not take it personally when I tell you we can't meet later. And it's probably best not to call back tonight. I don't think I'll be available." She did the hasty hang up that she always did with her mom.

She did it because she had to. Whatever was going on inside that house, she did *not* want Harrison to be on the other end of the line listening. She slowly walked up the stairs and went to try the knob, but the door was already ajar—waiting for her.

Just like her mom to make the really hard things easy. It was going to be a long night.

She entered the house.

She flipped on lights as she went, trying to illuminate her own thoughts as well as her surroundings so she didn't trip or anything. A cursory look through all the rooms provided nothing. She searched each room again, checking under beds, behind draperies, inside closets, but her mom wasn't there.

"All right, Mom!" she shouted to the walls. "You got me! I can't find you! Come out!"

No response.

Her phone buzzed in her pocket, nearly startling her into a heart attack. She glanced at the screen, deciding she wouldn't answer if it was Harrison calling back. Not recognizing the number, she answered. "Hello?"

"Is this Emma Armstrong?" The man's voice sounded hard.

"Yes." Her mind shouted questions back to the man. *Who are you? What's going on?* "This is Emma," she said.

"This is Officer Cowan from the Seashell Beach Police Department. Is your mother's name Corinne Armstrong?"

"Yes." Emma slumped down on a chair in the kitchen, her legs unable to hold her weight any longer. "Do you know where she is?" she asked, feeling the tired in her bones rumble in her own voice.

"We have her in custody. We've already called her psychiatrist who confirmed she isn't a danger to herself as long as she is taking her medicine and in the care of a responsible party. We'll release her to you if you'll come pick her up and agree to keep watch over her, otherwise we'll need to hold her in the psych ward for three days for observation."

"Do I dare ask why she's in custody?" Emma asked.

"She tried to jump off the pier on Seashell Beach. Witnesses stopped her and called us."

Emma nodded in response, but said nothing.

"Miss Armstrong?"

"I'm here. I'll be there to get her soon."

She hung up the phone but continued to sit, unable to make her feet and legs shift to bear the weight of this new burden settling over her shoulders. She'd lied when she told Harrison she "had" this. She hadn't known she'd been lying, but not knowing didn't change the lie. She didn't have anything at all.

Her mom had found her way to Seashell Beach. The pier was a stone's throw from the restaurant Emma just left. The location was not an accident. It was one of her mom's lessons—her way of saying, "See? I control you. You don't control me."

After several minutes of shallow breathing, Emma forced herself to her feet. She closed the windows in the house, turned off the lights she'd turned on, and shut the front door behind her after locking it. "Yes, Mom, I see."

Seven

Emma paced the small pathway in her apartment between the boxes of books that went all the way to the ceiling. She blew her hair out of her eyes in exasperation as she shifted the phone to her other ear. "You weren't there, Rosalee. You have no idea what it was like." She no longer tried to hide her own irritation. If her sister insisted on being obtuse, then she at least had the right to be annoyed by it.

"I don't ever ask for anything!" Emma shouted at her sister. "Not once since Daddy died have I asked for you to help me with this, but she's your mother too! I only need one weekend." The evil, horrible part of her chanted how she should've left her mother in the psych ward for three days.

Rosalee whined and hedged and claimed to be busy even though Emma knew darn good and well that Rosalee didn't have anything actually going on. Rosalee didn't work a job because her husband was some fancy CEO of a soup company. She had two kids, but also had a nanny who took the brunt of the issues with child rearing. And she had a housekeeper who also cooked the family dinners. She had no hobbies, didn't read, didn't have any artistic endeavors, didn't make anything or fix anything or solve anything. Emma honestly didn't know what her sister did with her time, which was why Emma felt no guilt in not backing down from asking this favor.

"She's suicidal, Rosalee! She tried jumping off a pier at sunset. She can't be left alone right now because she won't take her medications unless someone is there to force it down her throat, and because the police made me sign a statement saying she would be watched over. If anything happens to her, I'll go to jail for neglect or something. And I *can't* be there this weekend. I have been there when she vomited all over herself in an effort to purge the medicine I made her take. I've been the one to clean that up. I've been there when she was sad and wanted to cry and cry and cry. I'm the one who had to go to the police station to pick her up. It is totally *your* turn!"

The fight over the phone took another twenty-eight minutes before Rosalee finally gave in and agreed to fly down for the weekend. She hadn't been down from Seattle even once since their dad's funeral. It was about time she visited her mom anyway.

With that taken care of, Emma glanced into her bedroom to check where her mom slept. The shallow breathing of sleep assured her that her mom hadn't overheard the fight. Emma didn't know if that made her happy or not. It might be a good thing for her mom to understand that Rosalee wasn't the sweet angel their mother believed her to be.

But her mom slept soundly. Which was just as well. Emma had a lot of books to sign and stuff in her preaddressed envelopes. Finally something to smile about. She was about to sign her very first book.

She went to work.

Eight

Harrison paced his parents' house, not quite knowing what to do. He felt like he'd been pacing for days. She'd hung up on him, and her voice had that haunted sound he remembered from back in high school. He knew it had something to do with her mom. He'd read the personal essays, the poems, and the short stories that hinted at something deeper and darker.

Emma told him not to call back. The task of not calling back required superhuman strength. He'd kept her wishes for thirty-seven hours. He wanted to show her that he respected her. But how far did he have to take that respect? He wanted to help. He wanted to smooth the worry from Emma's voice. He wanted to erase the tired wariness from her eyes.

He pressed her number on his phone's screen and held his breath to see if he'd waited long enough. She didn't answer. So he must *not* have waited long enough. Or maybe she didn't answer because she was at work. It was ten in the morning. Surely the café had a breakfast menu.

That made sense.

He grabbed his keys and went to The Fortune Café. Maybe her boss would let him wash the windows so that he had an excuse to hang out with her.

"She's not here," Jen, one of the other waitresses, said. "She hasn't been here since the other day when you were here before."

"Is everything okay?" he asked, thinking about how she had sounded before she'd hung up on him.

Jen lifted her thin shoulders in a shrug. "Doubt it. Her mom's a piece of work. Emma's a slave to that woman. It's really sad actually. Emma needs to get a life of her own."

"What's wrong with her mom?" he asked, feeling bad for shaking down Emma's coworkers for personal information.

"Crazy. More than the usual crazy. Even more crazy than your date from the other night. Emma puts up with a lot of abuse from that woman."

"Thanks for the information," Harrison said, mentally forgiving her for bringing up his crazy date. He headed to Emma's apartment. If she wasn't there, then he planned on camping out on her doorstep. At her apartment, he knocked on the door and waited. He heard noise inside and felt immediate relief. She was home.

She answered the door wearing black yoga pants and a red t-shirt with Chinese characters splattered over the front. A ponytail holder kept her dark hair up off her shoulders revealing the long lines of her neck and the narrow slope of her cheekbones. She was so beautiful.

Her brown eyes widened in what could only be called an expression of horror at seeing him. She glanced behind her and stepped out to join him on the front porch, making sure to shut the door behind her.

She stared at him and appeared to be waiting for him to say something. His eyes trailed back to the closed door. What was she hiding? "Are you okay?"

She started to nod, then shrugged and let out a sigh. "I'm just really tired." She eyed him. "Why are you here?"

"I came to help," he said after a moment of her watching him.

She opened her mouth, closed it, and opened it again. "Harrison..."

"You have a book launch, and I know that has to entail a lot of work. I plan on doing work. Give me directions. I mean, you might as well because free labor is so hard to find these days."

"You don't know what you're asking." She looked exhausted, emotionally beaten.

"I think I might understand if you'd let me in." He meant the words on several levels.

She pressed the heels of her palms into her eyes and inhaled deeply before lowering her hands and giving him a tired, sad look. "Okay. Just be warned, though, my mom's inside and she's not..."

"Well?"

"No. She's not *nice*. My mom is not a nice person. I mean, she's not well either, but she's not a nice person. If you go inside, you will have to listen to things that are uncomfortable—things that are... really *awful*." Her voice trembled. "Do you still want to help?" Her red rimmed eyes grew glossy with tears.

He couldn't stop himself. He stepped forward and wrapped his arms around her, pressing her into him as if somehow he could press his energy into her through a simple embrace. What had she been going through? And why had he waited so long to make contact when she obviously needed someone?

At first, she remained stiff and uncertain, maybe even afraid of his touch. But she melted slowly into him until her arms were around him too, clinging to him as if he was the rope keeping her clear of the alligators and spikes at the bottom of a ravine.

She fit against him so well, like she belonged there. Her tears soaked through his shirt, and he tightened his arms just a little. "You're okay, Emma. I'm here. It's all going to be okay."

Not nice. She'd called her mother not nice. But Harrison remembered the hurt layered under words in her assignments. If he remembered correctly, *not nice* was a very mild way of putting it.

But he determined that his hero from the first day of high school deserved a little payback. Today, he would be her hero. He would protect her from the cruelty of another person. Today, he would save her. He'd save her every day for as long as she would let him.

He pulled back from her enough to gaze into her brown eyes glossy with her tears. "Hey. We got this. Let's get it all done."

She sniffed but opened the door.

She let him in.

He stood facing the wall of boxes and books and envelopes, but he stepped forward. He was right to think she had an overwhelming task in front of her.

"My sister is supposed to be here already," Emma whispered. "Her plane arrived four hours ago. But she's not answering her phone at all, so it's been hard to get work done while—"

"What are you whispering about in there?" A voice came from the other room. "I hear you talking about me. Is Rosie here? It's about time I get to spend time with someone competent. Listening to you nag has worn down my nerves to their bare roots. Rosie?"

"Rosalee isn't here yet, Mom." Emma's face had darkened with the blush of shame. "Told you," she whispered to him. "And it'll only get worse."

"Then who's here?" The woman's voice demanded to know. "Who are you whispering to? Or are you talking to your dragons again?" A hissing sort of laughter sounded. "It's ironic that you have me seeing a psychiatrist when you're the one talking to dragons, don't you think?"

"I have a friend here to help me, Mom. Please . . ." But Emma didn't add anything further. It seemed a world of unsaid requests hinged on that one word *please*.

Noise, shuffling, and rustling came from the other room as someone stumped toward Emma and Harrison. An older woman appeared in the doorway. The severe bun pulled her hair so tight that her eyes slanted a little. Makeup and jewelry dripped off of her in a way that made it difficult to tell what she really looked like underneath it all. He hadn't expected someone who looked tidy and made up. He'd expected snarled hair and missing teeth. He'd expected wildly shifting eyes instead of an imperiously cold and level gaze. "Who are you?" the woman said with a suspicion that made Harrison take an actual step back.

"I'm Harrison Archer, Emma's friend."

A slow, deliberate show of disbelief formed in the arch of her eyebrow. "Emma doesn't have friends."

He worked hard to keep his features smooth as anger welled up inside him. "Not to argue, but you're wrong about that. I am definitely Emma's friend," Harrison assured the woman. "I'm here to help her with her work."

"Work? You mean her scribbles that she put into a book? I told her she might as well make furniture out of all those books because no one wants to buy her scratches. Dragons! What a waste of time."

He truly understood why Emma chose to draw dragons after meeting this fire-breathing sort of person. How had Emma grown up so *Emma* with someone like this woman?

"I'm actually really impressed with her web comic. She's created quite a franchise. She's likely to be as successful as Calvin and Hobbes."

Emma put her hand on his arm and murmured, "Don't bother. It's not worth it."

The woman narrowed her eyes and opened her mouth as if about to speak, but a knock came at the door before anything more could be said. Emma looked like she might collapse with relief at the interruption. Her sister had finally arrived.

Harrison was surprised at how much older her sister appeared. He hadn't known there was such an age gap between the two sisters. She seemed to be working hard to hang onto youth, but the platinum blonde hair and the perfectly tweezed eyebrows looked unnatural and forced.

Her mom practically tripped over her feet to throw her arms around Emma's sister, proclaiming herself to be rescued and begging to be taken out of Emma's matchbox-sized apartment immediately so she could finally breathe.

"Where've you been?" Emma asked her sister.

"I had my own errands to run. The world doesn't revolve around you, you know."

Emma's eyes tightened, and she handed off a bag and quiet instruction to her sister who had yet to apologize for not showing up on time. They were gone in a flurry of veiled and not-so-veiled insults from Emma's mom to Emma.

"Wow," Harrison said, watching her carefully to gauge her reaction. But she walked to the stacked boxes as if nothing had happened.

It took Harrison a second longer to recover from listening to a mother eviscerate her own daughter, but apparently Emma was moving on to the next task.

"Are you okay?" he asked, hardly believing anyone could be capable of brushing off such a verbal abuse.

She glanced at him. "She was actually pretty well-behaved. And you were warned." She turned her back to him and tried to wrestle a box from the top.

"Hey, Armstrong. Quit trying to live up to your name. Let me do that." He pulled the box down for her and tried to get the encounter with her mother out of his mind as he listened to Emma explain the process of her needing to sign the book and then place it in the corresponding padded envelope, and then prepping the envelope to be mailed.

He looked dubiously at all the boxes and then to her rather extensive list of names for mailing. She smiled softly. "I had really good presales," she said, the pride in her voice evident.

He loved to see her smile. "I guess you did!" He laughed. "But you're never going to get through this before you need to be at your convention tomorrow."

She smiled wide. "I stand a better chance with you here. Thank you. You don't owe me anything, and yet here you are. I can't begin to tell how much that means to me."

"You're more than welcome." He leaned over the waist-high stack of boxes that she'd been using as a seat and rested his knuckles on the cardboard on both sides of her. He hadn't planned to kiss her, not when she was so vulnerable from her mother's attack, but she leaned forward as if pulled by his gravity. Her eyes fluttered closed just as his lips met hers, soft and yielding. He closed his eyes as well and deepened the kiss, wrapping his arms around her. She scooted closer to him, tucking against him.

He'd thought about kissing her a million times in high school, but the fantasy was a poor shadow in comparison to this reality. He pulled back, leaning his forehead on hers, knowing that kissing her didn't exactly make her work load any easier. "That's not exactly what I meant when I said I wanted to help," he whispered.

"Weird, because it seems to be helping . . ." she whispered back.

Was he dreaming? Did she know what it did to him to have her, the girl he'd secretly loved during the entire unbearable years of high school, sitting before him with her arms around his neck? "Can you do me a favor?" he asked. She nodded against his head. "If this is a dream, don't wake me up."

She took a shuddering breath. "I've lived through enough nightmares to know that we're standing in reality."

"That's not true."

She frowned. "It isn't?"

"You're sitting."

She gave him a playful shove.

"But we really need to get to work. I don't want you panicking in a few hours because I sidetracked you and didn't help at all. But even with me here, we need reinforcements." He pulled out his phone.

She watched him curiously. "Who are you calling?"

"My mom and sister."

Her eyes went wide, and she tried to snatch his phone away, but he was tall enough that it allowed him to evade her attack. She stopped trying to steal his phone once he said hello. He couldn't help but think that Andrea would have kept trying to steal the phone.

He eyed Emma after he hung up with his mom.

"You really didn't have to do that," she said.

"It was the kiss that convinced me."

Emma laughed, and for a second he thought she might kiss him again, but she went back to work, not willing to allow herself to be idle for too long. He breathed a sigh of relief knowing his mom and sister would come to help. Emma needed them. And he had always known how much he needed her.

Yes. He was definitely glad he came home.

Nine

Since she couldn't stop him from calling in his personal cavalry, Emma went back to work. She couldn't believe he'd shown up, couldn't believe he was in her house, couldn't believe the fire still coursing through her at his kiss. Harrison Archer had kissed her.

She'd been kissed before, but never had she felt glacier-melting heat. After he made the phone call, they settled into an easy routine of him opening boxes, getting books ready for her signature, her signing the books, him putting them in the right envelopes. He didn't seal the envelopes but instead set them aside so, "Kristin has something to do."

His mom and sister arrived shortly thereafter, introducing themselves as Lily—his mom, the person who was evidently responsible for Harrison's startlingly blue eyes—and Kristin—his sister, who sort of looked like a slightly shorter girl version of Harrison with her brown hair and blue eyes. They must have inherited the hair from their dad because Lily was blonde. Emma felt a considerable amount of apprehension in meeting the people who'd been described as in-love-with-the-ex-girlfriend.

And though Kristin gave her an interested once-over as if doing a rigorous inspection, she also gave Harrison a thumbs-up. *Does that mean I passed?* Emma wondered. It must have, because Kristin smiled and acted friendly. Lily did no such inspection but rather acted as though the fact that Harrison liked Emma was more than enough information for her.

They formed an assembly line where all Emma did was sign books and take part in enjoyable conversation. This was the family who had wanted Andrea to marry Harrison, yet neither woman acted with malice toward Emma's obvious takeover. Instead they laughed and asked questions about the web comic. Harrison had to get after Kristin for reading the book instead of packing it away in an envelope.

"I can't help it!" Kristin defended herself. "It's really good."

Emma swelled with the compliment until she felt like she might float away. Her own sister had never said anything to her about the comic. Neither had her brother. Obviously her mother thought it was a big waste of time. Emma had not received a compliment on *Dragon's Lair* since her father had died unless that compliment came from her fans or her coworkers.

Kristin's enthusiasm toward the web comic felt personal as if she'd not only approved *Dragon's Lair*, but she had approved *Emma*. With four people, the workload still took well into evening, but not too late. Everyone would be able to go to sleep at a decent hour. Emma would be able to enjoy a good night's rest. She'd planned on showing up at the convention red-eyed and worn down, not well-rested and calm.

Harrison even went so far as to offer his mom's suburban to help haul the remaining boxes to the convention without Emma trying to figure out how to make it all work in her car. He also informed her he'd be attending the convention with her, insisting that selling herself was hard and that it was always a good idea to have an additional salesperson to add credibility to the brand. The argument was that if you can afford lackeys, then you must have some modicum of success.

The greatest part of being with Harrison, his mother, and his sister for the entire day was Harrison's mom. His mom seemed like a thing of myth. She loved her children. She laughed with them, *complimented* them. Even their bantering insults didn't feel tense as the insults in Emma's life always were, but instead they were fun and lighthearted. Lily adored her children.

Lily also adored art. She spoke at great length about lines and color with Emma, treating Emma as a peer, not a child with a silly hobby, but a professional equal. She offered for Emma to come and see her studio and to let her dabble in oils anytime she felt like practicing with a different medium.

Then the two women left with all the books to be mailed packed into Kristin's car to be taken to the post office. Kristin refused to allow Emma to do the mailing because Emma had enough to worry about in getting to her convention.

Soon, it was only Emma and Harrison left in her apartment that was considerably less crowded with a good portion of the boxes gone.

"I get it," she said.

"Get what?"

"The word 'help.' It means to assist, comfort, aid, relieve, support. I didn't know what it meant before today."

"Kind of nice, isn't it?" he asked.

"Kind of nice," she agreed.

The difference between the feelings in his family and the feelings in her family were so entirely opposite, she could scarcely comprehend how she'd partaken of both in the same day. "I don't know how to thank you," she said.

He drew her in as if he'd been waiting for this moment all day. He kissed her, carefully as if she might break. When he pulled away, he said, "Don't thank me until we have the rest of these books sold and another printing ordered." He stretched and glanced at his phone. "Get some sleep, Emma Armstrong. I'll see you in the morning."

It was the strangest thing. She still felt that support, that comfort, that help, even after he'd gone.

Harrison arrived at her apartment bright and early the next morning to drive her into LA with the books. The three-hour drive gave them lots of time to talk and get to know each other again. But as soon as they arrived at the convention center, Harrison was all business.

The convention was enormous. People dressed in Star Wars, Harry Potter, and Doctor Who costumes. People wearing T-shirts with dragons and pointed elven ears stopped by her booth. Harrison had done the setup, organizing all the display props she'd brought, and *designing* the space so it felt inviting. She realized how she never could have pulled it off without him. And she found she said very little to try to sell herself. She'd been worried about the selling part. Emma had never been good at putting herself out there, but Harrison with his earnest appeal called people over to the booth and did all the talking. She only signed.

But she signed a lot.

She signed all day, and into the next, and into the next. Sunday night, when they packed the remains away, she found she only had five and a half boxes left. "I nearly sold out," she kept saying on the drive back from LA. She couldn't keep the awe out of her voice.

"Of course you did. And you have a bunch of new contacts on your email list. Even people who didn't buy this weekend are likely to visit your website and become fans."

"I couldn't have done this without you," she said.

"Sure you could've. It just would've been harder." He grinned. "But don't act like I'm all heroic for going. I got some business out of this endeavor as well."

He was right. There were many authors and companies needing designs. As they waited in line for Emma to sign their books, Harrison talked to them. He was good at mentioning what he did for a living, which usually ended with the other person confessing how much he hated his logo, or how much she hated her website. Harrison had handed out nearly as many business cards for himself as he had for her. He already had two new clients on board with bigger projects.

When Harrison left Emma at the door with a kiss that held a promise of a future happiness, she knew nothing could dampen the perfection of the weekend.

Until she went inside and listened to her voice messages.

Ten

The note was in her sister's handwriting.

> *Emma, Mom won't take her medicine. She called it poison and flat out refused. So I decided she probably knew what she was talking about. She knows her own body and mind better than any doctor. If she doesn't feel like it's helping then she shouldn't be forced to take it. Just thought you should know. And turn on your phone every now and again. How hard would it be to make sure you're reachable?*
>
> *Rosie*

Rosalee had taken her mom off the much needed medication. Rosalee was an idiot. Emma would be the one stuck dealing with the issue once Rosalee left. She reached into her bag and checked her phone. It wasn't that she hadn't turned it on, but more that she'd left it on without charging it so the battery had died. It had died two days prior.

Feeling trepidation, Emma plugged the phone into the outlet at her counter and turned it back on. The fourteen messages started out mild enough. Mini rants from Rosalee about how Emma hadn't made sure their mom's fridge was stocked or how Emma had failed in making sure the gardener edged along their mom's driveway well enough. They grew into larger rants as they moved on, from the medication to the accusation that Emma was an abusive caregiver.

The eighth message was where Rosalee's tone changed from criticism to panic and pleading for help. "Emma! Mom's freaking out! I can't stop her from breaking things. She punches at me any time I get close enough to try to hold her down. Why is she doing this? You need to come home right now!"

"Emma! Where are you? I don't remember where you said you'd be! I can't handle this anymore! She's locked herself in the bathroom and won't come out!"

"Emma! Call me!"

The last one was the one that frightened Emma the most. Rosalee had calmed down considerably, but there was no mistaking the fury in her tone, as if everything she'd been through during the weekend was specifically Emma's fault. "Emma, I have no idea if I will ever be willing to talk to you again in your entire life so listen good, since this might be the last time you hear my voice. You are entirely irresponsible. Mom should have been placed in a mental institution a long time ago. For you to let her live on her own scraping by from day to day is just cruel. I've secured her a permanent home at the Gates Mental Center. What were you thinking, Emma? I called Blake, and he agrees with me. Dad would be furious with how you've failed. He would be eternally disappointed in you. Call me if you can figure out how to fit other people in your schedule."

Emma cradled the phone unsure of how she felt. Her mom was in an institution. Rosalee hated her. Rosalee called her irresponsible. Rosalee called her cruel. All of that evoked little to no feeling at all—just a sort of strange numbness.

But the last couple sentences ignited an explosive rage in Emma. *Dad would be furious? Dad would be disappointed? She didn't know how to fit people into her life?*

Emma screamed. Screamed until the sound clawed her throat raw. Then she did the irrational thing. She grabbed her keys and went back out into the night. She drove to her mom's house to have it out with her sister. She was tired of being stepped on and overlooked.

She stomped up the stairs of her childhood home and tried not to think about all the times her dad had carried her up those same stairs so that she could touch the peaked porch soffit. She pushed through the front door, which wasn't locked because Rosalee wasn't as paranoid as her mother. Emma tried not to think about how her dad used to go outside and knock on the door as a game to her where they spent the better part of an hour sharing knock-knock jokes through the wood.

"Rosalee!" She called from the entryway—the same entryway where her mom had once laced flowers in her hair before Rosalee's wedding and declared her a lovely little bridesmaid. Her mother had placed a soft kiss on top of a young Emma's head and said the words, "I love you, sweetie."

Emma froze. The further shouts demanding justice turned to ice in her throat and melted back down into her soul. The day of Rosalee's wedding had been good. Her dad had made her mom take her medicine. Their family had all been together. They had been happy—for that moment at least. And it was enough.

Rosalee appeared in the hallway. Her eyes were red, and her face looked grey with grief. "Emmy?" she said, her voice small and as sickly as her skin.

Emma stared for only a snatch of a moment before rushing to her sister and throwing her arms around her. "It's okay, Rosie," she said, calling her sister by the pet name that she hadn't used since before their dad died. "You're okay."

"She told me she hated me." Rosalee's shoulders heaved in her great sobs. "She told me—"

"I know," Emma interrupted. "But it wasn't her. It was the illness. Not her, Rosie. The illness." The two sisters stood like that a long time, crying and assuring each other that it wasn't their mom who hated them. Emma breathed air that felt clean going into her lungs and out of her lungs again. Emma was no longer alone. Her burden suddenly felt lighter.

She wanted to talk to Harrison, to tell him in person that everything had changed for her in that brief moment, but the next four days were a whirlwind of her brother coming into town as well, of the three siblings visiting their mom together to show that they supported her. They packed up many of her favorite things and decorated her mom's room to look like home for her. She spit out venom and anger while they worked to arrange the care center room, but with each biting remark, Emma's siblings would exchange a glance of understanding and solidarity. They were in this together.

Emma had a hard time breaking away from her brother and sister. She went to work only once when Jen needed to take her daughter out for her birthday and there wasn't anyone else to cover her shift.

While at work, a woman sat at her table who had claimed to have ordered takeout. The news was odd because not many people did takeout from the café. She asked the woman about her fortune, curious if Cái's voodoo extended to takeout. The woman seemed to not believe that her fortune cookie was magical, which made Emma need to duck her head to hide her smile. *See, Cái, no magic.*

That had been the only time she'd been able to go into work, and she was grateful Cái cared enough to be understanding about giving time off. She communicated a lot of what was going on to Harrison through text. But text was a clumsy way of having a real conversation, brief and clipped as it was. He didn't always respond right away, and his responses were fairly brief half the time, but she figured he was likely as busy with his family as she'd been with hers. She worried a little when his texts were one word responses that barely made sense in context to the questions she asked. She worried that maybe after discovering her mom was being institutionalized, he had decided that Emma wasn't worth the bother. Or maybe he was afraid her mom's condition was genetic.

And then she wondered if maybe her mom's condition *was* genetic since she was acting stupidly paranoid.

Friday morning came, and Emma remembered that Harrison said he'd be at the seaside reception center not too far from midtown Seashell Beach. She drove over, hoping to surprise him. She wanted to make his last couple of days count before he left back to Boston. She even toyed with the idea of taking an extended vacation to visit him there so they could explore their relationship further. She had the money now that *Dragon's Lair* had sold out and was on back order for the second shipment. At Harrison's advice, she was looking into getting a distributor. But she wanted to talk about that possibility with him personally rather than over text. The last thing she wanted was to show up in New England and have him horrified to see her there. She needed confirmation that they were still okay, that he wasn't freaked out by her mom.

She entered the reception center excited and energized to help Harrison's family the way they had helped her. But she stopped as soon as she passed through the doors and blinked several times to be sure she saw what she thought she saw.

Andrea was up on a ladder hanging lights while Harrison held the ladder and looked up at her. They were in deep conversation, one that looked natural and easy. "Oh," Emma whispered, feeling stupid for just showing up without announcing herself. Andrea was a family friend. She'd helped plan the party. It made sense that she would be there.

Andrea looked up at that moment, as if sensing someone watching her and saw Emma standing there. She whispered something to Harrison, and he nodded and hurried away. Andrea returned her gaze to Emma as she methodically made her way down the ladder rungs. Emma felt an instinctive need to run—probably similar to what a lone zebra felt when facing down a lioness.

"Hi, Emma. It is Emma, isn't it? I think that's what you said at the restaurant. I just wanted to say that I'm really sorry about what happened. It was a really off-day for me. Harrison and I worked things out. He promised he'd patch things up for me with you. I hear he helped with all the book stuff you're doing. Congratulations on that, by the way."

Harrison had done that to patch things up for *Andrea*? No. That wasn't right at all. Emma reevaluated everything she'd believed over the last two weeks. After the convention, his only communication with her was via text, but that was because he was busy . . . *she* was busy. Then she looked around the garden themed room with its fountain and lights. Harrison hadn't even mentioned the reception to Emma as something she should attend. It was always just something *he* was doing. She had assumed that he'd take her, but now she realized that if he'd meant for her to go with him, he would have at least brought it up.

And he had been so distant since their weekend in LA.

It made a sort of twisted sense for him to protect Andrea, to make amends and apologies the way he did. Isn't that what Emma's dad had always done for her mom through the years? "Oh," Emma said, the word starting out deep in her stomach and tearing free from her throat. "I just . . . I . . . tell him thank you for me."

Andrea smiled. "Of course I will. And truly, I am so sorry about that whole mix up at the restaurant. I have no idea what came over me. You're a really great person and didn't deserve to deal with my bad day."

Emma nodded and turned to leave. She didn't know what she felt or thought about the whole situation, but she knew for a fact she couldn't be there standing next to Andrea. Emma felt flayed and scoured by the ordeal with her mom and brother and sister. Her emotions were so unsteady, it was possible she'd misread Harrison's intentions. She tugged on the heavy, leaded glass door and tried to squeeze her way through it when she could only make her rubbery muscles open it halfway.

She made it to the parking lot, but no matter how hard she breathed in and out, she couldn't seem to get any oxygen. Where did all the oxygen in the world go? "Emma?" It was Kristin, Harrison's sister, coming from the parking lot to which Emma fled. "You okay?"

"I just . . . think I misunderstood. Thank you so much for helping me the other day. I know you don't owe me anything, and that was a really nice thing to do for a stranger."

Kristin snorted. "To hear Harrison tell it, you are the furthest thing from a stranger to our family. Besides, it was fun. And Harrison paid me back tenfold in several days' worth of anniversary work."

"Harrison's like that, paying off debts."

She gave Emma a strange look. "Why don't you come inside? Harrison will be thrilled to see you."

"Oh, no. Andrea . . ." She trailed off not knowing what to say about Andrea.

"Oh, don't let Andrea scare you. I promise she won't throw any food or dinnerware at anyone. Everything's been explained. She's totally fine."

"Yeah. She said that."

Andrea. She seemed to fit in that garden room with Harrison and Kristin. How had Emma imagined that *she* could fit into Harrison's life? Her mom was in a mental institution. Emma was a dragon-drawing waitress.

"Hon, you look sick. Do you need some water?"

"Water. Right. There's water in the ocean. I'll go to the ocean." Emma turned and headed to cross the street to the beach. She didn't know why she didn't get into her car to leave, other than she felt unsafe to sit behind the wheel. Was this what an emotional breakdown felt like? Is this how it all started for her mom?

"Emma?" Kristin called after her.

She didn't turn back to face Kristin. Emma crossed the road, and on the other side, at the bike trail, she broke into a brisk walk until she was well out of sight of Harrison's sister. She felt better walking. When she reached the water, she took a deep cleansing breath. "I'm not crazy. I'm not my mom," she said to the waves and was relieved to find that the words felt true. She wasn't crazy, just stressed, overtired, and confused.

She'd gone for several minutes when she heard the smack of footsteps on the hard, wet sand behind her.

"Emma!" Harrison's voice.

She couldn't ignore him, not after all he'd done. She realized that she was going to be okay if he didn't really want to be with her. It would hurt, but she'd live.

He took a second to catch his breath. "What. Are. You. Doing?" Each word came like its own bewildered sentence.

"Look, Harrison, I'll make this easy," she said. "I know I'm a big hot mess right now with my whole family drama and everything, and I get that it's a lot to take in from a male perspective. Andrea said you were back together. I don't want to make things weird or awkward or anything. So you know, it was great. You were really nice to help me, though you probably shouldn't have kissed me if you didn't mean it, but—"

He grabbed her arms and pulled her into him, pressing his lips urgently against hers. Her legs nearly buckled with the intense flaring between them and around them until there was nothing but heat.

She forced herself to pull away before she became consumed into ashes. "What are you doing?"

He looked baffled and ticked off. "Did that feel like I didn't mean it?" he asked.

"No. I . . . I don't know." She couldn't answer because she couldn't think.

Harrison raked his fingers through his hair. "Look, I don't know what Andrea told you, but whatever it was, it obviously wasn't true. I told her that you were important to me. I explained that you would be at the anniversary party as my date."

"We haven't had a vocal conversation in days," she said. "You seem distant. It feels like you might have been avoiding me."

"I was giving you space! Trying to be respectful because of all you've got going on."

She frowned, trying to unknot the different emotions swirling inside her stomach. "But Andrea said—"

"Whatever she said," he interrupted, "you know in your heart isn't true. You know me. You know better. So what I'm not getting is why you're running away from me?"

Emma stared at him, believing his sincerity entirely, which left her with an important question. Why was she running? Was she ashamed of being a dragon-drawing waitress? No. Was she really worried that she didn't fit with Harrison? No, not when she looked at the situation honestly. Did she worry about being like her mom? Yes. That was the problem—the reason she didn't date, the reason she pushed people away.

But she wasn't like her mom. She knew that. Her little overreaction to Andrea and running off wasn't because she *was* like her mom, but because she was *afraid* of being like her mom—which was its own brand of crazy, admittedly, but not the certifiable kind of crazy.

Look around. Love is trying to catch you.

She gazed at Harrison, his chest heaving with the exertion of chasing her. Was she afraid because of her mom and dad and their relationship? Was she so insecure that she bolted at the first test of her faith?

"You're right," she said. "I'm sorry. You're right. It's just all this is so big and scary, but you're right, Harrison. I do know you. I've always known you. From the first time you offered to make a cut into the frog during our biology lab so I didn't have to. I'm sorry . . . I . . ." Emma thought of her fortune and Cái's smug grin. Love truly was pursuing her; she might not get another chance. It was time to stop running and let him catch her.

"I know you," she finished and grabbed at the collar of his button-down dress shirt, pulling him into another fervent kiss, a fire hotter than before, a melding between the two of them, a decision made and understood. She pulled away more slowly this time and looked at him with a small smile. "Yeah. That actually does feel like you mean it," she said.

She felt the warm whisper of his words breathed into her as he said, "All those years ago at graduation, I told you I loved you. I didn't think I'd ever see you again. But now you're here, and nothing's changed. I love you, Emma Armstrong."

No more fear. Not for her. "I love you too," she said.

Who would've guessed?

Cái really did have a magic restaurant.

And love had finally caught her.

Part Two

Love, Not Luck

One

Lucy Dalton stepped into The Fortune Café and took a breath of fresh air. Really, the breeze from the ocean outside the quaint restaurant's windows should have been fresh air, but not with Blake around. And he'd be rejoining her and her parents any moment now. Whatever was making her fiancé cranky clung to him like a fog that even the Seashell Beach breezes couldn't blow away.

Her mother touched her back, the light touch she'd used to say "I'm here" ever since Lucy was little. She turned for the hug Beth Dalton would give without being asked. Her mom smelled like Beautiful, the perfume she'd worn since forever. The scent soothed Lucy's frayed nerves better than a Xanax until a loud clatter sounded behind them, and they both jumped.

"Oh my gosh, I'm so sorry." A waitress, her brown eyes crinkled in major distress, bent to yank an overturned platter out of the way. "I've never done that before. It's lucky you moved right then, or you'd have sweet and sour sauce all over you right now." She restacked the tray while waving a busboy over to help her contain the mess.

"Lucky," Blake said. "Yeah. She's definitely that."

Lucy hadn't heard him come in. "Hey. You find a parking spot okay?" She looked past him for his parents, trying to gauge how many moments she had before they walked in and the tension ratcheted up again.

Blake nodded and jammed his fists in the pockets of his golf shorts. "We can't all find the spot closest to the door every single time, but I did all right."

It was a dig. *She'd* gotten a spot right by the door. For a split second she'd considered passing it up because she didn't want to annoy him, but her parents would have wondered why she was parking farther away.

Her dad cleared his throat, but her mom put her hand on his arm to keep him from saying anything. Lucy hoped her mom could read the thank you she was trying to send with her eyes. Her dad should probably be sainted based on how often he'd bitten his tongue since the Seftons showed up, but she needed her dad to keep the peace just a little longer. The Seftons would get on the road, and they could all breathe easier. The door opened again and admitted Deborah, looking like she'd caught a whiff of something rancid despite the hints of sweet and spicy wafting from the kitchen, and Calvin, tapping out something on his phone like he was trying to punish whoever the message was for with his angry fingers.

This would be so much nicer if Blake's parents hadn't come. Guilt churned her stomach for a second. The Seftons had decided to fly in for the venue walkthrough when they heard Lucy parents were driving up from LA. It was good they were taking an active interest, even if Lucy's dad looked like he wanted to choke Calvin Sefton every time he voiced an opinion. And Calvin had a lot of them, from how liberals were killing America, to how the sky was the wrong shade of blue in Seashell Beach. Seriously.

It's just wedding stress, she reminded herself. The Seftons would be different when the wedding was done. They all just had to get through it, and they'd settle down to a good groove with each other. Right now, the best policy was overlooking their . . . quirks and surviving the weekend without any drama. She smiled at the server, faking enough of her famous perkiness to set the waitress at ease. "No problem. Accidents happen."

The other girl's expression relaxed a fraction. "Let me get you guys to a table." She scooped up an armful of menus and led them to a table with an ocean view. Lucy thought she heard Blake's mom, Deborah, say something about "low rent" places, but Lucy took a deep breath and kept walking, glad her parents weren't close enough to hear the unfair comment.

The Fortune Café wasn't a Michelin-starred bistro with menu items she couldn't pronounce, much less pick out of a lineup. But the café wasn't trying to be that kind of restaurant. It was a sweet little place with an eclectic blend of beach chic and clean Asian lines that appealed to her need for order. The reviews had been outstanding, and she didn't feel like letting Deborah's snobbery ruin it for her.

Her stomach churned again. More guilt. Deborah was used to a high standard of living and always getting her way, but she'd had to make a lot of compromises for this wedding, namely not having any control over it. If Deborah indulged in some passive-aggressive remarks here and there—or even about every single thing they'd done so far that morning—Lucy would overlook it.

Blake had begged Lucy to let his mom do more, but as much as Lucy wanted to please her future mother-in-law, she couldn't let go of the reins of the most important event in her life. She spent all her time making other peoples' visions a reality in the opulent ballrooms of the San Francisco Duchess hotel as their staff event planner; there was no way she could give up control of her own wedding day and trust someone else to make her dream come true.

The waitress set their menus on the table. "My name is Emma, and I'll be right back with some ice water and hot tea while you look over our wine selection. Is there anything else I can get for you?"

The Seftons ignored Emma, but Lucy's parents assured her that water and tea would be fine.

Two minutes of quiet followed as everyone looked at the drink menu or their phones and tried to avoid conversation. So few of them had gone well today that Lucy couldn't blame them, but it was a loud silence. She rubbed her lucky jade pendant, hoping for some miracle that would allow her parents and her future in-laws to find common ground. If they didn't, the next couple decades could get sticky. Crap.

She wished she could go back out and breathe the ocean air for a minute. Apparently, fresh air for her was wherever everyone else was not.

Emma returned with a tray of ice waters and a hot kettle. The shuffle of everyone moving tableware around to accommodate the water glasses made the silence less painful. Deborah didn't even complain that the tea wasn't whatever brand she normally overpaid for at Teavana. Lucy patted the jade.

Emma rattled off the day's specials—both local fish—describing them so well Lucy had no idea how she was going to decide.

"This all looks good," Lucy's mom said when Emma left with a promise to return soon for their orders. Lucy appreciated the effort since her mom preferred Mexican food to Chinese.

"How does the song go? Try some of column A, try all of column B," her dad joked.

"Do they really have columns?" Deborah asked. Her mouth pinched as if she'd already tasted something bad as she picked up the menu to investigate.

"No, not really," her dad said, and it sounded an awful lot like he'd ground the words out through gritted teeth.

"I wish they did," Blake said. If only he'd interrupted to smooth the waters. But no. "This is all that pretentious fusion crap that you can't get away from in San Francisco."

"Damn straight," Calvin Sefton added. "None of these new 'chefs' are much more than cooks with ADD, and no one to tell them when an idea is bad. No one trains in the classic French tradition anymore. This place needs a Hubert Keller."

Lucy refrained from pointing out that a French chef doing Chinese food would definitely be considered fusion.

"I don't think that's what they're going for," her mom said, keeping her tone conversational. "And I see all my favorites here—mu shu, cashew chicken, beef, and broccoli."

None of those were her favorites, but Lucy appreciated her mother's efforts to calm the Seftons. Blake didn't.

"If you're going to make beef and broccoli, just make it. Why do you have to tell me it's actually handpicked broccolini harvested by little Enrique in the exotic fields of Santa Maria, who raised it from a seedling and cried when he plucked it from Mother Earth?"

Calvin barked out a laugh and slapped his son on the back. There was a flash of the humor that had drawn Lucy to Blake when he'd attended one of the swanky events hosted by his firm at the Duchess. But she didn't like the edge in his voice now. His sarcasm had outweighed his real jokes more and more lately.

She drew a deep breath. "It's got great word of mouth. I'm sure the lunch will be fine, and then we can spend the afternoon tackling the flower situation while the men golf."

The look on her dad's face almost made her laugh. It's how Yancey, her parents' beagle, might have looked when he had to get past Fluffers, the family cat, to reach his favorite chew toy. Her dad loved to golf, but the price of Calvin's company might be too high to pay for the opportunity.

The instinct to laugh faded. She'd wanted this weekend to be perfect since perfection was her niche, and she was having a hard time adjusting to the potholes they kept hitting.

It had started the moment the Seftons had climbed out of their huge Mercedes under the portico at the Mariposa Hotel. Blake had called to let them know they were pulling in, and she'd rushed down to meet the car, excited to begin showing them around. She'd been so sure Deborah would overcome some of her misgivings about the location once she saw it. She was wrong.

Lucy had dreamed about her perfect wedding since she was little, but Deborah had been dreaming even longer about the perfect wedding for Blake. And Deborah wanted a glamorous wine country setting, not a quiet, out of the way beach.

The complaints had started the second her foot had touched the concrete, always phrased so passive-aggressively that it was almost an art form. "Good morning, Lucy. Well, I'm sure your guests won't mind that there's no valet service here."

A valet hovered in the background, in fact. But Lucy had been so anxious to welcome them that she'd rushed forward to open Deborah's door herself. That was only the beginning. When they'd walked down to the small cove where the ceremony would be held, Deborah had kept her Tory Burch pumps on even after Lucy had offered to wait while she switched to sandals. Calvin had snorted, like the idea of owning sandals was ridiculous, and Lucy bit her tongue as she thought of her father's well-worn flip-flop collection.

Down on the beach when Deborah finally had to sit on a rock to dump the sand out, she'd watched it trickle out in a thin stream and said, "Sand has its own . . . charm."

Her mom had tried to run interference for Lucy all day. After the sand comment, she'd squeezed Lucy and turned her to face the ocean. "This is spectacular, and the only thing that could be more breathtaking is you standing in front of it in your wedding gown."

Even her mom was worn down by now. Lucy hoped the food would come quickly because it would be a miracle if a fight didn't break out over the ordering. "Blake, sweetie? Did you see the mu shu pork? Maybe they could put that in lettuce, and it will be like those lettuce wraps you like at the one place in Chinatown."

He set his menu down to stare at her, disbelief on his face. "Nothing in this place is going to be like anything in Chinatown."

"Which is fine," her dad said, his voice daring anyone to argue. "Is there anything you think you can tolerate on this menu, Blake? Maybe you should spend some quiet time studying it until you find it."

"Now wait just a minute," Calvin said, for once picking up on the mood.

"It's fine, Dad," Blake said, looking down at the menu. His tone was even, but the skin along his cheekbones had reddened, and Lucy's stomach clenched. Navigating this whole lunch was like steering the *Titanic*, knowing full well there was no way to get the ship off the iceberg that was sinking it.

Emma reappeared, and Lucy wanted to kiss her for the distraction. "You guys ready to order?"

"I suppose," Deborah said with zero enthusiasm.

"I'll have the lemongrass chicken," Lucy said. "It sounds good."

"It is," Emma said, her smile looking slightly forced in the face of Deborah's coolness. "It's a twist on the fried and breaded dish you'll find in most Chinese restaurants."

"Is this even a Chinese restaurant?" Blake asked.

"Fortune Café is . . . it is what it wants to be, I guess. And that's mostly Chinese food and whatever else sounds good,"

Emma said, her real smile back.

The rest of the table ordered without incident, although the Seftons sounded like they were requesting root canals.

Lucy wanted to keep Emma there forever so everyone would behave. The unofficial truce at the table was a bubble in her hand, ready to burst with one wrong move. But Emma left despite Lucy's telepathic begging, and she caught a look of relief on the waitress's face as she fled for the kitchen. Lucy couldn't blame her. She was surrounded by people she either loved or was supposed to love, and she couldn't understand how everything had gone so wrong.

She'd been drawing on her deepest reserves—the ones she had to rely on when she faced particularly difficult corporate customers at the Duchess—to navigate all the wedding logistics with her in-laws. It was hard enough pretending not to recognize Deborah's passive-aggressive comments, but Blake's mood had deteriorated as the day wore on. Instead of feeling like they were a team, Lucy had to spend more and more energy managing him.

And they still had a meal to get through. She'd expected wedding planning to be stressful, yes, but wasn't there supposed to be some kind of underlying joy?

"Excuse me. I left something in the car. I'll be back in a minute," she said, glad she'd insisted on driving separately from the Seftons. She didn't even care that it was an excuse as thin as a mu shu pancake; she needed a couple of minutes to compose herself before dealing anymore with Deborah's lemon face.

She reached her car and leaned against it, trying to sort out her head. She felt swampy, just a glob of sticky, unpleasant feelings, mainly toward Blake. This would have been a rough enough day if it was his first time acting like this, but it wasn't. Over the last couple of months this surly version of him showed up way more than the high-energy funny guy she'd fallen in love with the year before.

She'd seen this happen with some of her friends: wedding stress put everyone on edge, then the big day happened, it was beautiful, and everything settled back to normal. But she didn't remember any of her friends' fiancés staying in a permanent bad mood the way Blake was. Several times she'd gotten so tired of it she'd had to fight the urge to get up and walk out of whatever space they were sharing—his space or her space. The restaurant table with their parents, apparently. Shame she'd lost that fight.

She took a few deep breaths and focused on the objective for the rest of the afternoon: ignore Deborah's barbs, be patient with Blake's mood, and keep her dad from blowing up.

She rested her head on her arms on top of the car, glad she couldn't be seen from their table inside. She stayed that way for a minute or two, surprised that it helped to be still and quiet. The soft scuff of shoes on concrete sounded, and she looked up at her mom approaching, the worry her mom had been trying to hide all day written all over her face.

"You doing okay, sweetheart?" she asked, once again resting her hand on Lucy's back.

"I am," Lucy said. "I promise."

"This is not how you act when you're doing okay. Tell me what's going on."

Lucy sighed and turned to face her mother. "I'm sorry they're being kind of rotten. Deborah's still not over the location, and Calvin is . . . Calvin."

"And Blake?" Her mom said it carefully, the way someone might offer a breath mint to someone who needs it while trying not offend them.

"Blake," Lucy repeated, sagging against the car. "Blake is overwhelmed."

Her mom stepped closer and rubbed Lucy's upper arms like she had when Lucy had needed comforting after some kid trauma. "Is it the wedding planning? Or the wedding?"

Lucy shut her eyes as the words bounced around her head. *Is it the wedding? Is it the wedding? Is it the wedding?* Her mom had given voice to a fear that had been dogging Lucy for almost a month. What if this didn't get better after the wedding? And even scarier, why was it stressing him out so much? She was handling all of the details, so why was he getting more wound up the closer it got? She couldn't run away from the question with her mother asking it to her face.

"He's not like this, Mom. You saw how he was last summer." They'd been dating almost six months when Blake had told her he thought it was time for them to meet each other's families. They'd spent the Fourth of July with her parents in LA, oohing and aahing as the fireworks exploded over their neighborhood park and laughing around nightly meals of grilled carne asada from their favorite *carniceria*.

"Honey, I don't want you to think we don't like Blake. We do. I'm not comfortable with what we're seeing today, but we trust you. If this is what you want, I have no doubt you're making the right decision. I guess I'm just asking if you're sure."

Lucy straightened and smoothed her hair behind her shoulders, the fine blonde strands the same corn silk color as her mom's, sliding coolly over her fingers. "I'm sure. But I'm going to be really glad when this wedding is done and we don't have to stress about it anymore. I want my normal life back."

Her mom opened her mouth, closed it, and squeezed her arms again. "Nothing about your life has ever been normal, Lucky Lucy. And it doesn't have to be. Ready to go in and eat?"

Lucy eyed the restaurant door. "Ready as I'll ever be." And she hoped she had just told the truth.

Two

Emma was just arriving with their food when they reached the table. Emma set each dish in front of its owner, and everyone tucked into their lunches.

"This is excellent, sweetheart. Good choice," her dad said.

"I like mine," Calvin agreed, and the stress around her dad's eyes eased.

Maybe an afternoon of golf together would be doable after all. Deborah said nothing, which Lucy took as a victory, and she savored her next bite. It was as good as anything she'd had in the city.

"Mine tastes weird," Blake said, and Lucy's peaceful bubble popped. She rubbed her necklace, wondering what kind of luck it would take to turn Blake's mood around. It was rarely a conscious habit anymore, rubbing the necklace. She did it when something lucky happened, which it often did for her. And she rubbed it when she needed something lucky to happen, which it often would. And sometimes she rubbed it when she needed to steady her nerves, like now.

"Let me try it. Pork can be tricky." She speared a piece and took a bite. It was perfect, not fatty or dry. "What is it you don't like? It tastes pretty awesome to me."

His face darkened, and she tightened her grip on her necklace, the smooth stone warm from her fingers. The gold setting around the jade bit into her palm.

Suddenly Blake's fork fell to his plate with a clatter so loud that Lucy jumped, and her necklace snapped.

"You have opinions about everything," he said. "You want an opinion on the food at our reception, fine. But can we leave my lunch out of it today?" The plea was so tired she couldn't be angry despite her dad's reddening face.

She looked from him down to the stone in her hand, the one she'd worn next to her heart ever since her granddad had brought it to her after a business trip to China when she was twelve. She never took it off—had even chosen jade silk bridesmaids gowns to match it since she'd be wearing it with her wedding dress.

Tears pricked her eyes. She wasn't much of a crier, but she hadn't owned this necklace for sixteen years out of habit. It was like having her grandfather always near her, and staring down at the two disconnected pieces of the chain made him feel very far away.

She picked it up to study it more closely, mostly to avoid eye contact with anyone that might make her burst into tears. It backfired because now she could see that she had bent the setting too when she gripped it so hard. She sniffed. She couldn't help it.

Blake sighed and kept his eyes on his plate as he cut his pork into unnecessarily small pieces. "Does this have to be a situation? I'd love a drama-free lunch."

A dead quiet blanketed the table and he looked up, his eyes darkening as he saw the broken necklace in Lucy's hand and the tears trying to escape her. "Oh no. Can I see it?"

He held out his hand for the necklace, but she pulled her hand back. "No."

His eyebrow shot up at her terse answer. "I know you love that thing, but it's not an omen. I promise."

Her dad's hands curled into fists on the table, and he began to push himself up. "You don't underst—"

Lucy shot to her feet first, knowing her dad had hit his limit with Blake for the day. "It's okay, Dad. We passed a jewelry shop up the street earlier. I think those places usually do repairs. I'll drop this off, and when we get back Mom and Deborah and I can meet with the Mariposa catering manager."

Her dad eased himself back in his chair looking like he wanted to crush the table in the death grip he had on its edge, but he said nothing else.

"Go ahead and drop that thing off," Calvin said. "We'll finish up lunch."

"Lucy's not finished, Dad," Blake said.

His dad frowned. "She isn't eating anything anyway. She can grab something later if she's hungry. Let her go handle her necklace, and I'll settle the check."

Normally her dad would have waved him off and insisted on paying—he loved to treat people—but he only stared at Blake's dad in stony silence, and her mom made a subtle shooing motion.

"I'll be back in a few minutes," Lucy said, scooping up her handbag and escaping outside. On the sidewalk she straightened her Lily Pulitzer sheath, chosen to impress Deborah who had an eye for designer pieces. An odd hollowness had ballooned in Lucy's chest when the necklace broke, heightening every sound around her. It was fear, and it made no sense. Standing in the sunshine, she paused to take a couple more deep breaths. *It's a necklace, and it can be fixed. It's not an omen.* Blake's words didn't comfort her.

Anyway, maybe it *was* an omen. So what? She walked up Tangerine Street toward Spyglass Jewelry, feeling better for taking the steps. She was in control of this now, and she would make things happen. If it was an omen, she'd had a thousand good ones to this single bad one. Didn't everyone say she was the luckiest girl they knew? Something would happen to offset the broken jade piece, but it was smart to get it fixed quickly no matter what. She picked up her pace and pushed the door to Spyglass open with a sense of relief.

A woman her age looked up from behind the counter with a smile. "Hi. Beautiful day, isn't it?"

"Yeah." The weather was great even if she hadn't had three minutes of uncomplicated time to enjoy it. "Do you do jewelry repairs?"

"If it's fixable, I can do it," the woman said. "What can I help you with?"

"I just broke my necklace. It's got a ton of sentimental value, and I want to get it fixed as soon as possible."

The woman held her hand out. "Let me take a look."

Lucy tried not to fidget as she looked it over, turning it slowly to study it from every angle.

"What's your name?" the woman asked.

"Lucy."

"Hi, Lucy. I'm Stella. This is a beautiful piece."

"Thank you. Can you fix it?"

"I have a similar chain I could replace it with, so that's no problem. The setting will be a little trickier. I can do it, but if you want it done right, I need to take my time with it."

"I'd rather stay with this chain. I've had this since I was twelve. My grandfather gave it to me and nicknamed me Lucky Lucy. Ever since he did that, it's kind of come true. Using a different chain, even if was identical, wouldn't feel the same. Am I being insanely high maintenance?"

Stella smiled. "No. I can fix the chain too."

"Thank you so much. I go back to San Francisco tomorrow afternoon. Do you think you'll have it done by then?"

Stella was already shaking her head. "I have other orders I need to handle first."

"I'll pay extra," Lucy said, desperation licking at her and forcing the words out in a wheedling tone that made her cringe. *This* was high maintenance.

Stella's eyes softened, but she only handed back the necklace. "I'm so sorry. I know it's important to you, but I can't push other clients' work aside to get to it. I can recommend a jeweler in San Francisco."

Lucy took a step back from the necklace Stella held out to her. "I'm sorry. I'm really embarrassed at making it sound like I think my stuff is more important. This probably sounds like the dumbest thing ever, but I was down the street having lunch with my fiancé and our parents when this broke. It already wasn't going great and when this happened, it freaked me out a little."

"No need to apologize," Stella said, her smile back. "I totally get it."

Lucy had a feeling Stella really did understand why Lucy needed the necklace whole again, not an imitation of it. She took a deep breath. As much as she hated the idea of leaving the necklace four hours south of home, she wanted Stella and only Stella to do the repair.

"I'm a grown-up. I can wait."

"Go ahead and fill out this repair slip, and I'll give you an estimate on time and cost." Lucy filled it out while Stella scrolled through her computer. "I have a couple of complicated commissions to do first, but then I'll move this to the top of my list. Should only be a few weeks."

A few weeks? Lucy leaned her hand on the counter for support. *Weeks?* She wished she could snap her fingers and have it repair itself. She smiled at the thought. Some of her friends would have sworn that the jade piece *was* magic, but Lucy wouldn't go that far. There was no denying her long run of spectacular luck since Grandpa Max gave it to her, but to call it outright magic was too superstitious even for her, and that was saying something.

She left with Stella's assurances to restore it to as good as new and pushed back through the door of The Fortune Café, proud she only paused for a second to consider walking right past it, but she couldn't abandon her parents to Deborah and Calvin. Emma had delivered a small plate of fortune cookies. Good. She needed a pick-me-up.

"You okay?" her mom asked in a low voice when she rejoined them. Deborah rolled her eyes, which did not seem like the classiest thing in the world to do for someone who prided herself on sophistication. Lucy pretended she hadn't seen it and mustered a smile for her mom.

"Sure. It's just a necklace, right?"

"It's not," her dad said, squeezing her hand. "I know you love that necklace. And I know you feel like it's your good luck charm, but I'll make sure you have enough other good luck charms until you get it back. Start with this. I can tell it's the best one." He plucked a fortune cookie up and handed it to her.

"Watch this, Dad," Blake said, his first true smile of the day appearing. "We'll all get those lame 'advice' fortunes, and Lucy's will say something that actually comes true. It's wild, but it happens every time."

Even Deborah looked interested in that and scooped up a cookie.

"I'll start," Calvin said. "'The wise man hears more than he speaks.' That's not a fortune."

Deborah went next. "'Kindness is the greatest commodity.'" Another eye roll. "Maybe fortune means something different in Chinese."

Lucy couldn't help thinking that her future in-laws had gotten the perfect piece of advice for themselves if they ever bothered to listen.

Her mom cleared her throat and read, "'There is no greater treasure than the love of a child.' Well, that's the absolute truth. I'm a rich woman," she said, leaning over to drop a kiss on Lucy's cheek.

"Mine says 'Look no further than your own home to find your greatest gifts.' Sounds to me like whoever wrote these fortunes knows us well," her dad said.

Lucy snuck a glance at Deborah. Calvin wouldn't have caught the dig, but Deborah's eyes had narrowed as she tried to figure out if Lucy's dad had insulted her.

Yikes. Evasive maneuvers. She prayed her fiancé would cooperate. "What about yours, Blake?"

He scanned the slip from his cookie, his eyes widening in surprise. "Check it out. Mine says I'll get a promotion soon. This is usually the kind of fortune Lucy gets, and then hers come true. What does yours say, babe?"

Lucy pulled the slip from her cookie. "'True love is for the brave, not the lucky.'" More anxiety washed over her. It was the kind of fortune her friends had gotten by the fistful over the years, but not Lucy. Hers were always specific. She'd been told once that a large sum of money was coming to her, and the next week she'd gotten ten thousand dollars from a winning ticket she'd pitched in to buy to appease one of her staffers. Twice she'd gotten fortunes promising her promotions that came almost immediately. She'd even gotten a fortune predicting she would find love by nightfall, and three hours later she'd met Blake at the Duchess.

Blake laughed. "I guess I got your cookie. It's good to know you're human like the rest of us."

To get a generic fortune like anyone else's was more than a little disturbing, but Blake disliked her superstitions, and she wasn't interested in upsetting his first good mood in days. "Words to live by, I guess," she said, her smile still in place. She tucked the fortune into her wallet.

"You keep them?" Deborah asked.

"Yeah. She plays the lottery numbers on the back. She wins a couple hundred dollars at least half the time. It's crazy," Blake said.

"We better go," Lucy said, pushing back from the table, embarrassed that Blake had told Deborah she bought lotto tickets. It was just something Lucy did for fun with her staffers, but Deborah's expression made it clear that Seftons and those marrying Seftons did *not* play the numbers. Even more than wanting to make their appointment at their hotel, Lucy wanted to be done with this lunch. So, so done.

Back at the hotel lobby, the men separated to go change into their golf clothes, and Lucy took a deep breath before slipping each of her arms into those of the women beside her and plunging into a long afternoon as Deborah and the catering manager went the rounds.

She could *not* wait until this wedding was over and life got back to normal.

Three

Lucy had never been so glad to be at work than when she walked in Tuesday morning. The long weekend at Seashell Beach had defied the laws of physics. While the time with her parents had sped by so fast she was sure it was violating some of Einstein's principles, the same time with Blake's parents had dragged so slowly that she wondered if it were possible to age a lifetime in a single afternoon. But she was back at the Duchess, and this was her groove.

She'd bought a lottery ticket from the newsstand nearest her BART stop, and she scratched it off before officially starting her day. A couple hundred dollars to buy her staff lunch as a thank you for covering for her would go a long way toward restoring order to the universe.

The scratcher turned up zeros. She stared for a full minute before crumpling it and dropping it in her trash can. She drowned the lick of fear in her stomach with a long swallow of coffee and waded into her voice mail. The day would turn around. It always did.

Not this time.

It only got worse by lunch time. The Ladies of Nob Hill semiannual brunch was a disaster when the chairwoman wanted documentation that the poached salmon had been sustainably fished. The chef had no answer to that, and the one hundred person brunch was served without the premiere dish to the grumbling of the ladies present. But somehow it was the Duchess's fault even though documentation had not once been raised by the chairwoman during the menu selection weeks before. But these were ladies with a great deal of influence in San Francisco society, so Lucy sent several of her staffers on a desperate run to the flower market to gather bouquets for the women.

She'd presented them herself with her apologies. The brunch would now end up costing the hotel because the chairwoman felt they shouldn't pay for the fish, but Lucy could only hope the move with the flowers was enough to offset any complaints that might filter through the ladies' social set and put people off from future bookings. The hotel needed the opulent wedding receptions that came out of this bunch, and Lucy couldn't burn any bridges.

By the time her work day ended, she felt more like she'd just failed to broker peace with Sudanese war lords than like she'd managed the events office. A high-end luxury import company had hosted a preview for its biggest Bay area buyers and the A/V system had glitched so badly that the trainer had stormed off the stage in protest. And she'd had a cancellation for an event in the fall that would have earned the hotel into the six figures in revenue.

On that call, she'd reached up to rub her lucky jade to remind her that it was going to be all right and almost broke into tears when her fingers found nothing.

Now she was walking the two blocks to her apartment from her BART stop with her shoes in her hands because one of the heels had snapped off. She alternated between trying not to think too hard about what the stains on the sidewalk might be and trying not to cry.

When she limped into the vestibule of her building, it was all she could do not to collapse in front of the mailboxes and stay there until she mossed over. Instead, she fumbled her mail key from her purse and shoved it into her mailbox. It would no doubt be full of notices that owed money to the DMV or the IRS, but she'd drop them on her foyer table and deal with it later. This night called for crawling into bed for a *New Girl* marathon.

The mail key stuck, and she cursed. The refined ladies of the Nob Hill Society would have fallen over their perfectly sauced eggs if they'd heard the words coming out of her mouth, but she *did not care*. She couldn't take one more thing going wrong, and she would bend this mailbox to her will if it was the last thing she did. She jammed the key into the lock again and swore even louder when her hand slipped, breaking her middle fingernail. She stepped back and held it up to inspect the damage.

"Seriously, I said I was sorry about the milk delivery, but it wasn't my fault," a warm voice said from the lobby entrance. "No need to flip me off." It was her neighbor, Carter, and he approached the mailboxes with a grin.

She dropped her hand and laughed. "At least now you know how I really feel."

"What's up, Lucky Lucy? I feel like I never see you around anymore."

"Probably because I'm never around anymore," she said, barely stifling a sigh. "Wedding planning? Not my favorite."

"Even for the event queen extraordinaire, huh? If you can't hack it, the rest of us are screwed."

She smiled again. "Hack. Good word. I'm hacked off. I would like to hack a few people."

He stopped short and backed up, pushing his hair out of his eyes. On his best days it looked like a nest of vaguely related cowlicks, so it fell back exactly where it had been. "I'll just be going now."

"You're not one of them. Stay, get your mail, enjoy the lovely surroundings."

"How gracious of you. This must be why they pay you the big bucks."

Lucy only shook her head. Whatever tech thing he did paid him enough to live on the same floor of the medium-niceish building that she did, but he still liked to tease her about her "high roller job." Ha. It was a good job, one she could parlay into a great job, but not if she had too many more incidents like today. She'd parlay herself right into the street whether it was her fault or not. The thought depressed her again, and she decided her mail could wait.

"Where you going, Lucy-Lou?" Carter called after her, his brown eyes crinkling at the corners. "I'm not scaring you off with my bad luck funk, am I?"

It was a running joke between them. Carter had been a disaster since he'd moved in the summer before. Anything that could go wrong for him did. Broken pipes, missed deliveries, birds breaking his window, and a bedbug problem that never seemed to affect anyone else. All of those incidents had bypassed Lucy, but they'd still made her wary of pushing her own good luck too much by association. She hadn't said it in so many words, but one of her girlfriends, tipsy on wine, had told Carter all about Lucy's luck as they chatted over the balcony. He'd teased her about it ever since.

Lucy mustered another smile for him. "You're not scaring me off. In fact, you should maybe run from me. I've never had such a bad day at work."

"Sorry to hear that." He looked up from his envelope shuffling. "Want to talk about it?"

"Everything that could go wrong did, plus a dozen things that shouldn't have, all the way down to this." She stuck her broken nail up again.

"I said I was sorry."

"Sometimes a girl just needs to flip someone off, you know?"

"Yes. Do it again. I'll even act offended to make you feel better."

She lowered it instead. "I don't remember ever breaking a nail before. I'll have to cut them all off so they don't look completely stupid with one stubby nail. Or maybe I can get just one acrylic nail on Stubby for my wedding. Can you even do that?"

"Not my area of expertise, sorry. But I know a lot about being unlucky. I can tell you some of the perks."

"Yes, please," she said, realizing that more than crawling into bed, she needed a good laugh. "Meet you on the balcony?"

"See you there in ten."

"Deal."

He gave her a salute and headed up the stairs. She gave the mailbox a final try and got it open to find three bills. No party invitations or thank you notes or even really good coupons. Oh well. At least this day was almost over.

Lucy climbed to her third floor apartment and opened her door on the first try with a disproportionate sense of relief. What had her life become in one short weekend that opening a door lock without difficulty felt like a major victory?

Inside the door she dropped her new bills on the small accent table she'd found one weekend while hitting garage sales with her friends. They'd gone on a whim because none of them had done it since they were kids. While her friends all laughed at the kitschy stuff they found, she'd picked up this embellished table. Her friends had teased her for spending fifteen bucks on it, but she got the last laugh when it turned out to be an authentic Art Deco piece worth almost a thousand dollars.

Minutes later, in her comfiest pajamas, she slid open her back door and stepped out onto her tiny balcony. It was barely big enough for two chairs and a café table, but she loved it anyway. Any time the San Francisco fog lifted, she could see the Golden Gate Bridge, especially when it was lit up at night. It would still be a couple of hours before it shone, but sitting out here with Carter to make her laugh felt like a pretty decent consolation prize. Running into him at the mailboxes—minus the accidental flip off—was her first piece of decent luck all day.

He emerged on his identical balcony and smiled at her. "You didn't have to get dressed up on my account."

"Says the guy who lives in shorts and free T-shirts."

He looked offended. "Hey. I like—" he stared down at his chest, "Boom Tax. One of my favorite . . . programs?"

"You don't even know what it is?"

"It's one of my favorite programs," he said, his tone full of fake conviction.

"Tell me about them."

"Um. They will, um, see, you give them, um. I don't know what they do."

"Blow up your taxes, maybe."

"Like I need help with that," he said, and it made her laugh.

"Aren't you supposed to be out here telling me why being unlucky is going to be the awesomest thing that ever happened to me?"

"The perks are substantial. I'm not sure I want to share them. I don't want you in this club."

She shrugged. "I'm here for a while whether either of us likes it or not. Might as well show me around."

His sigh was the same sound Blake's mother had made at least a dozen times over the weekend. "Fine. First of all, it'll get you lots of women. They feel sorry for you, and it brings out their nurturing instincts."

"Not sure I need helping pulling chicks, neighbor. Got anything else?"

"Yeah. Free massages and new outfits are a pretty regular deal if you have bad luck. Every time you fly now, you're going to get picked for a TSA pat down, and the airline will permanently lose your luggage."

She tried to keep a straight face. "I'll stick with carry-ons."

"Doesn't help. They've lost my carry-on. Twice," he said, holding up three fingers and making her laugh again. "Just focus on the shopping you'll get to do to replace everything. Several times."

"That sounds pretty fabulous. What else?"

"I meet new people almost every time I leave the house. Granted, they're paramedics, but depending on how complicated the extrication is, they can be pretty nice."

"Extrication? What—wait. I don't think you're joking about that one." She'd seen him in an orthopedic boot and an arm cast at different points in the last year.

"I'm not joking about any of it. People really don't understand all the advantages of bad luck. It gives you super powers. Like all I have to do to make it rain is go on a bike ride, and it'll be pouring before I'm halfway done."

A bubble of laughter rose up in Lucy's chest. "Poor you."

"Poor me? Did I mention the increased popularity? Once people catch on that you're one of us, you're going to double your friend circle. They think it's super handy to have us around. Try going to the movies with your friends. If they get in a different ticket line, no matter how long it is, they'll get in twice as fast as you do."

By now, she couldn't stop laughing. "I get it, I get it."

"I didn't even get to your improved cardiovascular health because you will never get a close parking spot. Anywhere. Ever."

That one stung. She sat up. "I think I want out of this club."

"How'd you get in, anyway?"

Her hand crept up to the empty hollow at the base of her neck. She wondered if this felt a tiny bit like phantom limb pain. She couldn't process that her lucky jade was two hundred miles south. Today's string of crappy events was just an aberration, she knew. Everyone had bad days, even if she couldn't remember having one like this before. But she'd still feel better when her necklace was back. "Guess I just got lucky."

He choked on the drink he'd brought out with him. "Good one."

"Thanks."

He set the drink down and turned to face her, his shoulders squared like he was bracing himself to ask or tell her something, but his cell phone rang and a saved-by-the-bell look crossed his face. "Sorry, I might need to take this." He glanced down at the call display, and his eyes flashed almost as brightly as the glow of the screen. "Hello? Yes, this is Carter Mackey." He listened and his lips went from upturned edges to a Cheshire-level grin within seconds. "You're kidding. That's amazing. No, thank *you*. You won't be sorry."

Lucy wondered if she should step inside to give him some privacy, but Carter shot her a smile that suggested he had no worries in the world, least of all her presence on the balcony.

"Holy crap," he said when he hung up, and it was the exact same way she'd said it when she won the ten thousand dollar lottery.

"Everything okay?" she asked.

"Everything is beyond okay. What's the word for that?"

"Splendiferous?"

He made a face, but his grin wouldn't have come off with a jackhammer. "Less girly."

"Super fantastic?"

"Awesome."

"Stupendous?"

"Incredible!"

"Crazy cool!" she said, getting into the spirit.

"Life-changing!" he shouted and threw his arms in the air like he'd just won an Olympic sprint.

"Hooray!" she shouted back. "What are we celebrating?"

He shoved his hands through his hair. She hadn't thought it could look any crazier, but the strands poked out through his fingers like his hair had done meth.

"I can't believe it," he said, and his hair was a wild nest of exclamation points, testifying to his shock. "I won. I won!"

"What'd you win?"

"I pitched an idea for an educational app, kind of an interactive game version of the Khan Academy. I just got the grant that's going to let me work on it."

"Wow. I don't think I knew you did that kind of thing."

He smiled, and a look she couldn't read crossed his face. "I think there's probably a lot you don't know about me."

"Fair enough. And congratulations. Seriously, that's awesome."

"Thanks. I've developed at least a dozen apps that do all the new economy stuff like connecting users with services, and that's kind of fun. I know a couple of them have been great for small businesses. But I've been wanting to do something educational for a while now. I just couldn't afford to not work on the profit-driving apps while I developed it. Now I can get it done way faster and not stress about making rent."

"That's huge." Their medium-nice building by San Francisco standards meant they had really high rent. "Lucky guy."

"Yeah. I think I like this role reversal."

She smiled, glad for him but not able to say the same of their switch without it tasting like a lie on her tongue. "Your app will be amazing."

"You sound pretty confident for someone who's never seen my work."

She shrugged. "I know quality people when I see them. And quality people do quality work. It'll be great. And on that note, I think I'm going to go in and sleep off this day. See you around, Carter."

"See you around," he said, watching her more intently than usual.

She slid open her door and was halfway through it when he called her name. She poked her head back out. "Yeah?"

"It was great hanging out with you."

This time her smile came easily. "Yeah, you too." She closed the door and shook her head. It hadn't taken her long after Carter moved in to realize he was a lightning rod for bad juju to strike, and she'd always kept a polite distance, but her parting words to him were true. Her former bad luck neighbor had just become the only bright spot in her day.

Four

On Thursday, Lucy trudged home in even worse shape than she had two days before when she'd had to carry her shoes in her hands. She hadn't thought that day could be any worse, but Thursday was making Tuesday look like a good dream.

She reached the porch and stared up the five steps to the main door of her building. Might as well be Everest for all the energy she had. But if she didn't go up the steps, she couldn't fall into bed and let the huge tank behind her eyeballs drain its salty tears. She needed her bed for that—her bed and a full day off work. Or two. What was the standard amount of personal leave for someone who had just been dumped by her fiancé? Because right now staying in bed for the rest of her life sounded fan-freaking-tastic.

Borderline mental breakdown aside, no way was she going to stand on the sidewalk looking as blank-eyed as the street people who regularly wandered by. She forced herself up the stairs, counting them down like they were the end of her hundred daily crunches. "Four more, three more, two, one." She shoved her key into the lock and turned it. Nothing happened.

She held up the key ring and squinted. She'd definitely used the right key. She bit back a growl and inserted it again. It turned halfway then the tumbler resisted. What the . . .? After a dozen more attempts she let out a frustrated yell that made her look as crazy as Shoe Man, the homeless guy who staked out their corner and fondled the same old pink Reebok like a bunny for hours a day. She pounded the locked metal door with the side of her fist. It rattled and stayed locked.

For two seconds it felt good to lose control and hit it. Then it hurt like hell, and once the first tear leaked out, the tank broke wide open, and she sank down on the top step, too worn out to even make noise as she cried. She knew she should care about whether the tears stopped before one of neighbors came home. But she didn't.

She leaned her head against the wall and let them flow, too tired to hold her head up, too tired to even hold her eyelids. She had no idea how long she'd been sitting there by the time Carter called her name.

"Lucy? What's wrong? Are you hurt? Lucy?"

He stood at the bottom of the stairs, one of his hands reaching out like he was ready to brace her if she slid off the top step. She blinked and processed the question. Was she hurt? A laugh-sob escaped her. Yeah, she was hurt. But not how he meant.

"I'm not hurt," she said, and her voice came out thick and swollen.

He climbed up to sit beside her, careful to leave several inches between them, like he was approaching a wild animal he didn't want to startle. "You going to be okay?"

She liked that he hadn't asked her if she *was* okay. Just if she was going to be okay. Why did people ask if someone clearly in the throes of their world crashing down was okay? His was a much smarter question.

She hadn't answered it, she realized. "No."

He nodded. "All right. I'll just sit here for a while."

She shrugged. She had no energy for talking. She had no energy for moving, or explaining. She wished she had no energy for thinking, but Blake's face across the table two hours before played in her head on a loop.

She leaned against the wall again and tried to keep her mind blank, but Blake wouldn't stay out. His face popped up in every Blake-less image she tried to conjure, wearing the same sad expression he'd had at dinner.

Ocean waves? Blake in Seashell Beach appeared. Blue sky? Color of Blake's eyes. A flower? She could only see the pink peony that was supposed to have been in her wedding bouquet.

Supposed to have been. Past tense.

The tears fell faster, and she sniffed, the inside of her nose as sore as if it had been sandpapered.

Carter cleared his throat and spoke in that same don't-spook-the-wild-animal voice. "Can I do anything for you? Call your fiancé for you?"

And that did it. That turned the quiet tears into noisy, ugly sobs and pulled them right out of her—way scarier than any noise Shoe Man had ever made.

"Oh man, I'm sorry. What did I say?"

"Blake broke up with me tonight."

She heard a long intake of breath and then a quiet, "Damn." She could almost feel him thinking about what to say, but nothing came out of him. Instead he rested his hand against her back, light and steady, exactly the way her mom would have.

After a few minutes, she was able to breathe through her wet-sounding hiccups. "Sorry," she said once she thought her voice would stay even. It wobbled anyway.

"I appreciate that," Carter said. "I've been getting an epic number of dirty looks while I sit here. An apology is the least you can do."

She didn't smile. But she thought about it. She flashed him her broken fingernail, and he was the one to smile.

"I'm going to walk you up to your place now, okay? And then you can tell me who to call to come stay with you for a bit."

That finally made her smile. "I'm not a danger to myself, Carter. I just need to crawl into bed, let work know I'm not coming in tomorrow, and sleep for a couple of days."

"Uh, so parts of that sound healthy. The rest of it sounds like you really need to give me a friend's number so I can get them over here." He rose and held his hand out to help her up.

Standing so close to him on the top step, she was surprised by how tall he was. Most people were tall to her since she was only five feet three, but Carter had a slight build, at least compared to Blake's gym-sculpted muscles, and she'd thought of Carter as smaller. But he was maybe only an inch or two under six feet.

Six feet. Six feet under.

That's where she wished she was at the moment—not that she would be taking any steps to put herself there. But it sounded quieter and less painful than the here and now. Anger stirred inside her beneath the white noise of hopes collapsing in on themselves. She pushed deeper to find it and cling to it.

"The lock's jammed," she said. She wanted to pound the door again. And again and again.

Carter's key slid into the lock and turned easily. Of course it did. Why wouldn't it? Why would one single thing go right for her this week when everything had been going wrong since Seashell Beach?

She climbed the stairs behind Carter, concentrating on putting her feet in the right place, then plodded down the hall behind him. When they reached her door, he held out his hand. She looked at it, trying to understand its purpose lying there palm up in the space between them.

"Your key?" he said.

Right. She picked out the correct one, and he opened the door and followed her in.

"I'm serious about calling someone for you. Do you have any friends nearby who would come over?"

She pulled her phone from her purse and blinked at it, not even registering the crack she'd put in the screen the day before when she'd tripped over an extension cord at the Duchess. The contact list scrolled past, a blue blur. It stopped and she blinked at it some more. Sherri. Slade. Sophie. Spyglass Jewelry.

Spyglass Jewelry. More than sleep or a babysitter or her next breath, she needed her jade piece back. She'd thought it was like missing a limb, but it was more like missing an organ. She mashed the button, and relief crossed Carter's face.

The phone rang and rang on the other side before a voice mail message informed her that she was calling two hours after closing but that she could try again during normal business hours. "This is Lucy Dalton," she said, and Carter's eyebrow quirked like he was trying to figure out why she'd need to identify herself to any of her good friends by first and last name. "I dropped a necklace off on Saturday, my jade one. I was just wondering what the repair status was. Please call me back as soon as it's convenient." She left her number and hung up, not caring that it was days too soon for the jeweler to have gotten to it.

Carter pointed at the sofa. "Sit." She walked past him because her legs weren't going to hold her up much longer anyway, and he snagged the phone from her hand before she plopped herself down. "I've seen your mom here before, haven't I? Petite blonde, a slightly older version of you?"

She nodded.

"You guys seem to get along."

She nodded, tired now, wanting to leave her head down with each nod. "She's awesome, but don't call her. I'll be fine in the morning, and I'll tell her what's up when I don't sound like a wreck."

"You sure? I found her number."

"I'm sure. She's going to worry all night when she can't do anything about it. I just want to go to sleep. Can I have my phone back?"

He handed it to her. She dialed work to leave a message for the hotel manager that she would be out the next day. At the rate the last few days had gone, he'd probably be relieved anyway. When she hung up, she looked at Carter and blinked, surprised that she wasn't more surprised that he was still there. "Tomorrow or the next day, I'm going to think the me right now is really, really stupid. But the me right now feels as bad as I've ever felt."

He took the phone from her and set it on one of the sofa end tables. "Then the you right now needs to go to bed. Go. I'll let myself out."

She trudged to her bedroom door. "How are you going to lock it behind you?"

"I'm going across the balcony."

"Am I going to be able to argue you out of that?"

"Nope."

"Good night, Spider-Man."

He wiggled his fingers to shoo her toward her room. "See you in the morning."

He didn't though. When she stumbled out around noon with her eyes still swollen to slits, it was her mom waiting for her on the sofa. Without a word she collapsed next to her, and her mom gathered her into a hug so tight she couldn't breathe for a second. It made the world stand still.

Lucy curled up beside her and laid her head in her mom's lap, knowing her mom would sit and run her fingers through Lucy's hair, gently picking out snarls and smoothing it better than any conditioner.

"Why are you here?"

"Your neighbor called me last night from your phone. He explained the situation, and I grabbed the first flight out of LAX."

Lucy's eyes flew open. "I'm going to kill him. Don't you have the AP tests coming up? You didn't need to come up."

Her mom taught high school history, and the last six weeks before the AP tests involved intense review with her kids.

"This is more important." She stroked Lucy's hair. "He was on the sofa when I got here this morning. I guess he fell asleep keeping an ear out for you. Nice guy."

Prickles of guilt at the thought of Carter squishing himself into a sofa proportioned for her eroded the numbness she'd woken with.

She wasn't in the mood to feel, so she snuggled further into her mom. A half hour passed before her mom patted her back. "You need to eat. I'm going to whip something up."

"I'm not hungry."

"I don't remember asking," her mom answered in the tone that had guaranteed every chore of Lucy's childhood got done in the time and manner that her mom decreed. Her mom rummaged around the kitchen and within minutes the scent of sautéing onions floated out to the sofa, making Lucy's stomach grumble. Maybe she could handle breakfast after all.

"Mom? Thanks for coming. I'm going back to work tomorrow. You should too."

"We'll see how you're looking tonight. In the meantime, eat." She set an omelet down in front of Lucy. "I figured we'd better focus on protein because you're going to need some endurance for talking through this breakup."

Lucy nodded and ate, cleaning the whole plate. When she was done, she pushed it back and turned to face her mother who had waited quietly beside her. Lucy opened her mouth, and her phone rang. For a second, her stomach lurched. What if it was Blake? What if it wasn't? She snatched it up. Spyglass Jewelry.

"Hello?"

"Hi, this is Stella at Spyglass. I got your message last night. I'm sorry, but it's not done. It really is going to take at least a couple of weeks. I promise I'll call you when I start working on it so you know what to expect, okay?"

Her voice was gentle, and Lucy swallowed, feeling guilty for hounding her. "Thanks, Stella. I swear I'll be patient from now on. Thanks for calling me back. That was nice of you."

Stella assured her that it wasn't a problem. Lucy hung up and dropped her face in her hands. "Nothing's gone right since I broke my necklace, Mom."

Silence met that, and she glanced up to catch a look on her mother's face similar to the one she wore when grading her students' essays and not buying their interpretation of historical facts.

"Let's start with what happened last night," her mom said.

"Blake called me yesterday and said he wanted to go to dinner. He took me to our favorite café. I was going on and on about how good the stupid salad was, and then he said, 'We need to talk.' And since nothing good has ever followed that, I wanted to puke up the salad."

"Did you?" her mom asked, looking alarmed.

"No."

"Good. That would have been a waste, especially since the right thing to do would have been to throw any remaining salad at your fiancé."

"Mom!"

"I'm sorry, sweetie. I'm already breaking my own rules. It's hard to be nice when he's hurting you."

"You didn't like him?"

"We want whatever is going to make you happy. If that was going to be Blake, then we loved him."

"But I didn't make him happy. He said that he'd been unhappy for a long time. I told him that it would be a lot better when the wedding was done. A lot of the tension between me and Deborah would go away. But he said," and here she gulped, afraid that the next words would come out on a sob. She took a deep breath and tried again. "He said that he'd been unhappy before the wedding craziness started and that he didn't want to put either of us through any more of it. How could I not know that I was making someone I love unhappy?"

"Come here, baby," her mom said, pulling her back into a hug and rubbing her back. "You couldn't make him unhappy if you tried. You couldn't make anyone unhappy. You're not wired for it." She pushed Lucy away enough to fix her with a stare that wouldn't let Lucy look away. "What I noticed about Blake right away is that he's deeply unhappy in a way that some people are doomed to be."

Lucy couldn't make sense of the words. "I know he wasn't great this weekend, but you saw how he was last summer. Laughing, joking, having a good time with everyone. He's a life-of-the-party kind of guy."

"He is," her mom agreed. "And a lot of those guys need that, the constant party where he can shine. Every joke they make, every funny story they tell, is about keeping him front and center. I'd bet he doesn't spend a lot of time alone, does he?"

No. He didn't. Whether it was going to the gym or buying groceries, he liked her right there with him. "I think that's pretty normal for two people who love each other, right?"

"It can be. But you have to add up all the parts to see the whole. Dad likes to do stuff with me because he likes my company, not because he dislikes his own."

"Then why would he break up with me? Wouldn't it make more sense for him to stay in a relationship?"

"Maybe. Except you have such a strong sense of self. I think that started coming out more and more as you got into the wedding planning."

Lucy stiffened. "You're saying I railroaded him?"

"No! Oh sweetheart, absolutely not. I think he realized you weren't going to disappear inside this marriage, but that's a good thing."

Lucy rubbed her palms into her eyes. "How did I get it so wrong?"

"Well . . . he's a pretty good-looking guy," her mom said, mischief twinkling in her eyes. "You wouldn't be my daughter if you didn't have an appreciation for that kind of thing."

Lucy laughed for the first time in hours even though it hurt her throat. "You're awful."

"Maybe. But this is my advice for any future relationships. If he's pretty, keep him around for a while to look at, maybe a little longer if he makes you laugh, but if the guy isn't the kind you would let hold your hair back while you're vomiting at two in the morning with the flu, cut him loose sooner than later, okay?"

Lucy's smile faded. "I can't even imagine a future relationship. I can't even process that I'm not in one at the moment. Yesterday I was, and now I'm not."

"Blake's not a bad guy. Just an unhappy one. You're definitely going to find a guy who is happy to be with you." Her mom patted her leg and stood, gathering up her dirty dishes and depositing them in her tiny kitchen. "I'm going to jump in the shower. Then you're going to take a shower. And while that happens, I want you to think about what's most upsetting to you about this engagement being called off. We'll go for a walk and talk some more."

Lucy nodded. She couldn't think of anything she wanted to do less but needed to do more. An hour later, she emerged from her shower feeling about twenty percent more human, mainly from washing gallons of dried tears off her skin. Lucy decided on Golden Gate Park for their walk because Blake, for some perverse reason, had hated it. She and her mom sat on rocks in the sunshine, and Lucy talked. And she talked. And the longer she talked, the more of her frustrations with Blake flooded out—the way he always decided where they would eat because he had more "food moods" than she did, the way he told jokes as if he'd practiced them for maximum effect, the way he'd refused to take sides between her and Deborah, saying they'd have to figure out how to work with each other.

Her mom listened through it all without interrupting. When Lucy finally wound down, she sat quietly as her mom scrunched her forehead and thought hard for a minute. "I thought the wedding planning was getting to me too, but maybe I just . . ."

Her mom waited and when Lucy didn't finish, she rested her chin on her hands and smiled at her. "You never answered the question back at your house. What bothers you the most about the engagement being called off?"

"What doesn't?" Lucy asked on a groan. "A massive amount of work went into this. I'm going to lose some deposits. My friends are going to pity me, which is never fun."

"How do you know?" her mom asked.

"How do I know my friends are going to pity me?"

"No. How do you know how it feels? Have you ever been in a position where people would have a reason to pity you?"

"Of course I have. Everybody has."

"Name it," her mom said, a small smile playing around her mouth. "Name the time when people pitied you."

But Lucy was stumped. There had to be something, of course. Right? Who didn't have incidents like that? But she couldn't think of a single example. "I'm drawing a blank."

Her mom's smile widened. "I kind of thought you might." She scooted over until she could put an arm around her daughter and press Lucy's head down to her shoulder. "You've had a pretty charmed life." Lucy started to lift her head and object, but her mother held her head in place. "That's not to say you haven't worked hard for everything you have. And you deserve every bit of it." Lucy quit straining and leaned into her mom, comforted again. "The truth is, though, you haven't had anything really hard happen to you since your grandpa died. And in my heart of hearts, I've always believed when the first big challenge of your life came, you'd rise up and meet it, but there's no way to tell until it happens."

She dropped her head against Lucy's, and the vibrations of her next words traveled down through Lucy's skull and shivered her spine. "It's here, Lucy. The hardship that's going to test your mettle and show you who you really are. It's here. So the question is, what are you going to do about it?"

Lucy ran the question through her mind, feeling out the truth of her mom's observation. It felt pretty damn true. Yes, she'd run into obstacles in her job and other things, but she'd never for a single second doubted that things would work out. And they always did. Hard work and luck tended to go like that.

But hard work couldn't fix this. And her luck was long gone. So what was she supposed to do? Tears stung her eyes again, and she straightened, refusing to let them fall. What she would *not* do is sit around feeling sorry for herself. "I'm going to wash that man right out of my hair?" she said, quoting the song she'd sung when she'd won the lead in her high school production of *South Pacific*.

If relief had a sound, it would have been the musical scale of her mom's laugh. "That's what I figured. None of the reasons you listed for regretting that breakup had much to do with Blake and missing him or loving him. This is a good thing, even if it doesn't feel like it." She patted Lucy's thigh, and it was more reassuring than hot coffee on a foggy San Francisco morning.

"It's not that easy, Mom. I already miss him. I mean, the last few months weren't great. But it's not like I fell for him for no reason. He was pretty amazing when I met him. Funny and good-looking, ambitious, smart. And he's been a big part of my life for the last year and a half. Now he's not going to be in it at all? I can't just snap my fingers and be okay with that ending by bed time."

"Of course not. But when you say he was funny, did he make you laugh?"

"Yes."

"But when it was just the two of you, and he wasn't trotting out one of his perfectly polished jokes, did he make you laugh? Don't answer," she said, holding up a hand. "Just think about that for a while. And when you find the answer, ask yourself what you're really missing."

Lucy sighed but nodded.

"Good. Now. The plan. I'm going to get you jump-started." With that she pulled her cell phone out and made a call. "Carter? It's Beth Dalton. We're on."

Five

Her mom wouldn't give up any details on the way home. All Lucy could get out of her was her mom's opinion that Carter was a really nice guy.

When they reached the front stoop, he was sitting there waiting for them. He smiled at her like it was a normal run-in and not like he'd slept a whole night on her couch because she was a crazy person. "Hi. You probably don't know this about me, but the whole reason I moved here last year was because I was getting away from a bad breakup. So I've got ideas for your plan."

"I have no plan," she said. What was going on? It felt like being on a moving carousel without anything to hold on to. She was keeping her feet, but barely.

"Not yet, but your mom says you plan like a boss, so I'm sure one will kick in. I'll just give you something to start with."

Her mom squeezed her arm. "I know you love a good plan, and Carter's is great."

Lucy rubbed her temples. "It's okay. I can think of my own. It'll just take me a day or two. And I don't want you sticking around until then. I'm so thankful you came up here, but I want you to go back to work, Mom. You can go home tonight if you want to because I'm absolutely going to be fine. Here's what I know so far: in a disaster, I'm not a pouter or a whiner. I'm going to be a doer. So I'm going to work tomorrow, and you should too."

Her mom smiled. "Love the can-do attitude, daughter. Carter, you ready to take over on Friday?"

Lucy shook her head. "That's another thing. Carter, you don't have to babysit me. I can do this."

"I'm not babysitting you. You're more like a mentoring project."

"You're going to train me to be an expert in bad luck?"

He grinned. "No, even better. I seriously have the perfect strategy for getting over a gnarly breakup."

She rolled her eyes. "You going to write me an app or something?"

His expression grew thoughtful. "Now that you mention it . . ."

"Mom, make him stop."

"Sorry, honey. I approve his plan."

"No one's telling me what it is."

Carter smiled. "You'll find out when you get back from work tomorrow. In the meantime, enjoy your day with your mom." He waved and headed up the stairs.

Lucy gave up. "Can you at least tell me the plan for the rest of the night?"

"Lots of chocolate, watch *Just My Luck* for the billionth time, and then more chocolate. Or maybe ice cream. No, both."

"Make all Carter's plans be about chocolate too," Lucy said, already heading in to dig up her copy of the old Lindsay Lohan movie she'd loved since college. Her real life had no resemblance to anything Lohan, but she'd always seen a ton of parallels between herself and Ashley Albright, the movie's main character who lives a charmed life until all her luck goes bad. She'd just never shared the *full* experience with Ashley until her jade necklace broke. And if given the choice, that's definitely where she'd have drawn the line at life imitating art.

The next day at work was hard, but Lucy survived it with a pasted-on smile and vague excuses about food allergies to explain her slightly puffy eyes. Nothing bad had happened at the Duchess, and given the last few days, she'd count it as a victory.

When she got home, she found Carter sitting out on the steps. "I'm going up to bed," she said.

He caught her wrist in a grip light enough to break with a tiny tug. "You can't. It's time for my plan. Sit."

She sat. "You're absolved, Carter. I hereby emancipate you."

"Sorry, you don't have the authority. Only your mom can fire me or otherwise remove me from duty."

"She stuck you with a bad job. Why would you even say yes?"

"It's at least six weeks until the funding comes through for my math app, so I need a fill-in project." He rested a hand on her shoulder and gazed deep into her eyes. "Thank you for saving me from boredom, Lucy."

"Knock it off," she said, as she pushed his hand aside, but she barely smothered a laugh. "Do I get any details today?"

"Yes. Today is the first day of the Take Your Mind Off Of It Rampage."

"Do I get a T-shirt for playing?"

"No."

"Then I don't want to do it."

"Sure you do. You get something way better than a T-shirt. Revenge."

Lucy's eyebrow went up at that. "Tell me more."

"You ever hear that expression that the best revenge is living well? That's what you're going to do. Flake is going to wonder if you even miss him."

"Blake," she corrected him.

"That's what I said. Flake."

That made her grin. "What's step one?"

"Food. It makes everything better, and that goes double for good food. We're going to the corner market and picking out at least five things you've never tried, and we're making them for dinner."

"If I haven't tried it, how do I know if it's good food?"

"I'm a good cook. We'll make it work."

"I'd rather just grab Italian. Then I *know* I'll like it."

Carter nodded, like he was considering that option. "You want to know something about you? You come off as carefree but careful, like you're happy as long as everything is going according to plan."

"There's nothing wrong with that," she said, surprised that he'd noticed that about her. "People say I'm lucky, but they don't realize how much of that comes from hard work and careful planning. You get extremely lucky when you live like that."

"Yeah, like that Edison quote? 'The harder I work, the luckier I get'?"

"Exactly, smarty pants."

"I'm not that smart. Statistically it was going to be Edison, Einstein, Lincoln, or Twain. Try this quote: the secret to happiness is goofing off in your kitchen with stuff from the corner market and no real plan."

"Abraham Lincoln?" she guessed.

"Eleanor Roosevelt. Can I trust you to go in and change into something that is not flannel, or do we need to go straight to the store?"

She looked down at her wrap dress and heels. Not exactly slumming-at-the-market clothes. "I'll change."

"See you in fifteen?"

She nodded and climbed to her feet, unsure how he'd convinced her to go along with his plan. Two flights of stairs later, she walked into her apartment to hear a Skype alert from her mom. She answered and smiled at the sight of a David McCullough book thick enough to brain a yeti sitting beside her mom. "*Truman* again?" she asked, squinting at the spine.

"It won't be the last time, either," her mom said. "How are you doing?"

"Hard day, but I survived. And if I get through tonight with Carter, I'll do it again tomorrow."

"That's my girl. What are you doing with Carter?"

"Going on some sort of fun-having rampage that will fix all my problems. But I'm overdressed," she said, glancing down at her dress. "I have to change." She signed off with a promise to call if she got too sad and went to her room. She eyed the bed, wishing she could collapse on it and stay there until approximately December, but she didn't figure either her mom or Carter would let her get away with that.

She stared at the closet for a minute, trying to figure out exactly what one wore on a rampage. She'd spent a lot of time and money investing in high quality wardrobe pieces that would translate well from working with corporate event planners to evenings out with Blake at his cocktail parties. He liked when she played up her femininity, calling her his pocket girlfriend and his doll.

Why had she ever thought that was cute?

She must have let it slide because he also seemed to have a healthy respect for her intellect, but . . . doll?

She shuddered and pulled out something far more casual than Blake would have liked. His idea of dressing down was a collared shirt with a tasteful Tommy Bahama print. Deborah had probably never taught him to even dress himself in the kind of shirt he could pull over his head.

Carter always dressed for comfort, and as she slipped into a tank top she normally wore for yoga, a pair of shorts that were the veterans of countless washings, and flip flops, she decided Carter was onto something, and Blake, with his stupid button downs, was an idiot.

A knock sounded on the front door, and she opened it to Carter.

"You ready?" he asked.

She took a deep breath. Yeah, she wanted to be done with his self-pity more than Truman had wanted to be done with Stalin. "Let's go shop for our dinner abomination."

♡ ♡ ♡

Fruits in sizes and colors she'd never imagined filled produce tables in lush pyramids. She picked up something that looked like a spiny lemon crossed with an anemone and sniffed it. "How can this even occur in nature?" she asked, turning it over.

"That's a dragon fruit," Carter said, taking it from her hand. "Maybe it didn't occur in nature. Maybe it's actually laid by a dragon."

"You're a dork."

"Hardcore, and I don't deny it. Check this out," he said, setting the dragon fruit down to pick up a squash, a green one with a neck that curved over on itself. It looked like the offspring of a swan and a hand grenade.

"What is it?" she asked.

"I have no idea," he said. "We're definitely getting it."

"I guess we can always Google how to cook it. You know, right after we Google what it is."

"As long as it's a squash, we can work magic on it with enough butter and brown sugar."

"And if it's not a squash?"

"Then I still don't see a problem. Butter and brown sugar. What else do we need to know, really?"

The rest of the time in the store went like that. By the time they reached her apartment, they had gone way over the five unknown foods goal, but she was far more worried by the partially open front door that greeted her. Carter stepped in front of her and handed her the grocery sacks. "You locked up?"

She nodded, her heart pounding.

He pushed the door wider and called, "Hello?"

Someone answered from inside, which in a weird way made her feel better. A robber wouldn't answer back, would he?

Carter stepped in and poked his head back out a minute later to gesture her in too.

She walked in to get an eyeful of the building manager's plumber's crack. She squeaked. The manager, John, grunted but didn't look up from where he was prying away drywall near her baseboard.

"We had an incident while you were out. Got a call from 2B below you that they had some water leaking from the ceiling."

"I've only been gone an hour," Lucy said.

"Pipe leak," Carter said. "It's probably been going on for a while."

"How do you know that?" Lucy asked. "He hasn't said what's going on yet."

"Had one last year. Even in a well-maintained building like this, sometimes the old pipes will do their thing."

John heaved himself to his feet. "Yeah, looks like this one's been going for a couple days at least. The only reason it's not worse is because the unit above you has been empty for two weeks. Lucky for you they weren't up there running water every day or your place would be the new third floor pool."

Lucy looked down at the pieces of drywall littering the floor. "Yeah, lucky," she echoed, wondering when that word had come to mean something so different in her life. "I guess if that's the worst of the damage then you're right."

John snorted. "Nah, that's just the start. We've got to tear out the drywall all the way up to the ceiling so they can replace the pipes. Then they'll have to repair it. And I'll have to shut off the water to the unit while they do the repairs, but that won't be before tomorrow. But it could've been worse." He knelt back down and resumed whacking at the wall.

Lucy's grip on the grocery sacks loosened, and an ostrich egg nearly paid the price, but Carter snagged it before it hit the floor.

"Lucky catch," he said, straightening and lofting the bag to show her it was safe.

"Yeah, lucky," she echoed for the second time in minutes.

"We're not going to be able to cook in here tonight," he said, flinching when an extra hard whack sent a piece of wall flying. "Better cook at my place."

"What are we making again?" They had a scaly green thing, persimmons, red bean paste, and a lettuce she never heard of. "Mishmash Surprise?"

"Let's just call it the chef's special."

He took the bags back, and Lucy followed him next door. "I've never been here before," she said, stepping in to check it out.

Blake's place looked like Deborah had copied it straight from a GQ article on "Contemporary Furnishings for the Modern Man," because she had. Dark leathers, square angles, perfectly on trend gray walls hung with expertly spaced photographs of vintage cars shot from artsy angles.

She didn't figure Carter's place would be anything like that, but neither did she expect to step into his living room and feel like she'd been swallowed up by the world's most comfortable library. She'd thought she might find his bike hanging on the wall and an IKEA desk full of computers, cables, and papers, but instead she met two walls full of bookshelves. A big corduroy sofa sprawled in the middle of the room. He even had potted plants—herbs, it turned out, when she wandered over to investigate.

"I like your place," she said. A muffled thump sounded from her apartment, and she winced. "I can't believe they have to tear my wall out. The streak continues."

"You thought that was bad luck? Nope, it was good luck. Now you get to repaint it any color you want."

"I could have done that before."

"Yeah, *you* could have. But now you can make John do it. See? Good luck. Now let's cook."

An hour later, her side hurt from laughing over Carter's beyond stupid narration of their food prep, *Iron Chef* style. "He rips the guts from the green thing like he's taking its smell personally."

"That squash is never going to mess with you again." She stared down at its stringy guts spread over the counter. "Actually, I'm totally creeped out now. I'm going home." Another loud bang sounded next door. "Never mind."

"Remember, your mom said you have to go along with my plan," Carter said, as if that were totally normal.

"Carter? I can't even believe I have to say this, but it's possible she's trying to set us up."

Carter's brow wrinkled. "That's too bad. I want your mom to like me, and I already have to disappoint her."

"Good. I mean, not that I want you to disappoint her. Good that we're on the same page about not dating."

"I definitely don't want to date you, Lucy-Lou," Carter said, a statement that managed to reassure and peeve her at the same time.

"Why not? Am I suddenly un-dateable now too?"

He rolled his eyes. "Do you want me to want you or to not want you?"

"Us dating is a terrible idea. I'd just like to think at some point when I'm not a mess that I may be considered worth asking on a date again."

"You're dateable. In fact, I was getting up my nerve to ask you out last fall when you showed up at the mailboxes with an engagement ring on your finger."

The tips of his ears turned red. He got busy chopping vegetables, his knife flying so fast it was almost a blur. Lucy had to duck a piece of squash, but Carter didn't notice. He'd wanted to ask her out? She did an accelerated slide show of the times she remembered interacting with him. She'd never gotten a vibe that he was interested. He'd always been friendly and talkative but not in a flirty way.

She didn't know whether to comment on his admission or move on to something else, and just as she was about to open her mouth to find out what would come out, he spoke again. "Did you ever notice how much time I spent out on my balcony?"

"Not really?" she said, not sure what answer he hoped to hear.

"Good," he said.

"I mean, it seemed like I was always running into you out there, but I thought you were digging the view. I was out there a lot the first year after I moved in too."

"Hi, my name is Carter, and I'm an underachieving stalker."

"I guess if waiting for me to wander out on my balcony was the worst you did, that's not so bad." The tips of his ears were still red. "In all honesty, if I wasn't already dating Blake, I'd have probably wandered out on my balcony to see if my cute new neighbor was on his." She bumped him with her hip. He smiled.

"Dating who?"

"Blake."

"Who?"

"Blake," she repeated, a little louder.

"Who?"

She grinned. "Right. No one."

"*Now* you're understanding how the Rampage to Take Your Mind Off It works," Carter said. "I need all your attention on the recipe and none on Flake. Deal?"

"I live to cook."

"Good. Let's throw this together and see what happens when we add a little heat."

Blake would have made that sound flirtatious, and she wondered how she'd never noticed how rehearsed his lines were before. Blake was an A + B = C kind of guy. Flirt *this* way, girl reacts *that* way, the result is a hook up or a date or whatever Blake was angling for. He was like that about everything; he approached every situation with an outcome in mind and a plan for achieving it. It had made him excel in business. In a lot of ways it had made them a good fit. She was a big believer in planning like crazy and getting a predictable result. Predictability got a bad rap, and it shouldn't. It's why she'd been so successful too.

Carter had been rummaging around in his cupboards and turned to face her, holding plates and bowls. "Time to eat."

She helped him set the table for two, aware that somehow doing this here with Carter seemed way more intimate than the dozen times she'd cooked for Blake at her place, probably because she was hyperaware of the new surroundings.

Fifteen minutes later they'd decimated the food. She groaned. "I'd lick the plate, but I scraped it clean."

Carter only gave a sleepy grunt that made her smile. A couple minutes passed before he found the energy to push himself to his feet. "My stomach says as far as rampages go, Achievement Unlocked."

"Thank you, Chef Neighbor."

"You made at least half this dinner."

"No, I mean for taking my mind off of things. I know I've got some rough days ahead, but thanks for helping me through this first part. They say the first seventy-two hours determine how the rest of your breakup goes."

"I think the seventy-two hour thing is for kidnappings. Or solving murders, maybe? But not breakups. You'll need more time than that. We've got rampaging left to do."

"Rampage sounds so violent. I mean, it makes sense as a guy thing to do, but I think I want to name it something more feminine."

"Girl words are all too nice for the amount of getting-it-out-of-your-system that's called for here."

"I was thinking maybe I should call it the binge-and-purge. You know, binge on fun things to purge Blake out of my life."

"Who?"

She smiled. "Right."

"Wrong. About the name. I'm the expert. Your name idea is disturbing, and we're sticking with the Rampage."

"Moot point. I don't need more rampaging anyway. But thank you. This was so much better than staying in."

He gathered up the plates and headed to the kitchen. "Don't get up and try to come do dishes," he called over his shoulder as she stood to do exactly that. "Also, the Rampage can't be over. I figured out great stuff to do when I was outrunning my issues last year, and you can't be done until you cross them all off your list too."

"I *can't*," she repeated, and the note of warning in her voice stopped him cold.

"Let me rephrase that. You can do whatever you want. But if you want a tried and true recovery plan, I'd strongly advise you to finish the Rampage."

She had a plan for emotional recovery she'd been working up between putting out fires at work earlier. It involved soul searching and listening to soothing music, self-betterment, reading a few classic novels, and vigorous exercise. "What does the rest of the Rampage involve?" she asked, nearly comatose just thinking about her plan.

"Tomorrow it's eating at Emmy's Spaghetti Shack, and next Saturday it's going to the Exploratorium."

"Those sound like things for little kids."

"What's your point?"

She laughed. "No point. Let's do it."

"I don't hear any more thumps next door. You're probably safe to go burrow now if you want."

"That's allowed during the Rampage?"

"It's inevitable. And it's kind of good to have the moments of self-pity, so you can contrast them to how much better you feel when you're not burrowing." He walked her to his door. "Want to knock on my door when you get home tomorrow?"

She nodded right as her phone beeped with a text from her mom. *Did you hang out with Carter?!*

She held it up for him to see. "Notice she didn't ask if I'm okay? Or how I'm feeling? Just if I hung out with you. I'm not kidding about my mom trying to fix us up."

He shrugged, his smile real and easy. "I don't do rebounds. So this is me helping out my neighbor while I wait for funding to kick in on my new development project. If you're okay with me using your crappy situation to drag you out of the house and entertain myself I guess we're even. You know, in the interest of full disclosure."

"Sounds fair to me. See you tomorrow."

"Looking forward to it."

She slipped out, surprised to realize that she was too. A lot.

Six

Lucy glared at Carter, who was holding his sides and laughing. She poked him, hard. "This isn't funny."

The light wind got extra playful with her hair, and she pushed the strands out of her face to glare again, but it didn't help. Carter was almost wheezing by that point.

He tried to stop long enough to check on her. "You didn't hurt anything, did you?"

"My pride. I think I gave a pigeon a heart attack. What have I become that now I'm spending my afternoon terrorizing birds?" She redirected her glare to her rented rollerblades. "This is your dumbest idea so far. Who even rollerblades anymore? Why did I let you talk me into this?"

Carter only laughed harder, and she shoved him. "Sorry," he gasped. "It's just . . ." And he quit talking so he could do an imitation of her from three minutes before, his arms flailing while his feet competed to take him different directions. That's probably what his imitation of a kitten on roller skates would look like too. She'd never understood how fast breakneck speed really was until she, in fact, felt in danger of breaking her neck. She clenched her fist a couple of times, trying to figure out how much it would hurt her if she punched him for real, but he let out a high-pitched whine that was such a spot on imitation of her that it broke her, and she collapsed on the grass in giggles. He dropped down beside her.

"I didn't sound like that," she said between gasps of air.

"You did," he said, his voice strangled with more laughter.

"I hate you."

"You love me. Who else buys you spaghetti meatballs as big as your head?"

That was true. On the night Blake had dumped her, she'd been overwhelmed by how her structured life had suddenly become riddled with holes where Blake was supposed to be. She'd dreaded having to go through that initial stretch of time without him. All the time they used to spend together would be hers to spend alone.

Alone.

She didn't do alone. And when she'd thought about how long that aloneness might stretch into the future, it had made her ill—pounding head, churning stomach, the works.

But Carter had come around every day that she let him, pulling her to this museum or that gallery, or this weird little shop, or that hole-in-the-wall restaurant. When she'd complained that her waistband couldn't survive any more food adventures, he'd decided they should rent rollerblades and sacrifice themselves to the gods of stupidity.

She'd still noticed Blake's absence, but in ways she didn't expect. She hadn't realized how much energy she'd spent in managing him and his moods. Or how much brainpower went into making everything perfect for him. She'd seen it as a challenge, an extension of the work she did at the Duchess, another chance to flex her skill set.

Running around and doing things with Carter just because they were there to be done had made her realize how little downtime she'd had from her work mode. Even the socializing she and Blake had done had mostly revolved around him networking, buttering up new clients, or schmoozing for work.

Carter shifted beside her, lying back on the grass with his arm over his eyes to shade them. The smile still playing around the corners of his mouth wrung a return smile from her, even though he didn't see it. She stretched out too and stared up at the blanket of blue above her, unbroken by clouds.

Carter was all about the hard work of playing. For three weeks now, these adventures with him had made everything bearable because she could forget it all. She could forget that work was still going wrong as often as it went right, that her kitchen had only barely been patched up, that a hundred things fell apart each day until Carter whisked her off to play.

But it was going to catch up to her. At some point, the sheer suckiness of the situation, all the feelings she hadn't worked through about Blake, were waiting to come crashing down. She couldn't outrun them forever, and it didn't seem fair to hang on to Carter and let him drown too. She didn't know when it would happen, but she had a nasty feeling it would be the day she'd highlighted in red on her calendar—June 2. Instead of walking down a petal-strewn sandy aisle to get married, she'd be at her desk at the Duchess with a million tasks to do, exactly as if she had never given up eighteen months of herself to a relationship that had gone nowhere.

Carter stretched his other arm out and nudged the top of her head, a wordless invitation to rest it on him instead of the grass. She hesitated. He was a touchy-feely kind of guy, but this was a step short of cuddling, not his usual teasing pokes and friend-hugs. He nudged her again, but it felt as absent-minded as a pat on the head from her grandmother, affectionate but not insistent, so she scooted up enough to accept his arm pillow. "You're a good friend, Carter."

He didn't say anything to that, but that's what she liked about him. He was comfortable with silence. Blake had used it as a weapon to let her know she'd screwed up somehow or to get her to knock herself out trying to find out what was wrong with him. She sighed. She didn't miss that.

"What are you thinking about?" Carter asked.

"Stagnation."

"Sounds nice."

She smiled even though he was studying the inside of his eyelids and not her. "I just realized I was stagnating professionally."

"This epiphany brought to you by rollerblades. And you thought they were stupid."

She elbowed him, and he laughed. "Anyway, back to my pathetic personal problems, I was saying I was pretty distracted with Blake. I figured I'd push hard at work *after* the wedding. I mean, I always work hard, but I had big plans for the Duchess once everything with the wedding settled down."

"Like what?"

She smiled again at the question. The curiosity was a Carter thing; he wanted to know about everything from how the chef at Emmy's had made the meatballs so big and still got them to cook through to why inline skate styles had changed in the last ten years. On the day they'd gone to the Exploratorium, a hands-on science center, he couldn't get enough of all the interactive exhibits. Within minutes she'd been playing like a nine-year-old right beside him, giddy over all the gizmos and whirligigs.

He nudged her, a reminder that he'd asked her a question.

"I want to make the Duchess the premiere venue for high profile events. We get a lot of those already, but I want to push it farther, tap business that hasn't considered us before by offering the most elegant high-tech setting they could imagine. And then I would be so amazing that the hotel group would beg to promote me to general management at one of their lead holdings. Maybe even at the Duchess."

"That sounds like a good plan," he said, his voice full of late afternoon sun, warm and lazy. "Do it."

"I wish it were that simple. But you've seen how bad my luck has been when I'm with you. It's actually worse when I'm at work. It's like Murphy's law on steroids over there. A promotion is definitely not in my future. I'm not sure even a job is in my future if this keeps up."

"You'll be okay." His lips grazed her hair in a kiss. She went still but nothing else happened. She slid a sideways glance at him, but his eyes were still closed, his face still turned to the sun.

He wouldn't have kissed a guy friend that way. But he had sisters, so maybe that's what he would have done to cheer one of them up? She hoped. Didn't she?

She cleared her throat. "Anyway, I need to get work under control." She tried to pick up the thread of the conversation, but the kiss was still distracting her. What was that? She should ask. But if he was going to act like it was nothing, then it must be nothing.

"You will," Carter said. "That's something I figured out about you quick. If you decide you're going to do it, it happens. So work doesn't stand a chance. They should give you the keys to the Duchess now because that's a done deal."

"I already have the keys to the Duchess." It had been a fast kiss, like he hadn't been thinking about it, so that was good. Right? She wasn't sure. Random kisses, even hair kisses, seemed like a bad idea.

"Then they should give you the crown and scepter or whatever it is you get when you're the boss of the Duchess. A special RFID badge? What is it? It's a crown and scepter, right? Say it's a crown and scepter."

"It is, but my boss never wears them because they don't go with his suit." Maybe that hadn't been a kiss. Maybe the wind had ruffled her hair again, and it felt like a kiss. But how did the wind make a kissing sound? She straightened, too fidgety to lie down anymore.

"You okay?" Carter asked, cracking an eye open to check on her.

"Fine. Except for not. I'm really stressed about work." *And about you kissing my hair.* "I think I liked it."

"Sorry, what?"

Her cheeks heated. She couldn't believe she'd said that last part out loud. She'd meant she'd liked him kissing her hair and *that* was the problem. *Focus, girl.* "Nothing, just saying I'm glad I like my work."

Work. She'd let Blake dominate her work-life balance, and it hadn't balanced at all; the wedding had gotten her attention, and the Duchess got what was left. She had to flip that, at least until her job was under control.

When she put all the pieces in place, luck had a way of happening. When she got distracted, let things get too spontaneous, everything went sideways—it rained bad luck. She caught herself reaching for her necklace again. "You think I should call Spyglass again?"

"You called her two days ago, right? I think she'll let you know when it's done."

That would have sounded so condescending coming from Blake, everything underscored with an unspoken but obvious "duh." But Carter's tone was reassuring, and it made her want to burrow into him and soak up more of his mellowness.

Hold up. Bad idea.

As much as the last three weeks with Carter had been fun, she didn't need the double awkwardness of getting caught up in some emotional rebound with a neighbor she couldn't avoid when her emotions inevitably flamed out, plus having her career fall apart due to lack of focus.

Carter was a cute guy. A really cute guy, actually. And if she quit distracting him, she'd leave him free for someone else to swoop in and snatch him up. In fact, her friend, Ally, had hinted more than once that Carter seemed pretty dateable. Maybe she should hook them up.

She pictured them together and wrinkled her nose. She couldn't say why, exactly, but something about it was off. It was the same sense of something being not quite right when she was eating chicken at a nice restaurant and it had been grilled too close to where they'd cooked seafood. Blake had always said she was imagining the fishy flavor, but she always asked the server, and she'd never been wrong yet. The picture of Ally and Carter in her mind had the same tinge of not-quite-rightness.

Wait. Did she think that because she wanted it to be herself in the picture with Carter? She gave that mental image a whirl. It looked totally normal in her head, and she frowned.

"You must have some deep thoughts going on in here," Carter said, startling her with the feather-light touch of his finger grazing the furrows between her eyebrows. Her eyes flew open to find him propped on his elbow and smiling down at her. His finger moved down to trace the frown tugging down her mouth. A devilish impulse to catch the tip of his wandering digit between her teeth and see what he did parted her lips, but before she could see what would happen, her phone shrilled, and she shot up.

"Hello?" she said, aware of Carter's gaze on her profile.

"Hi, this is Jolie at Eveline's Bridal. Your dress is here, and we're ready to schedule you for a fitting."

Lucy's chest tightened. "I canceled that order a couple of weeks ago. I canceled my whole wedding." Keeping her voice steady as she said it felt like walking a high wire without falling.

She listened to clerk's flustered apology on the other end that sounded as if it were coming from way below her perch on her high wire. Yes, she understood that she would still owe the cost of the special ordered dress, but they could attempt to sell it on consignment for her if she would like to do that. Yes, she would like to do that. No, there was no way she would be wearing that dress. No, Jolie didn't need to apologize for the call.

She hung up and scrounged up a smile for Carter. "I guess whoever called me last time didn't leave a note that I'd canceled the order."

"You still have to pay for it?"

She nodded. "Yeah. They might be able to sell it to someone looking for a deal."

He rested his hand on her back. "I'm sorry. Maybe we should ramp up the Rampage?"

She straightened away from his hand and climbed to her feet, fighting hard to keep her balance—emotionally and otherwise. "Carter—"

And whatever he heard in her voice shadowed his face as he climbed to his feet too.

She continued anyway. "You got me through the worst of it. The Rampage was a success, and now I need to focus on work. You made it possible for me to hold on to the status quo, but I really need to push ahead. I'm getting to the point where all this spontaneity is starting to go from being helpful to getting me off track. Not that it hasn't been amazing," she rushed to add when a flicker of hurt flashed in his eyes. "But the healthy thing for me to do is to take control of my life again. Besides, think of all the free time you're going to have now that you don't have to babysit me," she said, hoping to tease a smile out of him.

It worked. "You mean babe-sitting?" he asked, wiggling his eyebrows at her, dirty old man style. He ducked when she swung at him, and he caught her fist, using her momentum to spin her around and pull her up against him. He braced his feet on either side of her skates and steadied her. "Careful there, Sugar Ray. You steady?"

She nodded, surprised by how hard his chest felt against her back. He released her slowly, keeping hold of her hand until he was sure she'd found her feet. She was even more surprised by how much she missed his warmth against her.

"Let's go," he said, turning on his skates as easily as if they were his regular Adidas. "Let's return these before I deposit you back at the Lucy cave."

She clunked after him, relieved that he hadn't put up a fight.

Right?

For the millionth time, she reached up to rub her jade and flinched when she found empty space. Carter's gentle urging aside, it was time to call Spyglass again and see when it would be done. She needed all the help she could get to put her life back on track. Play time was done.

Seven

First thing at work the next morning, Lucy went through her wedding to-do list one more time to make sure everything was actually canceled. The call about the dress had been a lot like finding a fly in her morning juice, and she could do without those kind of karmic ripples on a regular basis.

It looked good until she got to the dates for the Mariposa Hotel. She'd canceled the reservation weeks ago, but she hadn't been able to bring herself to take the vacation request off the Duchess calendar. She hated the symbolism of it. What should have been a week of celebrating with friends and enjoying her new husband would officially become another week in the office.

She closed the to-do list. Soon. She would delete the time off request soon. Just not today.

Today was about pulling work out of a downward skid. It was about working smart and seeing problems before they could arise. It was about working so hard that it compensated for her missing luck. It was about making it happen. And with a final deep breath, she dove right in to fill some of the gaps that had opened on the Duchess event schedule.

That night and every night for the next two weeks she fell into bed like she'd been wrung out of energy and dropped there to dry. Some nights she dragged herself out to the balcony to see if Carter was around. She only saw him twice. Based on their conversations, he was winning life.

She rattled off a long list of new events they'd booked, new hires she'd made, new problems she'd solved.

He described some ridiculous thing he did that day that sounded more fun than anything she'd done all year, minus the weeks of the Rampage with him.

She refused to let it distract her. The progress at work had been clear and steady, but setbacks kept cropping up—a flower vendor who had decided on an unreasonable rate hike or an event liaison who was more interested in booking personal dates with tech guys than booking events for the hotel.

At the end of her first week of Operation Break the Slump, it had all come pouring out during her nightly call to her mom. "I don't get it," she complained, hating that she sounded like one of her mom's honors students whining about a B. "I'm giving this my full time and attention, and I'm running into problems like I never have before. When is this stupid bad luck streak going to snap? Because I will, if it doesn't soon. I'm going to lose my mind."

Her mom had sighed. "You're still convinced this is all going to be better when you get your necklace back, hm?"

"I know it will."

"Sweetie, you're having the same luck you always had. It's just that before you always expected things to work out, and they did. Now you're expecting things to go wrong, and they do. The truth is nothing's changed. You have the same amount of things going right as you do wrong, but your perception is different because of your expectations."

"But Carter's luck has definitely improved. It's not my imagination. Everything used to go wrong for him, and now it all goes right."

"Ask Carter about his luck some time. See if he agrees with your assessment."

She'd had to wander out on to her balcony four nights in a row before she'd had the chance. What had happened to the days when he'd hang out here waiting for a glimpse of her? It would have been a lot more convenient if he'd kept that up. She was smiling at the inner three-year-old that seemed to be controlling all her emotions when Carter's door slid open, and he settled into the deck chair on his side.

"It's good to see you smiling," he said. "Let me in on the joke?"

She shook her head. "I was just being lame."

"Not possible."

"I have a random question for you. Do you feel like you're having a run of good luck right now?"

He shrugged. "No more than usual."

"But didn't you feel like you were having a ton of bad luck last year?"

"Nah. I was having a lot of bad days, and now I don't. But that's what happens after a tough breakup. It's hard to see anything as going your way for a while. Doesn't mean the rest of the stuff in your life is better or worse, but when the biggest thing in it becomes a total wreck, sometimes it's hard to realize that the rest of it is the same as it always was."

She straightened and fixed him with the unwavering stare her mom had always used to pry secrets out of her when she was a kid. "Has my mom been coaching you on the phone?"

That startled a quick head shake out of him. "What are you talking about? I haven't seen her since she left after . . . you know."

She eased back into her chair. "You can say 'breakup.' I'm not fragile."

"Okay. So what made you ask if I talked to your mom? I promise to tell you if she's trying to check up on you."

"Don't worry about it. It wouldn't bother if me she did."

He stood and walked over to lean on his rail. If she did the same thing, they'd be face to face. Her cheeks heated. Stupid. This is what came of not having a fiancé around to kiss regularly.

She cleared her throat and stood up. "I'm sure she won't call you. Have a good night, Carter," she said, slipping through her door.

She closed it on his soft "Wait, Lucy-Lou" because she didn't need to stay outside any longer and wonder how soft his hair felt or if his biceps were as hard as his chest had been. She climbed into bed and fired up her laptop, determined to get a jump on the next day. Her mom was right; if she expected glitches to happen, they wouldn't surprise her, and if she expected them to work out, they would. Now she just had to figure out all the possible glitches, and since she couldn't think about them *and* Carter's hair, she pushed Carter out of her head.

The new approach helped the second week. Every time something went wrong, she tried to think of it as a problem that would solve itself, no biggie. And even though sometimes those problems did in fact turn into biggies, or none of them solved themselves, they did get solved. Eventually. After she finally managed to replace the conference that had canceled for September with a different event that grossed almost as much on the food and beverage service, the general manager stopped by her office to compliment her.

By the third week, she'd hit a groove. Her job didn't have the same feel of lighthearted fun like it had before her necklace had broken, but she was starting to crave the feeling she got when she finally worked through a particularly knotty problem. It was like a huge post-workout stretch, but inside her brain.

None of it helped in the fourth week. June 2 stared back at her from her work calendar in red, highlighted as urgent. It wasn't like she was going to forget when that should have happened, but she had forgotten to delete her time off request.

She went into the scheduling function and deleted Monday, Tuesday, and Wednesday. But the closer she got to Friday, her chest tightened. That was supposed to be the day where everything in her life changed for the better, when she took a permanent step into a new life. It deserved more mourning than a deletion from her calendar.

Instead of erasing it, she scooped up her cell phone and texted Ally, formerly her maid of honor. *Going to head down to Seashell Beach next Thurs/Fri & do something either symbolic or crazy. Probably both. You in?*

The answer came back in seconds. *Totally. Seashell Beach back on my calendar.*

Lucy didn't need a ten-day block off from work anymore, but those two days . . . Those two days would be spent reconciling her new path with where it had split with the old one, and proving to herself that she was truly okay.

Eight

Her alarm was set early for Thursday so she and Ally could beat the worst of the traffic before hopping on the coast highway to cruise down to Seashell Beach. But her phone rang even earlier than that.

"Hello?" she mumbled while squinting at the time display.

"Lucy? Bad news," she heard Ally say at a tinny distance until she fumbled the phone back up to her ear.

"What's going on?" She sat up and blinked sleep from her eyes.

"Food poisoning, I think. I feel like I'm going to die. There's no way I can make the drive this morning. I'm so sorry."

Lucy sighed. Ally sounded like death had reanimated her to use her voice box. "Don't worry about it. Hydrate and sleep."

"But I feel so bad."

"Don't. Maybe my mom can drive up and meet me. Or maybe I need to go down there and do this alone, so I can prove I'm strong enough. But whatever I do, you need to go back to sleep." She cut off another croak and ordered Ally back to sleep for the third time before hanging up.

She lay there for an hour, long enough for the sun to brighten her room, debating what to do. Her mom could drive up after school and get there by dinner. But she didn't want the weight of her mom's worry on her.

She could do this alone. She'd use the time to reflect, to come back from the weekend that should have been her wedding recentered and refocused.

She got up and changed into the cute sundress she'd pulled out the night before, trying not to think about how taking Ally's convertible would have been way more fun. She'd just keep her windows down and her radio high and it would be fine.

An hour later she'd polished off a grapefruit and some yogurt and had her bag in the car when her phone rang again. This time it was Stella at Spyglass.

"Lucy! I know your necklace took longer than you would have liked, but I promised it would be worth it, and it is! It looks as good as new. I can send it out to you today, if you like."

Lucy leaned against her car. It was done? And today of all days. It felt eerily full circle. "I'm heading down that way. I'll come in and pick it up." She ended the call and plopped down behind the wheel where she slumped and rested her head on her hands. It was the weakness of relief mixed with an emotion she didn't expect. Six weeks ago she'd been down in Seashell Beach without the faintest idea that everything was about to fall apart. And while she grew more sure each day that it had exploded only for her to rebuild something better, the reality of how hard this weekend might end up being for her sunk in.

Anger roiled in her stomach and chest as she thought about the box she'd forced herself into to fit with Blake. It was anger at him, but anger at herself too.

Prickles traveled up her chest and lodged on the inside of her eyelids, threatening tears. She sniffed and started the car, then pulled the key from the ignition again. She needed to go, to prove she was strong enough, but she wasn't at all sure she was strong enough by herself. So she called the person she knew could make her stronger.

"Carter? Are you busy for the next two days?"

Nine

Her mom checked in at lunch time. "You doing okay? Is it strange being there?"

Lucy glanced up at the redwood towering over her. She couldn't even see its leaves. "Uh, didn't actually get there yet."

"Traffic?" her mom said, sympathetic the way only an Angeleno can be.

"No, actually. Um, Ally got sick so I invited Carter along for the ride, but he keeps tricking me into detours. We're in a redwood forest right now, and I guess when we're done here," she pulled the phone down and called over to Carter, who was sniffing ferns, "What are we doing next?"

"The Giant Dipper."

"We're riding a roller coaster in Santa Cruz," she reported to her mom.

"Carter's with you?" her mom said, sounding way too delighted.

"Yep, he reported for *friend* duty this morning, but he's turning this four-hour drive into about twice that, so I don't know how much help he's being," Lucy said with a laugh when he turned to roll his eyes at her.

"I won't bother you anymore. Call me when you get there." Her mom hung up before Lucy could finish saying good-bye.

"What's after the roller coaster?" She used her annoyed tone of voice, but the truth was, these ridiculous detours were the exact reason she'd called Carter. Work had straightened itself out beautifully, but she couldn't remember feeling so bored. Having the wedding to look forward to had taken up a lot of her non-work time, and then Carter had stepped in to soak up that time when Blake dumped her. But once she'd scaled back time with Carter, she'd begun to realize she had phased out an awful lot of non-Blake interests in her life when he came along.

Carter shrugged. "I don't know. I'll figure it out when we're done with the roller coaster."

"Uh-huh. Do you figure on us actually getting to the hotel at any point?"

"Dinnerish."

"And when are we done with the redwoods?"

"When enough people get here to calculate out how many of us it would take to hold hands and wrap around that tree." He pointed at the hugest tree they'd seen so far, about a hundred yards off.

"We're literally going to be tree huggers? What if it takes forever for enough people to get here? That's a huge tree."

"Then it takes forever." He studied her face like it was the GPS display of her car. "You're getting twitchy. Look, you're doing me a favor if you do this. I can turn this into a word problem that's going to be great in my app."

She narrowed her eyes. "You just made that up."

"Yes. But it was true the moment I said it. I need to stay until we can do this big group hug."

It took an hour and a half before he pulled it off. A

busload of little old English ladies thought it was a "delightfully daffy" thing to do and helped them out. When Lucy and Carter climbed back into the car, he wore a satisfied smile. The answer had been seventeen senior citizens plus the two of them. "I can turn this into so many problems with variables. What if it was all adults or all kids? They'll have to find average arm spans by age and extrapolate. This is awesome."

Lucy shook her head and got them back to Highway 1. In Santa Cruz, Carter tried to chicken out of the roller coaster, but Lucy shamed him into riding it with his hands up the whole time.

He insisted they stop in Monterey to visit the aquarium and narrated the action in the tanks as if they were eavesdropping on high school girls.

He wanted to stop at Hearst Castle in San Simeon, but Lucy pleaded exhaustion. He did convince her to pull over and gawk at a beach covered in seals. "That's the cutest thing I've ever seen," she said, watching a baby nestle with its mother for a while. "Makes me miss my mom."

He grinned at her. "Yeah, I can kind of see that. She's pretty protective of you."

"She hasn't been bothering you, has she?" Lucy closed her eyes and turning her face up to catch the rays of the setting sun.

"Not bothering me, no."

Something about the way he inflected the word "bothering" snapped her eyes open. "Wait, she still calls you?"

"Yeah. Just to make sure you're telling the truth about how things are going, I guess."

She straightened and turned to face him, her knees caught up to her chest. "And am I?"

"I always tell her I don't really know. I haven't seen you much the last couple of weeks."

"Well, if she's checking to see if I'm adapting to life just fine after my breakup, the answer is yes, I'm telling the truth."

"Good." He flicked a glance at her. "Does it bother you that she calls me?"

"No." It surprised her. Her mom had never called Blake, but Lucy didn't tell Carter that. If it made her mom stress less to get an independent report, and Carter didn't mind the calls, Lucy was okay with it.

He cleared his throat. "So really? You're happy as is?"

She glanced over at him. He stared out at the horizon like he was studying it for the secret of life, but it was empty. "Sure, I'm happy."

"Happy like this-is-what-you-want-the-rest-of-your-life-to-be-like happy?"

"No," she said, drawing the word out like it had acquired ten extras vowels. "But it doesn't have to be that right now. I'm in transition. It'll take time to get back to that kind of happiness."

"So you've had it before."

"Yeah." She frowned. "No. I guess I've been happy in moments, but not ones where I want the rest of my life to be that and only that. Have you?"

He held her gaze for several heartbeats before he looked back out at the horizon. "I've had moments I wanted to freeze forever. But I think maybe being really happy is when you get to the end of a day and you never want it to end, but you also can't wait for it to be over because then you're that much closer to the next day, and you know it's going to be even better because that's how your days are going—each one is even better than the last."

She thought about how that would feel. Had that been what it was like for him with his ex before they fell apart? A sad pang echoed through her before she blinked and shoved one of his arms hard enough to knock him flat on the sand.

He sat up, laughing. "What was that for?"

"I'm supposed to be on a road trip. We're late getting to the hotel. What kind of Sherpa are you?"

"Sherpas are in the Himalayas."

"Then what am I supposed to call you? My cabana boy? My bellhop?"

He rose to his feet and held out a hand to pull her up, his easy smile in place. "You can call me your friend. Come on, Lucy-Lou. Let's get you down to Sad Town."

He turned back toward the scenic overlook they'd hiked down from and kept her hand in his as he towed her along the sand.

"I don't think it's Sad Town," she said. "It's more like What Might Have Been Town. And Put Things to Rest Town." Carter said nothing but squeezed her hand. She decided not to tell him that the rocks on the beach weren't big enough for her to need his help navigating them and left her hand where it was.

She thought about his definition of happiness. When had she last felt like that? Three hours before, she realized. It was when they'd left the sequoias, and she'd realized that Carter had no intention of taking a straight line anywhere. She'd been torn between wanting to stay and soak up the quiet of the forest forever and wanting to see where Carter would drag her next.

He always seemed on the edge of possibility, throwing himself into whatever project ignited his passion. She could do that—if she could find it. She liked event planning—she was good at it. But it didn't light her up inside the way her mom did when her students' AP scores came in, or the way Carter did when he explained some new modification for his math app.

So tomorrow the search would begin to find it—that thing that would make her light up inside too. And not the content glow she'd felt when Blake came along at the right time to fit her marriage timeline, either. She wanted the fire that sent her mom into her rough high school every single day with a determination to make a difference to those kids, that kept Carter's light shining through his balcony window at two in the morning when she stumbled to her fridge for a drink. She'd asked him once what he was up to. "Ideas," he'd said, the same way she might have confessed to a middle-of-the-night chocolate binge—with total happiness.

She drove the last hour into Seashell Beach. Carter watched the coast roll by out of his window, shooting her a smile and pointing now and then when something caught his eye, but he didn't talk much. She was thankful for the quiet. Her thoughts tumbled and slid like the seals on the beach had, bouncing off of each other and scuttling in a new direction.

When she turned into the stone-paved driveway leading to the Mariposa's entrance, she frowned. Last time she'd pulled up beneath the portico, her stomach had already been in knots over Blake, wondering what his mood would be like, which version of her fiancé would show up to meet her. How had she not seen it then?

Carter's hand brushed hers, and she looked up to read a question in his eyes.

"I'm fine," she said, looking past him to the hotel entrance. "Blake's mother would be pitching a huge hissy if she knew I was staying here with another guy on the night before my wedding."

Carter's eyes widened, and Lucy burst into laughter even as her cheeks heated. "Wow. That couldn't have come out more wrong. We're in the honeymoon suite, but you'll have a whole fold-out sofa all to yourself."

A look she couldn't decipher flickered over his face before he grinned back at her. "Good. I know how hard it's been for you to resist me. I need a buffer for my own safety."

"Ha," she said, putting the car in park and separating the key from the ring for the valet. "Seriously, are you okay with staying on the sofa? I was planning on having my girlfriend Ally with me, and she thought it would be more of a full-circle moment if we stayed in the honeymoon suite. I'm sure it's a comfy fold-out couch in a swanky place like this."

"Oh, I've done time on a sofa during your emotional trauma before. I'm sure I'll be fine," he said, a small smile still in place.

"Right. You know how people say 'I owe you one'? I think I owe you more like a million."

This time his hand covered hers on the gearshift and stayed there. She liked the sugar scrub friction of his calluses against her knuckles. She stared at their hands layered together and wondered where his calluses came from—the handlebars of his bike?

His gaze followed hers down, and he withdrew his hand. Cool air flowed over her skin where his touch disappeared. He turned to open his door. "You ready for this?"

"So ready," she said. Getting past the day felt like the final step toward being done with Blake. He'd be the picture in the back of her head when she eventually dated again, but only so she could ask herself if what she felt for someone was real, or just convenient. It wouldn't be about how easy it was to be with them socially or because of similar life plans; it would be about how easy it was to be with them sitting on a sofa in their sweats and being quiet and happy.

The desk clerk smiled at her when she pulled up the honeymoon suite reservation. "Congratulations, Miss Dalton. Hope tomorrow is wonderful."

"Oh, it'll be something, all right." The clerk's smile wavered, and remorse needled Lucy. She gave her a smile and took her key without another word, afraid only snark would come out.

Up in the room, Carter gave a low whistle as he took in the floor-to-ceiling windows. Sheer drapes fluttered in the ocean breeze blowing in over the balcony. "Wow."

"Yeah." She didn't have anything to add. *Wow* covered it.

"So what's the plan now?"

Ally had planned this part of the trip. Knowing her it probably would have involved ceremonial deletions of Blake's pictures from all Lucy's social networks, a little bit of rum, and a lot of nonsense. But all of that felt weird to do with Carter, so she shrugged and wandered out to the balcony.

The moon painted a silver path across the waves to where they met the sand a few hundred yards from her perch. "What time is it?" she asked when she heard Carter step out behind her.

"Almost nine."

"It's been a pretty full day. I think I'm ready for room service and then bed."

"I'll find a menu."

"Wait," she said, and Carter paused in the doorway. "Is that okay with you?" Blake didn't like staying in often. He was more about the scene and being seen in it.

"I'm up for whatever, Lucy. This is your weekend."

"Then I want to sleep," she said. Right after she spent a long evening taking the inside of her brain apart and making sure that she'd gotten the rewiring right. She'd need to be cloistered, nun-like, away from Carter and his distracting hair for that; she'd short-circuited a couple of times around him lately, and she didn't have time on this mini-retreat to figure out why when there were so many other things to sort through.

"Do you care if I order for us?" Carter asked, poking his head back out.

"More adventure?" she asked with a grin.

"You know me so well."

"Go ahead. And just so you know, I'm planning adventurous stuff for tomorrow. It won't be all working on our tans."

"Oh good," he said. "Watching people lay around in

swimsuits is low on the list of how I like to pass the time. Uh, although I'm sure you look awesome in a swimsuit, and it would be totally worth it."

It was a line on par with some of the worst she'd heard out at bars, and as if he sensed her surprise, he colored. "I'm trying to say that I didn't mean I thought laying out would be boring because you would look bad in a swimsuit. I wasn't trying to sound like a subclass Guido."

Her filter shut off and let the next words out of her mouth. "I rock a bikini, believe it."

He swallowed. "I definitely, definitely do. I'm going to go order some chicken breast." He squeezed his eyes shut on the word "breast." "Anyway, it looks really good. It's stuffed with some herb paste I've never heard of, and it sounds good. And I'm getting nachos because they sound good too. And I'm going to just do that now."

He disappeared. Something about walking into a hotel room with him had made her feel like an awkward fifteen-year-old, and she understood his blush. It'd be a relief to get a good night's sleep and reset. This day was playing more havoc with her brain than she'd expected it to.

She soaked in the moonlight for a while longer until she was sure it had unwound her then slipped back into the suite. Carter was bent over his laptop, the screen full of code.

"Working on your app?"

"Yeah. Funding is in so I hired a couple of other developers. I'm just gathering the requirements so I can call a design meeting next week."

"Cool." She shifted from foot to foot. Turned out she was still wound up, so she opted for escape. "I'm going to go sit and think for a while. Let me know when the food gets here?"

He nodded, his brow pinched into wrinkles, but he didn't stop her. Forty-five minutes later she heard the muffled sounds of Carter talking to the room service guy. She joined him on the still-folded couch for a more normal dinner.

They'd done this many times, eaten something new and laughed together. But at ten-thirty a yawn got away from her even after she clapped her hand over her mouth, and he stood and pulled her to her feet. "That's it, lightweight. You're done. Go to bed," he said, leading her to the bedroom and nudging her through the door before he stepped back and tried to pull the door closed.

She held it for a moment. "I'm not a lightweight. It's been a full day, that's all."

"Yes, and there are different kinds of tired. Go sleep today off. You're probably going to need even more energy tomorrow." He smiled as he pulled the door all the way shut behind him.

She changed into her pajamas and climbed into the bed, staring up at the ceiling instead of the inside of her eyelids like he'd ordered her to. This weekend was supposed to be about putting Blake neatly into his place in her life, a mental file box like the ones she kept at her parents' house, full of high school pictures and mementos—certificates, dried corsages. Tokens that proved it had happened, but nothing she needed to keep with her and explore regularly. And Blake was cooperating, staying where she tucked him.

But Carter? Carter wasn't cooperating at all. And she sensed a long night ahead of her, trying to figure out where he was supposed to fit, because the "benign neighbor" file wasn't it.

Ten

Lucy woke up the next morning and took a deep breath. It had taken her until well past midnight, but she'd decided what to do next. She'd take all the time she needed to sit with the idea and see if held up to the bright light of day. And if it did, well . . . the rest of this road trip was going to end up far more interesting than she would have guessed.

She crept out of her room in case Carter was still sleeping. He lay on his stomach, his hair poking out over the blanket. She wanted to touch it to see if it felt soft or bristly against her skin. She rubbed her palm against her pajama pants and padded over to the sofa, trying to decide how to wake him. He looked so comfy, his eyelashes lying long and dark against his blanket-creased cheek.

She climbed on the bed and sat next to him. He mumbled something but didn't wake up. She reached toward his hair—she couldn't help herself—but she pulled back short of touching it. What would he think if he woke up to find her in his bed, in her pajamas, fondling his hair? And what did she want him to think? She edged back toward the floor, just setting her foot down as he rolled over to blink at her.

"Hey. What are you doing?" he asked, the same way Ally had sounded when Lucy had given her a ride home after she got her wisdom teeth out.

"Nothing. Came in to wake you up, but then I felt bad. I'm going to change and go for a run. Take your time. Sleep more if you need to."

He pushed himself up on one elbow. He'd slept without a shirt and his chest looked as muscled as it had felt when they'd been Rollerblading. "No, I'm good. What's the plan for today?"

She narrowed her eyes at him. "Are you asking so you can change it on me, or are you really going to do what I planned?"

He smiled and lifted one shoulder. "Depends on if I think it'll make you happy."

She didn't know what to make of that. "I thought we'd rent bikes and ride down to Pismo Beach, poke around there to see what's interesting. You want to add any bells and whistles to that?"

"Yeah, breakfast and a shower. But I can do that while you run."

"Sounds good," she said, scurrying into the bedroom. Five minutes later she was out again, dressed to run. Carter was sitting on the side of his sofa bed looking like he hadn't connected all the way to reality yet, but he'd put on a Microsoft T-shirt. Lucy didn't know if that was a good thing or not, but she thought probably not. It seemed wrong to cover up that chest.

"See you in an hour," she said. Within minutes she was pounding down the boardwalk, but all the strange, jittery energy she'd felt around him had followed her out to fuel her run. Fine, then. She ran harder, trying to focus on the rhythm of her feet and her breathing. Thoughts of Carter intruded anyway.

She had a whole reel of Carter highlights she hadn't known about, and it played on a loop. Carter laughing as he diced vegetables like he'd been born doing it, Carter's eyes twinkling at her as he pulled her to her unsteady rollerbladed feet, Carter's forehead furrowed with worry when he thought she wasn't looking, Carter's gaze level and cool as he challenged her to the Rampage, Carter's easy way with her mom.

She glanced out at the water. Three hours from now she would have been stepping onto the sand to walk toward Blake and a minister. She'd expected him to be on her mind so much more today, but all she could feel was a sense of relief, like when she was nine and she'd knocked over her grandmother's prized vase but caught it right before it hit the floor. It was the bone-deep thankfulness of narrowly avoiding a disaster.

All the space she thought Blake would take was going to Carter. And the more time she spent with him, the more room he took up in her head.

She ran harder, racing toward a conclusion that she'd fallen asleep considering. She'd been ready for a relationship when Blake came along. She'd mistaken him as Mr. Right because he showed up at a convenient time. But she was still ready for a relationship. Now the timing didn't seem great, but the guy did. She wanted Carter.

She slowed to a stop and pulled her phone out of her sports armband to make a call.

"Hi, honey. Hanging in there?"

She smiled at the worry in her mom's tone. She loved being loved. "Yes and no. I might be losing my mind, but not for the reasons you think."

"Okay," her mom said, drawing the word out as a question.

"I want to talk to you about Carter."

"Ah." Her mom sounded about as surprised as if she'd announced that ocean still had waves.

"He's my friend, but I think I want to upgrade."

"To a new friend?"

"To benefits. No, to a relationship."

She could hear the smile in her mom's answer. "I vote yes."

"But Carter won't. He's been pretty clear that he will *not* be the guy to step in and catch me on rebound."

"Are you rebounding?"

"No."

"Then there's no problem."

"Yes, there is. He's never going to believe that, especially not if I bring it up here." Something about her mom's calm reaction nagged at her. "Wait, aren't you surprised? I thought you'd ask me if I was sure about this."

"Sweetie, I saw this coming from the first day I was up there. I think that neighbor of yours might be crazy about you."

The possibility made her heart pound hard enough to drown out the crash of the waves in front of her. "I don't know, Mom. He's always ready to help me out if he thinks I need it, but I don't want him to see me as some project. And even if you're right, I don't think the day and crime scene of my canceled wedding is the time or place to convince him that I'm not rebounding."

"I'm sure you've got a plan," her mom said.

"Time." It would take a lot of time actually, but she'd convince Carter that Blake was a misguided idea she'd had that was as much in the past as her untouched box of high school mementos in her parents' garage. Only Blake wasn't something she was interested in holding on to. "I'll play it cool, be his friend for a while, slowly add in some flirting until he can't miss the signals, and then I'll graduate out of the friend zone."

"Why not just say something to him—ask him where his head is at?"

"Because I really want this to work out, and right now I'm standing about three miles down the road from where I was going to get married at noon. He's not going to trust anything I say while we're here." She'd love to go back to the hotel, grab him, and kiss him as a wordless announcement of where she wanted them to go. But for now, no matter how many new discoveries she made about Carter's hotness and his fascinating mind, no matter how often he made her laugh until her stomach hurt, she'd be his friend until he understood that she was already over Blake.

"I think you should just talk, but I guess it never hurts to take things slow. But make sure you don't move so slowly that he can't even detect the forward motion, okay? I like that boy for you."

"Don't worry, Mom. I like him for me too. I'm going to play this right."

They hung up, and a half hour later, she was back at the Mariposa. It was a letdown to find the room empty, but she knew Carter had to be around somewhere. She stepped into the bathroom to shower. Steam and the smell of soap lingered from the shower Carter had already taken. It was an odd sort of intimacy that took her straight back to eighth grade when Aaron Wellberg had gotten up from a lunch table to go shoot hoops with his friends, and she'd slipped into his spot while it was warm just so she could feel the traces of his body heat on the bench.

She walked out of the room thirty minutes later in cute shorts and a tank top, a touch of lip gloss, and her favorite hoop earrings, but she hadn't done more than blow-dry her hair because Carter had said once that he liked how it looked when she let it go natural instead of straightened. The almost-curl in it seemed somehow more right here by the beach anyway.

"So . . . bikes?" Carter asked, looking up from his laptop to smile at her. His hair looked like he'd tried and failed to tame it, strands of it already trying to reclaim their cowlick status.

"We're going about twenty miles. Think you can handle it?"

He rolled his eyes, "Yeah, Lance Armstrong. Maybe you better hit up your secret sauce so you can keep up."

She grinned. "It's not a race. It's one of those days where I want to enjoy every minute because it was so close to being such an epically wrong turn. I want to savor every second of being back on track."

His eyebrow rose. "That sounds . . . um, much better than I thought you would."

"I'm taking my life back, no big deal."

He grinned back at her. "Yeah, no big deal."

"I want to swing by the jeweler and pick up my necklace first. Seems like a good way to kick all this off."

Worry crossed his face. "Is it a big deal if we don't go by until this afternoon?" He nudged a backpack that Lucy hadn't noticed. "I went and picked up some lunch for us. It's not going to keep forever, but I thought it would be fine if we got on the bikes right away."

Lucy shrugged. "Yeah, we can do it after the bike ride. She told me once that afternoons are less crazy for her anyway. What'd you get for lunch?"

"It's a surprise."

"Isn't everything with you?"

"Yes. Bring me to the bikes, woman."

On the way out of the hotel, she narrated the sites of canceled wedding activities in the serious tones of a news anchor describing an accident scene. "And there is where Lucy Dalton almost held her rehearsal dinner. It was a narrowly averted disaster since Dave Dalton would most likely have punched Calvin Sefton. Hard."

Carter smiled at her fake news voice, but it didn't turn the creases around his eyes into smile lines. Well, he'd see as the day went on how relieved she was to be here presiding over the ashes of her plans and *not* celebrating a misguided wedding.

They picked up beach cruisers, and Carter made Lucy laugh by insisting on a girly bike because it had a basket in front where he could put his backpack. For the next ten miles he played tour guide with fake information. "The house on our left was once owned by the millionaire who invented the bendy straw. His name was actually Ben D. Straw, so it's not like he could invent anything else. That large boulder on the right is called the Goliath Booger because, well, look at it."

"Gross. Goliath Booger? Are you twelve?"

"Sometimes I feel like I am when I'm around you," he said, grinning.

A couple of times he made her laugh so hard she swerved like she was trying to bike after a night of tequila. Around mile eleven, he settled down to study the undeveloped coastline stretching down either side of the highway. She took advantage of the chance to steal glances at him, at the way he watched the passing scenery with nothing but a smile, like enjoying the view was the only thing in the world he had to do.

She loved that smile. Whatever she'd seen Carter do, he did only that thing, whether he was deep inside a coding problem for his app or people watching at the park. He was so *present* in a way she'd never mastered. When he listened to her, he only wanted to know what she had to say. He wasn't parsing it so he could figure out what to say next.

He glanced over and she looked away, embarrassed to be caught. She wanted to hop off her bike right that second and drag him across the sand to play in the waves and then collapse and roll around in them with him *From Here to Eternity* style, hungry kisses and everything. Especially the hungry kisses.

She kept her eyes on the road ahead. How was she supposed to fake just-friends indefinitely?

A few more quiet miles slipped by. Every now and then Carter would ask her a question or point out a pelican or something. But to her it felt as if her whole mission on this bike ride was to keep him from catching her staring at him like Aaron Wellberg had often caught her doing in middle school—love-struck and hopeful.

She increased her speed, pushing the heavy beach cruiser bike to go faster. She was a grown woman, and she could keep it together, for pity's sake. She just needed breathing room to reset.

"We racing?" Carter called, close behind her. Too close. She needed more space and a few minutes to get it together.

"No race," she called over her shoulder. "Just getting some . . . stuff out. Feels good." And she poured on more speed.

He kept pace, and even if she hadn't been able to hear the hum of his tires, she would have sensed him there anyway. Her nerves had acquired intensely sensitive Carter antennae.

It didn't take long before Carter was even with her, but she kept pushing. Her calves burned from the strain of powering the heavy bike until she morphed from a hurts-so-good to a just-plain-hurts situation. She pulled into a scenic outlook and climbed off to stretch.

Carter stayed on his bike. "Let's call it a tie," he said. The wind had destroyed any remaining order to his hair, and the sight of it paired with the satisfied grin on his face was so adorable that it stopped Lucy's breath for a few seconds too long. She remembered to quit staring and inhaled on a gasp.

"You okay?" Carter asked, his smile fading.

"Yeah, I'm good. Winded from that sprint." She turned toward the water. This was ridiculous. *Pull yourself together, girlfriend, because you aren't going to convince anyone you're emotionally stable like this.* "I think I need a few minutes alone. Is that okay?" she asked, daring a glance back at him.

His laugh lines had all been dragged downward with worry again. "Of course. Yeah, go ahead. Take as long as you need. I brought my camera, so I'll just stay up here and shoot."

She trudged through the sand until she was a few yards short of the tide line. It was warm enough for people to be out flying kites or running, but still too cool for many of the locals to be in the water. Her research on an ideal date for a beach wedding had been dead on. This would have been a perfect day, but not one molecule of her regretted that she was sitting here in shorts and a tank instead of a wedding dress.

She dug into her front pocket for the slip of paper she'd taken from her purse before leaving the hotel. *True love is for the brave, not the lucky.* Flecks of dried soy sauce speckled it, a reminder of the disastrous lunch where she'd gotten the cookie. It had bothered her so much then—the fact that she'd gotten her first generic fortune right after breaking her necklace.

Maybe it was possible to make this is as true as any fortune that had ever predicted her promotion or winning lottery numbers. "Just talk to him," her mom had said. And Lucy had told her she was afraid of ruining a good thing. That wasn't brave.

What if she were brave enough to ask Carter if she was more than a project to him? She thought she was more. At the very least she was someone fun for him to hang out with.

Was that all? If she had the courage to ask, would "love" really favor her?

It would be a lot easier to try if she knew her bravery was backed by luck, and her hand fell away from the spot where her necklace should be. She wished she had insisted on them stopping by Spyglass.

A trio of seagulls to her right scattered and flew away. She looked up and found Carter trudging toward her, his backpack slung over one shoulder and his hands in his pockets. He dropped down beside her. "Sorry. You're just making me too sad. I brought you something."

"Lunch?" she asked, eying the backpack.

"Eventually. Something else first." He rose to his knees to dig in his pocket.

"Why am I making you sad?" she asked. "I'm not sad."

"Then you do a good imitation of it," he said on a grunt as he freed a small box. "Here. I think you've been wanting this."

She took the white box with a picture of a Spyglass stamped on it and her eyes flew to his.

"Open it."

Her fingers fumbled over each other in her hurry to check inside. There on a bed of cotton was her necklace, but it didn't look the same. She frowned in concentration and pulled it out, letting it hang from her finger to study it more closely. The jade and its setting looked like they had the day her grandfather gave it to her, but something else hung with the pendant.

"You can take that off," Carter said, the words flying out of his mouth faster than their bikes had sped over the highway trail.

"You know what this is?"

"Yeah. It's an aspen leaf. I made a call a couple of weeks ago and asked Stella to add it, but you can remove it, and your necklace will be exactly what it was before."

Lucy studied the intricate leaf done in the same gold filigree as the jade's setting. "I don't understand."

Carter drew his knees up to his chest and clasped his arms around them. It was casual, but in a very deliberate way. He cleared his throat and looked somewhere past her head. "I've always paid attention to you. I've seen you wear that necklace a hundred times. I did a little research and the aspen leaf symbolizes determination. Sometimes I think you think that your luck thing makes you who you are the way that your eye color and your laugh do. But it doesn't." He met her eyes and took a deep breath. "I thought you should remember that the best parts of you have nothing to do with that necklace."

She let the chain pool in her hand and touched the aspen leaf again. "I can't believe you did this," she said, awed by what he saw in her.

"I'm sorry," he said.

"I didn't mean—"

"No, it's okay. I shouldn't have done it. At least I didn't have her fuse it on, right?" He rose to his knees again and dug through his backpack.

She tried again. "I meant that—"

He groaned at something inside his bag. "Man, I thought I had such a great idea to help you today. I was going to reverse engineer that whole day when you were down here with Flake and make this place a better memory for you, but I think I really, really suck," he said, pulling out a dripping plastic bag with The Fortune Café logo on it. "Looks like now that you have your necklace back, our luck is reversing already. I can't believe this exploded. I was super careful when I packed it."

"Wait, you were trying to recreate the day my necklace broke?" she repeated, trying to understand his logic.

"No, reverse engineer it. I mean, that's where it all fell apart, right?"

She nodded slowly. She *had* thought that. She didn't now, but she'd put it that way to him when she'd told him about it one particularly rough night in the days after the breakup."

He shrugged, and set the bag down to rub at his sticky fingers with a napkin. "I know you're into signs and stuff. I thought I'd turn this day into a sign that things are getting better. New and improved necklace, lunch from the same place as last time, but I rigged the cookie with a different fortune." By now he was mumbling, whether out of embarrassment or in distraction as he tried to sop up the mess inside his backpack, Lucy wasn't sure.

"You rigged my fortune cookie?" she repeated.

"Yeah. That's hard, by the way," he said. "It took me like twenty tries to do it at my place. I'm just glad I was smart enough to try it at home instead of here. Because I was definitely not smart when I thought egg drop soup would be good on a bike ride."

She grabbed the bag and looked for the wax pouch inside where Chinese restaurants always put the fortune cookies and the soy sauce packets. Carter looked up when the bag rustled and his eyes widened. "You don't need that," he said, taking the pouch from her fingers. "It was a stupid idea. I'm going to get this mess out of here, and let you meditate or grieve some more or whatever I interrupted."

"I'm not grieving. Why was it a stupid idea? I think it's amazing. Let me see the fortune."

He froze for a moment so quick she wasn't sure she'd seen the hesitation. "No, it's fine. I'm sure it's trashed anyway from the soup spill."

"Should be fine inside that bag. I want it." He started to stand, and she tried to snatch it away from him again, but he jerked it out of her way and they both lost their balance. She pitched into his chest and knocked him flat on his back. She didn't apologize. She didn't even move. She stared down at him, into his eyes full of nothing but her. He wasn't breathing; if he was, she would have felt it against her lips. "I want the fortune," she repeated, propping herself up on her forearms but making no effort to move off of him.

His eyes flicked down toward her mouth, and he shook his head. "Lucy."

A tingle shot down her spine at the strain in his voice. "Yes, Carter?" she asked, relaxing into him even more.

His eyes slammed shut, and she grinned. "Lucy . . ."

"Yes?"

He hesitated. She didn't mind. She liked her perch.

"Carter . . ." She trailed off his name and swallowed, trying again. "Carter, I want to be brave."

That got his eyes open. He reached up and twined his fingers through her hair, giving it a soft tug. "Don't mess with me," he said, his voice soft as the breeze off the ocean.

"I'm not." She wiggled against him while she tried to reach behind her for the slip of paper she'd pulled from her pocket.

His eyes shut again, and he clenched his jaw. "Lucy-Lou, stop."

"I just need—"

His hands closed around her waist and held her still. "I mean it. Stop."

She tucked her worn fortune into his hand and slid her arms around his neck, loving the feel of the warm sand against her palms and his soft hair against the backs of her hands, her lips barely grazing his as she spoke. "Read it."

He held her gaze for a long moment, and the intensity of it only made her want to dip down and steal a longer kiss. He glanced at the fortune, his eyes scanning it then darting back to her face, searching again. They were so close she could see his eyes darken, and this time the look inside them sent another shiver down her spine. *Why wasn't he saying anything?*

She slowly righted herself and let him up. He reached into the wax bag for a homemade-looking fortune cookie, plucking the paper slip out, and handing it to her.

She straightened it and read the words. *Maybe what you're looking for is just a balcony away.*

He watched her so closely she wondered if he could see the pulse jump in her neck, and she blushed. He reached for her and settled her into his lap, turning her face up to his for a kiss that would have melted her if he wasn't holding her up, his arms tight and sure. He deepened it, confident in a way that sent tingles skittering through her stomach, hotter than she'd ever have thought possible, and tasting like sweetness that was purely Carter.

When he drew back enough to breathe, he rested his forehead against hers, and she wondered if he could feel how flushed her skin was. That had been good. So, so good.

He smiled and dropped a kiss on the tip of her nose. "If you're going to be brave, then I guess that means I'm very, very lucky."

But his next kiss only proved that Lucy's luck was back again.

Part Three

Takeout

One

Stella Novak ignored the incoming text. She didn't care if Andrew was "stopping in" at Seashell Beach and wanted to catch dinner together. The fact that she was now a stop along the way bothered her more than it should. Thinking of her ex-boyfriend used to hurt, it used to make her mad, but now she just felt . . . tired.

Besides, if Andrew really wanted to find her, he knew where she worked. He'd been to her mother's jewelry shop, Spyglass Jewelry, more than once. He used to tease her about how someone on a full-ride academic scholarship to Stanford had come from a touristy town.

"Did you even have to take tests in your tiny school?" Andrew's voice echoed in her mind. "Or did they let you out early to go cater to the tourists?"

At first, Stella thought Andrew was charming, witty, and cosmopolitan. He was from Seattle and was one of the most brilliant minds in the business entrepreneurial program. They were put on the same team in Marketing 410 while doing their undergraduate degrees. By the time they both graduated, they were a steady item on campus.

TAKEOUT

Stella aced the GMAT and had her application in for the MBA program when her world fell apart.

Or more accurately, her mother fell apart.

Her mother had suffered a mild stroke from her diabetes, and now Stella spent her days running her mom's shop, and her nights taking care of her mom.

Andrew had been sympathetic at first, but when he realized Stella was dead set on moving back home to take care of her mom on a long-term basis, he had walked away. Until the last three months. It seemed Andrew hadn't found any women to fawn over him during his MBA studies. And now he was back on her trail. Thinking of his persistence made Stella want to close the shop for a couple of hours and walk alone on the beach. Sand between her toes always seemed to help her forget Andrew and her former dreams.

Her phone buzzed again.

She looked at it simply because she had to. Most of her vendors texted her when they were running low on product.

Need 2 doz moon & star bracelets b4 weekend. ???
–Ronnie

Stella set down the silver bead she was crimping and texted back. *No prob. Pick up Fri a.m.*

Setting the phone back down, she scrawled a note on a lavender Post-it note. She had them all over the wall above her desk. It looked disorganized, but the method helped her prioritize. The note about the moon & star bracelets now went into position #2, right below Post-it #1 that read: *Order food.*

She kept that Post-it in first position always because if there was one thing she was forgetful about, it was eating dinner. She worked late after her mom went to sleep in their house behind the shop, and by the time she realized she was starving, the restaurants were closed. And her mom's special dietary food did little to satisfy Stella.

She grabbed her stack of takeout menus and fliers, then

glanced at her phone to check the time. 9:15 p.m. It was Tuesday, so the restaurants closed down by 9:00 p.m. That left the pizza joint. She dialed and ordered a personal size with pepperoni, olives, and mushrooms, then as an afterthought, she added a Diet Coke. She'd be up late starting on Ronnie's order anyway. She pretty much kicked her Diet Coke habit after moving back home, but it had been creeping back lately.

While she waited, she reviewed the orders of the day. A woman had come in earlier with a broken jade necklace. When Stella said it would take at least a week or two to fix, the woman was upset . . . the necklace meant a lot to her, she'd said. Stella reviewed the contact information on the Post-it: *Lucy Dalton*. Stella suspected that the woman put a lot more stock in the superstitious nature of jade—and the fact that it was supposed to be a good luck charm. People were certainly interesting.

The door chimed as it opened, and Stella looked over to see a teenaged kid, carrying a pizza box.

"Set it on the counter, please," she said, digging out her money from her purse. She handed over the money, then checked the pizza box. The order was right. "Thanks."

"Have a good night," the teen said.

The smell of the pizza made Stella realize how hungry she was. She carried it to the work desk. As she ate, she browsed through the other takeout menus. She stopped when she got to The Fortune Café menu. The restaurant was down the street, but she hadn't ordered from them in a while. She remembered them being good, so she'd have to try them again.

Stella was about halfway through the pizza when the door chimed again.

Maybe the delivery boy had left his keys or something. She rose from her desk and walked into the shop.

A man, with a little girl tugging at his hand, had just

entered. For a second, Stella stared. The little girl had blonde curls, reminding her of herself. And the girl was about six or seven, the same age Stella had been when her father was killed in a car wreck on the PCH.

Stella's throat felt tight, and she commanded herself to breathe until she started to relax. The man and the girl hadn't noticed her yet. "It smells like flowers in here, Daddy! Can you smell it?"

The man exaggerated a sniff. "Yeah, I smell it."

"Look at these!" the girl said, pulling her father toward the display of sun necklaces. The dark-corded chains contrasted with the polished brass suns. They were one of the more popular tourist buys. "Sunshines! Can we get one for Mommy?"

The man crouched next to his daughter and fingered the metal charm. "Do you think she'll like this?"

"Yes." The girl's blonde curls bounced as she nodded. "She loves the sun!"

The man smiled, then he looked up to see Stella.

She flushed, realizing she'd been caught eavesdropping—but it was her store, wasn't it? Yet for some reason, her standard "Can I help you?" didn't materialize. She was staring into the most incredible eyes she'd ever seen. She could only describe them as sea glass—a mixture of green and blue.

And the man's gaze had that *appreciative* look in it.

This was definitely not happening. He was good-looking, any woman could see that, but he was married with a kid. Stella ignored the awareness spreading through her body and looked down at his daughter. "Do you like that necklace?"

The girl clasped her hands together. "It's the most beautiful thing I've ever seen."

Stella laughed at the kid's dramatics. The man was laughing too. He straightened to his full height, and their gazes caught again. If Stella wasn't mistaken, he was checking her out.

Wow. She was flattered for precisely two seconds, then she was mad. What married guy checks out other women when shopping with his kid?

Not that there was a lot to check out. Stella's blonde hair had faded to a dirty-wash color the past couple of years from spending so much time inside, and she probably had pizza breath, not to mention her multicolored hippie blouse gave her no shape whatsoever. Still.

"It is beautiful, sweetheart." But he wasn't looking at his daughter. "We need to find out how much it is. Can you read the numbers?" His gaze finally went back to his kid.

The girl turned the necklace over. "There's no numbers."

He reached for the necklace and turned it over himself. "You're right. Maybe we should ask someone the price?"

The kid pointed at Stella with a grin. "How about the shop lady?"

Stella smiled at her. She had to hand it to the guy—he was an adorable dad.

"Great idea," he said, his tone low and amused. "How much are the necklaces? We don't see any prices."

That's because I don't label anything. Encourages customer interaction. And why are you looking at me like that? You're married. But Stella said none of these things. "They're $65."

The man's eyebrows lifted slightly. If he thought he was in a junky jewelry shop, he was mistaken. Stella had handcrafted everything in the store. And her mother had done it before her; it was what made the store unique.

"Can we get it, Daddy? Pleassssse?"

His daughter's begging tore his attention from Stella, and he looked down at his daughter, a half smile on his face.

What? Your wife's not worth $65? Stella wanted to say, but instead she said nothing. The man didn't look like a bum or anything. His daughter wore a cute sundress with sparkly sandals, and his casual clothing—a button-down shirt and jeans—was nice-looking.

"All right, Katie," he said. "It's a deal. Pick which one you want."

The girl named Katie squealed and started sorting through the metal suns, chattering to her dad as she did so. Each of the suns was a little different and the cord lengths also varied.

"I'll be over here when you're ready." Stella popped a piece of gum into her mouth and absently redid her messy ponytail. Her hair was probably a mess—the charming curls of her youth had become a pain to work with as an adult. If she didn't take the time to manipulate her hair with a flat iron, then it was hopeless, and she ended up pulling her hair up or winding it up in a clip.

It appeared that Katie had chosen a necklace, but now she was pointing out some other things to her dad.

Stella hid a smile. Married or not, she was interested in the man's response to his daughter. But Stella didn't allow herself to watch them and instead straightened the counter. She had Post-it notes on the edges of the counter as well, mostly with vendor supply numbers that she frequently called from her business line.

"We can come back again," the man's voice said, surprisingly near.

Stella looked up from the cash drawer that she'd impulsively started organizing. The man was standing directly across from her on the other side of the counter.

"Okay, Daddy," Katie said, her tone disappointed.

The man leaned down and kissed the top of his daughter's head.

Stella's heart flipped. He was a sweet father. Then his blue-green eyes were on hers, and her heart sank. He had no problem staring at her, and it made her want to yell at him to mind his own business. He wore a half smile as he leaned one elbow on the counter and held out the necklace.

Stella took the necklace from his outstretched hand, trying not to think about what it felt like touching his hand. She avoided looking into his eyes as she rang up the purchase. He handed over a credit card, and even though she told herself she wouldn't, she asked to see his ID. It was her policy after all. So why change it for a man who had gotten under her skin? The name on both the credit card and the driver's license matched: Evan Rockham.

"Thanks, Mr. Rockham," she said, handing back both cards, along with the necklace wrapped in tissue paper and slipped into a shiny bag reading *Spyglass Jewelry*.

"Thank *you*," he said. "You have great pieces in here."

Normally Stella would have launched into a few tidbits about how she made the jewelry and how she offered custom designs as well, but she didn't want this married man coming back to her store. He needed to focus on his wife.

She simply nodded and smiled at Katie, who was peering over the counter at her. "Hope your mom enjoys it."

Two

Evan Rockham stepped into the ocean-scented air and breathed in deeply. His daughter, Katie, was holding his hand and chattering almost nonstop. But Evan wasn't listening, even though he usually hung on her every word. He couldn't get the blonde woman with amber-brown eyes who worked in the shop out of his mind; she was pretty, but it was more than that. When he'd looked into her eyes, he'd seen vulnerability, as if she'd gone through some hard times. Yet he could tell the jewelry shop was a place where she was comfortable and that she knew her business well.

She had practically challenged him on the price with her direct gaze. But then she had hardly looked at him after that. As if she was being careful. He could have sworn he'd seen a spark of interest in her, but then there had been nothing. Like she'd retreated into place that was untouchable. This made Evan curious, and he didn't even know her name.

"Come on, Daddy." Katie pulled on his hand, and he realized it was time to cross the street. He tried to tune into what she was saying—something about going to the beach the next day, which would be impossible because they had to leave early in order to meet her mother in time. Evan knew he'd miss Katie as soon as he dropped her off.

Since the divorce, guilt and a few other things had driven him to really focus when he was spending time with his daughter. In fact, he didn't even answer his phone, allowing it to go to voice mail, and then calling his culinary students back after Katie was asleep.

Tomorrow morning, he'd be meeting his ex-wife, Michelle, to drop Katie off. It would be over a month before he'd see his daughter again for a two-week summer vacation. Evan paused at the street corner, waiting for a car to pass. He looked back to the jewelry shop, thinking again of the woman who worked there. He hadn't been this aware of another woman in a long time. He'd dated a couple of women since the divorce three years before. But they'd all turned out too much like his ex, high maintenance and prone to tantrums.

Evan wouldn't have ever guessed a grown woman could throw tantrums when he and Michelle were dating. And when she'd thrown the first one, he figured it was his fault. And it probably was. As long as he never contradicted her, then everything went fine. When she'd decided they had to move into a specific neighborhood before Katie was born, he said nothing. When she enrolled their three-year-old daughter into an exclusive private preschool that cost nearly half their mortgage, he went along with it. But when Michelle insisted that Katie needed to live abroad for a year in Japan with a foreign-exchange family so she could become bilingual, Evan had put his foot down.

Thus, the divorce.

Fortunately, the judge had agreed with Evan. He and Michelle had joint custody, which meant that without Evan's permission, his daughter wouldn't be living in Japan or any other foreign country without his consent.

They'd been divorced for three years now, but he still had to deal with her obsessive needs when working out Katie's schedule. Any time a woman he dated showed any signs of being like Michelle, he made a beeline for the door. Maybe he attracted the wrong type of women.

They reached his truck, and Evan loaded Katie in, making sure she did up her seat belt.

His phone rang as he started the engine. It was his new boss, the manager of the Mariposa Hotel, a brand-new five-star resort at Seashell Beach. "Hang on a minute, Katie. I've got to answer this."

The phone call lasted only a couple of minutes, but it had Evan's mind spinning. As he drove back to his newly-rented townhouse a few streets above Tangerine, he was already planning out menu ideas. The governor of California was coming with his family for a couple of days—his daughter was planning a wedding in Santa Barbara. And with Evan being the new head chef of the best hotel in the area, he was now in charge of feeding the governor.

This job was turning out better than expected. The move from Los Angeles to Seashell Beach had gotten him out of the traffic and the daily grind, and the Mariposa had given him a ton of flexibility. He was allowed to use the back kitchen to teach the culinary arts course that he'd started to develop in LA. He had a few students from his LA courses get jobs as assistants or head chefs at resort hotels all along the California coastline.

Those students inspired him to seek out a hotel of his own. It was one thing working as a chef for a high-end restaurant in the city, but another when cooking for people who were on vacation and expected the dining experience to be an event in itself.

"Can we go to the beach tomorrow, Daddy?" Katie asked from the backseat as he pulled into the driveway of his townhouse.

"We have to leave right after breakfast to go meet your mom." He shut off the ignition and turned to face her. Katie had her arms folded and her face pushed into a pout. "But I'll see you soon, and we can go to the beach every day if you want."

Still, her pout remained, and Evan wanted to laugh at her adorable expression.

"How about I make your favorite breakfast tomorrow?" he asked.

"Smiley-face pancakes?"

"Is that what you like now? I thought it was a veggie omelet," he teased.

"No!" she said, her eyes wide.

Evan laughed. "A smiley-face pancake it is." He didn't really want to copy IHOP, so he'd have to come up with something better.

It wasn't long before Katie went to sleep, after her customary hot cocoa, of course. Evan had spoiled her with homemade hot chocolate before bedtime since the divorce, and now it was a tradition between them. He didn't mind it a bit.

He warmed up a second cup and sat down at the kitchen table with his laptop. He'd been building his website, and it was nearly finished. In LA, his students came by word of mouth, but in Seashell Beach, he was only starting to get to know people, and he hadn't been too proactive in handing out his business card. Maybe he'd ask the jewelry store lady if he could leave a stack on her shop counter.

Before he realized what he was doing, he'd Googled Spyglass Jewelry. A professional-looking website came up. Who would have thought a tiny tourist shop would have such a nice website? He clicked first on the *Contact Us* page, but was disappointed when there was no name listed, just a phone number, address, and business email.

Then he loaded the *Our History* page, and seconds later, he was immersed in reading about a woman named Leslie Novak, who started out selling her homemade jewelry on the beach twenty-five years before. The story continued, describing the grand opening of Spyglass that took place a few years later when Leslie's products garnered more demand. Spyglass became the name because Leslie's daughter, Stella, had called the colored glass that washed up on the beach spyglass.

At the end of the article, there was a picture of Leslie and her daughter, who looked to be about twelve. Evan enlarged the black-and-white photo. The young girl was the woman from the shop. About ten years or more years had passed, but it was definitely her. That meant her name was Stella Novak. He read through the rest of the website, growing more and more interested and impressed at the same time.

Three

"Here's your phone." Stella set it on the small table next to her mother's recliner.

Her mother smiled up at her, and Stella hid a wince. Diabetes had ravaged her mother's face, and her delicate, vibrant features were now swollen and jaundiced. Her silver-blonde hair had been cut short, and she could only wear light, loose-fitting clothing because anything fitted made her uncomfortable.

Stella leaned over and tweaked her mother's breathing apparatus that she'd been on since the coma that had destroyed her respiratory system. Her mother had been diagnosed with diabetes ten years before, but with not taking care of herself properly, the disease had taken over her body. Getting that phone call at college that her mom had had a stroke and fallen into a coma had made *her* life pass before her eyes.

Looking at her mom now made Stella realize that she'd done the right thing coming home and take care of her. "Do you want to come into the shop today?" Stella asked. Even though her mother could no longer make jewelry, on her good days, she liked to interact with customers.

"No, sweetheart," her mother answered. "Not today."

Stella blinked back tears and smiled. "I'll close down for lunch and come home. If you need anything before that, call me."

She adjusted the afghan over her mother's legs, then kissed her on the cheek. Before Stella was out the door, she heard the volume of the television go up a few notches. It would be another predictable day. Her mother would watch TV, maybe knit a little, and fall asleep until Stella woke her for lunch.

Stella ate lunch with her mom every day, but there was only so much of the diabetic food Stella could take. Hence the takeout every night in the shop. She'd learned the hard way that her mom had little self-control when it came to food choice. And it was too cruel to cook or bring something in the house that she couldn't eat. Her mom followed her diet to a T now and sincerely regretted the poor choices she made that took her down this path, but Stella knew she might still cave to temptation.

The walk to the shop was only a few dozen feet. One of the things that had attracted Leslie Novak into leasing then eventually buying the shop was the small house behind it. Stella strolled along the cobbled pathway, another endearing feature. The early summer flowers were in full bloom, and Stella knew she'd be weeding soon.

She still had about thirty minutes before opening for business, and so she bypassed the shop and crossed Tangerine Street to the beach alley almost directly across from the jewelry shop. It led to the boardwalk, and Stella slipped her shoes off there then stepped onto the beach. It would warm up within the hour, but for now, Stella enjoyed the cool granules slipping around her toes as she headed for the waves. She turned before she hit the wet sand and walked north, toward a group of tide pools.

The serenity of the waves, the rising sun, and the sound of the early gulls calmed Stella in a way little else could. The texts from Andrew no longer bothered her, and she could see her mother's illness with a better perspective. If they followed the right diet and kept up the doctor appointments, her mom would have a lot of good years left.

When the angle of the sun told her it was time to open, Stella walked back to the shop, feeling refreshed. She went around to the back and unlocked the rear door, and as always, the first breath of air as she stepped inside sent a thrill through her. It felt like home and tasted of memories. All of the best kind of memories any little girl could have of growing up at her mom's side, doing everything together. The nostalgia was stronger today for some reason. Maybe it was the walk on the beach or seeing the bright flowers along the pathway to her house.

Stella moved through the shop, opening the blinds, unlocking the front door, and sweeping the wood floors. The routine reduced the ache in her heart. How many times had her mother done this in the past twenty years? How many times alone while Stella was away at college?

Her mother told her time and time again that she needed to finish her MBA, but Stella regretted staying away so long as it was. Maybe if she'd taken that last semester off and finished online, her mom might not have gotten so bad. One part of her brain told her, *It's not your fault*, but the other part was full of what-ifs. Had Stella seen the signs earlier but just ignored them on her visits home? She should have clued in sooner when her mother shortened the store hours so that she could sleep in each morning.

Stella's phone buzzed, and she checked the incoming text. It was from Andrew.

I'm on my way. Are you at the shop or at home?

She definitely didn't want him to go to her house. Her mom was in no condition for visitors, and besides, Stella didn't want Andrew to see her. Stella knew exactly what would happen. Her mother would feel like she was keeping Stella away from dating, and Stella didn't want her mom to worry about one more thing.

Stella exhaled, standing in a ray of morning sun that filtered through the shop window. She just wanted peace, and she wanted her mother well. She didn't want Andrew or any reminders of what her life might have been if everything hadn't crashed around her.

The text mocked her, reminding her of everything she'd given up. She didn't want Andrew's pity. She didn't want to allow any hope that maybe he'd changed, that maybe he'd move to Seashell Beach to be near her, or that he'd share her burdens.

No, that wasn't who Andrew was. He'd try to draw her away. He'd insist on sending her mom to a care facility. He'd make Stella think about *her* needs for once. And that was the last thing she wanted to do. Once that box was cracked open, Stella would have to feel again.

But . . . maybe, just maybe, Andrew had changed. The power of *maybe* was too great, and with trembling fingers, Stella texted him back. *I'll be at the shop.*

The morning was slow as far as customers went, which was fine with her. She had quite a few online orders to fill, along with Ronnie's bracelets. But her heart was pounding, and predictably, right before noon, Andrew walked in.

Stella's breath hitched. There was no doubt he was hot. Tall, dark, handsome—it was all a cliché, but definitely true about Andrew. His half-Italian ancestry magnified his good looks.

"Stella," he said, his voice low and familiar. He crossed to her where she'd stood from her workbench, and kissed both of her cheeks, then lingered, his hand at her waist as he whispered, "You're gorgeous."

His words started to melt her hardened resolve, and she had to focus on not letting the compliment weave its way to her heart. She stepped back, and he released her. He didn't seem bothered by the distance. Instead he glanced about the shop. "How's everything going?"

"Fine, things are fine." She wished she didn't sound so breathless. "I've actually been really busy, although it doesn't look like it now."

His dark eyes swung back to her face. "Let's catch some lunch, and you can tell me more about it."

"I can't," Stella said. "I need to fix lunch for my mom, and I can't close the shop up for very long."

Andrew cast another glance about the empty shop, then settled his gaze on her, making her stomach flip. "I can bring lunch here for you and your mom." He stepped closer, casually taking her hand and threading their fingers together.

She'd forgotten how naturally affectionate he was. Every time they were together, he was touching her, and he was already tempting her. Making things too complicated. She needed to spend time with her mom at lunch or she'd be alone all day, and she didn't want Andrew coming over. It would be so easy to start dating him again, to let his affection be something real again. But she couldn't.

"Thanks for the offer, but my mom depends on her routine," she said, withdrawing her hand from his.

One side of his mouth lifted into a smile, as if he wasn't swayed one bit. "Then I'll go find lunch on my own and meet you back here." His voice was smooth and tugged at her middle.

Stella swallowed, her pulse racing. How could she be reacting like this—after all this time and after all the pain? "Do you have time for that?"

He leaned close, and she could smell the cinnamon on his breath. So familiar.

"I always have time for you," he said.

Stella took a step back, jarring her senses away from him.

He winked and said, "See you in an hour."

Four

Evan slowed down as he approached the jewelry shop. It was early afternoon and he'd just returned from dropping Katie off with her mom. He didn't mind the four-hour round-trip so much, but he did mind having to see Michelle in person.

She was a beautiful woman—almost too perfect, if truth be told. That should have been a red flag when Evan had first met her at a restaurant he'd worked as head chef. Even now, it always took him a couple of hours to shake off the Michelle-effect. A lot of memories, a lot of betrayal and hurt.

Evan parked by the curb, feeling lucky to find a spot this time of day. The tourists were out in full force, eating at the cafés and browsing through shops. He sat in his truck for a moment, wondering what excuse he could come up with for going into the jewelry shop. Maybe he could browse, but that would seem too obvious.

He could look for something to send to his mom. Her birthday wasn't until July, but Stella didn't need to know that. Evan climbed out the truck, knowing if he didn't go now, it would be several days until he had time off during business hours.

Evan walked into the shop. A couple of women stood near the front trying on some bracelets. He scanned the place, but didn't see Stella. As he neared the counter, he could hear voices coming from the back room. The door was cracked open, but he couldn't see through it. The voices were male and female, and it sounded like an argument.

At first, Evan tried to ignore the conversation. He recognized Stella's voice, but he had no idea who she might be talking to.

When she said, "No, Andrew. Please leave," Evan couldn't ignore the conversation anymore. He walked to the office door, knocking and pushing it open as he did so.

Stella was facing him and glanced at him as he stepped in.

"Sorry to interrupt," Evan said. "Is everything okay?"

A dark-haired man turned around, his equally dark eyes narrowed.

"Evan!" Stella said, stepping toward him. She slipped her hands to his waist, lifted up and kissed him on the mouth. He didn't even have time to decide how to respond before she pulled away and released him. "You're early."

"I—uh." He glanced at the other man, noting the curiosity mixed with suspicion on his face, which was exactly how Evan was feeling. He could still feel Stella's kiss; it had been unexpected, and he decided it was unexpected in a good way. "I finished up and thought I'd come over to see if there's anything I could help with."

Stella smiled at him, although her eyes were rimmed in red as if she'd been crying.

He casually draped his left arm across her shoulders. "Is this . . . Andrew?" He extended his hand.

Andrew shook his hand briefly. "Evan?"

"That's me," Evan said, hoping he didn't sound like the

confused idiot he felt. But when Stella looped her arm around his waist, he knew he'd done the right thing.

"So you are . . ." Andrew looked from Evan to Stella. "You could have told me, Stella, instead of coming up with other excuses."

Stella shrugged. "I'm sorry. We haven't been dating long, and I didn't want to put Evan in the middle of our past."

"*Past* . . . yeah, I think I get that now." Andrew inhaled sharply, his jaw working as if he was trying to hold back what he really wanted to say. "I'm going now, just as you wished." He directed an appraising scowl in Evan's direction, then looked at Stella. "I'll call you later."

Stella's arm tightened around Evan. "Don't call me, Andrew."

He paused mid-turn and stared at Stella, his face red. Then he left, pushing past the customers who were standing at the sales counter.

Stella released Evan. "Sorry," she whispered. "Don't leave. I need to explain."

She left the office and helped the two women who'd been waiting.

Evan looked around the workspace. Post-it notes covered half of one wall, and he couldn't help but read some of them. They were everything from "Try The Fortune Café" to "Order two dozen gold clasps." On the other side of the room were a row of shelves. Jars filled with candy sat on the top row, then plastic tubs with jewelry pieces lined the second row.

"Sorry about that," Stella spoke, and Evan turned around to face her. She smoothed back her wavy hair that had come loose. "You're probably wondering what happened." She glanced toward the shop, then took a deep breath. "I thought maybe if I acted like we were together, Andrew would finally stop calling me."

"Your ex-boyfriend?"

She nodded. "We went to school together, and I haven't seen him for a year. I guess he decided to change that."

Evan leaned against the desk. The vulnerability was back in her brown eyes. "Glad I could help." He smiled, but she didn't smile back.

"You can tell your wife I'm sorry." Her face went red. "I should have considered that before kissing you."

"I don't have a wife," Evan said. "I'm divorced."

Stella nodded and turned away, moving a Post-it note. "Well, again, I'm sorry. And thanks for your . . . help. I think Andrew was convinced."

"I think so too," Evan said, straightening. They were silent for a moment, and to prevent it from becoming too awkward, he said, "I came in to find something for my mom's birthday."

"Oh, right." Stella looked over at him. "What does she like to wear?"

Evan shrugged, shoving his hands in his pockets. "Maybe gold—she wears a lot of that."

"Does she like big earrings? Small ones?"

"Small."

"Come on," Stella said. "I can show you a few sets she might like."

Evan followed her out, appreciating how her tone had brightened when they started talking about jewelry. For the next while, she showed him different pieces. When he asked how she'd made them, she seemed surprised at his questions, but then started to explain.

Evan realized he enjoyed watching her talk. She used her hands a lot, and her tone was animated. She obviously loved her craft. "So you've made everything in this store?" he asked.

"Most of it by now. Some of the inventory was created by my mom awhile back." Her tone softened when she mentioned her mother.

"Does she still work here?"

"Not anymore." There was hesitation in her voice. "She's been really sick—diabetes."

Evan had developed a few recipes for people on dietary restrictions, but now wasn't the time to drill Stella about her mom's eating habits. "Sounds pretty serious if she can't be in the shop anymore."

Stella blinked her eyes, tears forming. "It is. I moved back home to take care of her. Andrew wasn't too happy about that."

One look at Andrew had told Evan that he wasn't a small-town guy. "He doesn't seem like the type of man to settle in a place like this."

Stella's eyes widened. "You're pretty perceptive—for a stranger."

Evan smiled. "It doesn't take much perception. I know his type. I serve guys like him all the time."

Her brows lifted. "Serve? You're a waiter?"

"Chef."

Stella laughed, and her gaze moved over him. "Oh, wow. I'll bet chefs get all the women."

"Not really," Evan said with a smile. "I'm pretty much behind doors the whole time, and besides, with a young daughter, dating is not on my priority list."

Stella nodded, smiling now. "Yeah, I can understand that. Katie is adorable."

Evan decided he loved her smile and that she remembered his daughter's name.

The door chimed, and a woman with a couple of sunburned kids came into the shop. Evan checked the time, surprised that he'd been talking to Stella for so long. But it was time well spent.

"I should let you go," Evan said. "I think I'll go with the Inspired set."

"That's my favorite." Stella picked up the necklace and matching earrings, then carried them to the counter. "Thanks again," she said as she rang up the purchase.

Evan pulled out his credit card and handed it over. Lowering his voice, he said, "Can I borrow a Post-it?"

Her eyes were curious as she peeled one off for him.

Evan wrote his name and number on it, then stuck it next to a group of Post-its on the edge of the counter. Stella's gaze followed every movement. "I'd love to cook for you sometime," he said. There, he'd made the obvious first move. There was no backtracking now.

Her eyes met his, then slid away.

"Call if you want to," he said quietly. "No worries if you don't."

She nodded and made no offer to commit. Evan wasn't surprised. He might have helped her out of a bind, but that was as far as it went.

He took the wrapped jewelry set and walked out of the shop, feeling like he'd just put his heart on a bright orange Post-it.

Five

Stella called the number for The Fortune Café, feeling like she was starving yet again. When a woman answered, Stella placed her order for cashew chicken, fried rice, and an egg roll. It was 7:30 p.m. and the shop would stay open until 9:00, but it felt like this one day had been two.

First Andrew, then Evan.

She couldn't believe she'd kissed a stranger whom she thought was married. Relief had flooded through her when he'd said he was divorced. Maybe too much relief. She wondered what Evan had thought; his lips had been warm and she couldn't get the memory out of her mind. Although that was probably from doing something so daring. Yet, she couldn't get Evan's sea-colored eyes out of her mind, and it was making her crazy. That and the fact that he *wasn't* married when she had thought he was.

Gazing at the Post-it for the umpteenth time since he'd left, she wondered what he'd meant by "cooking for her." Maybe he wanted her to come to his restaurant—which made her realize that she didn't even know where he worked. What if it was The Fortune Café? She laughed to herself, although she couldn't picture him inside a tiny Chinese restaurant frying up chicken pieces and stirring sesame glaze toppings.

Maybe he meant his apartment. She assumed he lived around here—or why would he have given her his number? She moved the Post-it to the far corner, so that it wouldn't glare at her so much. Evan was nice . . . but that might be the problem. She didn't want to hurt a nice guy's feelings—especially one who looked a bit haunted when he mentioned that he was divorced.

And he had a daughter. Dating Evan would be too involved—too many other people were already a part of the equation. Stella's heart pounded as she realized she was even considering calling the number he'd left.

She hadn't dated since Andrew, but she also had more than one person in her own equation. And she didn't want to do anything that would make things worse for her mom.

The front door chimed, and Stella looked up.

A short man had entered, carrying a large white sack. "Takeout," he said.

Stella crossed to him and handed over the money, then took the sack. "Thank you! Smells great."

The man bowed his head and left.

Stella set the food on her work desk, keeping the office door open so she could watch for customers. She hadn't had Chinese in a while, and by the smell of the food, she knew she'd be a frequent customer. Halfway through her meal, she unwrapped the fortune cookie. She'd never been very good at waiting to read a fortune. Not that she'd ever had one come true.

She cracked open the cookie and laughed to herself as she read the tiny red words: *Do the thing you fear and love is certain.*

Like calling Evan? I fear that. Too complicated and all.

And nothing is ever certain. She'd learned that lesson well when Andrew dumped her. Even when he'd been practically groveling at her feet earlier that day, he was still telling her how to live her life and that she'd given up too much to run a tiny jewelry shop. The first time she'd heard it before leaving college, it had hurt deeply. This second time, it had made her angry that he felt like he could have a say in her life now. As if she was so desperate and missed him so much that she'd take him back and quickly agree with everything he said.

Stella pushed the paper aside and took another bite of the cashew chicken. *Do the thing you fear and love is certain.* Did she really fear calling Evan? No. She feared what that one phone call might *start*. Logically, she knew a single phone call wouldn't make love certain. But what would it lead to? She already couldn't stop thinking about Evan. Would going on a date with him fix that? She doubted it. And she wasn't looking for love anyway—maybe someday, but her mom's health was her focus now.

And Stella was more than happy with that decision.

She eyed the phone number again, and finally added it to her contacts. Then she opened a drawer and set the Post-it note inside. There. That would help her concentrate better on her work. She logged into her computer and entered a couple of orders for supplies.

By 9:00 p.m. she was emotionally drained enough to close up the shop and head right home, but the moment she stepped outside, the scent of the ocean tempted her. A quick walk, then home. She strolled along the boardwalk passing couple after couple until she started to feel really painfully single. Had she never noticed how many couples went out walking at night on Seashell Beach?

Annoyed, she turned and went back home. The light in her mother's room was still on, so she tapped on the bedroom door and opened it.

Her mom glanced up from a novel.

"How was the shop today?" she asked, closing the book and setting it aside.

Stella smiled. Times like this, her mom looked almost healthy. "Getting pretty busy now. You're up late."

"I was hoping to talk to you," her mom said.

Stella walked into the room and sat on the edge of the bed, worry tightening her stomach. Maybe she shouldn't have gone to the beach. "What is it?"

"I've asked my cousin Amelia to come up for a few days. She'll run the shop while you take a break."

"Mom," Stella protested. "I'm fine. We're fine."

Her mom gave her a half smile. "You look exhausted every time I see you, and Amelia knows the shop inside and out."

Even though Stella wanted to protest, taking a break did sound nice. Especially after a day like today. Amelia had helped out whenever her mom went on vacation, and at one point she'd offered to take over the store when things were getting tough. But Stella felt it was her obligation first to take care of her mom.

"When will she be here?"

"Early in the morning," her mom said. "So sleep in, then go out to breakfast. Eat a lot of pancakes and plenty of syrup for me."

Stella laughed and reached over to hug her mom. As she drew away, she did a mental check of the items on her mom's bedside table—finger stick, insulin, and bottled juice.

After saying good night, she left her mom's room and decided to take a bath, something she rarely indulged in because she'd probably fall asleep in the water. As she soaked in her favorite bubble bath scent, she thought again about the number she'd saved into her phone.

The relaxing heat of the water caused her mind to wander. She closed her eyes and replayed the scene in the office when Evan walked in and she'd kissed him. She wondered what it would be like if she kissed him again, only this time, he returned that kiss. He looked more than capable of making a woman melt.

Stella slid lower until the water touched her chin. With a few days off of work, it would be tempting to take Evan up on his offer.

Six

*E*van walked past the jewelry shop, trying to talk himself out of going inside. It had been twenty-four hours since he'd given Stella his number, and she hadn't called. A day wasn't all that long, but it was long enough to constantly think about her, he decided.

He shoved his hands into his pockets and stopped in front of a bookstore two shops down. Maybe he could buy his sister a gift. Her birthday was in November. Pretty soon, he'd have the next three years of gifts picked out and purchased. He turned and walked toward the jewelry shop. His lunch break would be over in about twenty minutes, and it was a ten-minute drive back to the Mariposa.

Without second-guessing himself again, Evan walked into the shop. He scanned the place, ignoring the customers, and looking for Stella. An older woman sat behind the counter, leafing through a magazine.

Was it Stella's mom? The woman looked like a modern-day gypsy, wearing a row of bracelets up each arm and several necklaces. He didn't even try to guess how many rings were on her fingers. The woman didn't look ill, and, he realized, she didn't look like the picture that was on the website. Of course, the years could have changed her quite a bit.

He walked up to the counter and said, "Mrs. Novak?"

The woman looked up, her brows raised. "No, I'm Amelia—just filling in for a couple of days. Can I help you?"

Evan glanced toward the office. The door was open, but the light was off.

"Were you looking for Stella?" Amelia asked, propping her elbows on the counter and leaning forward. Her bracelets clinked together, and her eyes assessed him. "I can take down your number."

"She already has it," Evan said, before realizing he probably shouldn't have said that.

The woman smiled like a Cheshire. "She does? That's wonderful. But I think it would be better if you talk to her in person. She's down at the beach, a straight line from here. She doesn't vary from her favorite spot much." She gave him a wink.

Evan was about to protest, but suddenly he wanted to laugh. "Are you related to her?"

"Her mother is my cousin." The woman's eyes stayed bright with interest. "And who are you?"

"Evan," he said.

"Well, Evan," Amelia said, her voice sugary. "If she turns you down, I'm single." She waved her left hand, flashing rings on every finger but the one that should have sported a wedding band.

Evan smiled. "Uh, thank you."

He turned away, and Amelia sang out, "If you don't find her, I'll let her know you stopped by."

Which might not be such a great idea. In fact, finding her on the beach might not be either. It wasn't like he could ask her for recommendations on what to get for his sister. Evan exhaled as he crossed Tangerine Street and found an alley that led to the sand. The closer he got to the beach, the more he tried to talk himself out of it.

He stopped on the boardwalk and scanned the sunbathers. It took him only moments to spot Stella. Her blonde hair was knotted into a bun at the top of her head, and she wore a red bikini top and a sarong tied around her hips. And she wasn't alone. She was standing, talking to some man.

Evan laughed at himself. Obviously Stella didn't lack for admirers. He might as well get in line. First Andrew, then him, and now this man at the beach. Stella probably didn't have a spare moment to call him.

He walked away before he could be caught staring like a fool. As he headed to his truck, he wondered why he was so eager to get to know her better. With a daughter in his life, opening his heart to another woman would be complicated.

Seven

Stella watched a man who reminded her of Evan leave the boardwalk and disappear into one of the alleys that led to Tangerine Street. She must be imagining things because what were the chances of running into him on the beach?

"Are you interested in coming to the BBQ tonight?"

Stella turned her attention back to Dave, a friend from high school. He had the day off of work and was there with his son. Dave was part of her graduating class who had stuck around, living and working in Seashell Beach. A group of them got together about once a month.

"I have to fill orders at night. It's too hard to get much done when the store is open and busy," Stella said.

Disappointment crossed Dave's face, but Stella figured he was being polite. He was married with a kid, and when Stella had first moved home, she'd gone to one of their gatherings. She had felt totally out of place. Everyone was either married, dating someone, or just wanting to play around.

She was suddenly anxious to get back to her sunbathing. She told Dave she'd call if her plans changed, and then she went back to the beach chair she'd carried from the house. The temperature was perfect, and although the beach was crowded, the sun was worth it. She'd grown too pale and her hair too dull.

Stella wasn't into tanning like she was as a teenager. Now she used sunscreen, but that didn't stop her from a bit of worshipping. She settled in her chair and closed her eyes, listening to the sounds of the waves, the seagulls, and kids running up and down the sand, yelling and laughing.

She was half asleep when her cell phone rang, startling her out of her reverie.

"Stella! Did Evan find you?" Amelia's voice boomed over the phone.

Stella sat up, blinking at the brightness of the day. "Evan?"

"Yes, that nice man who came in looking for you. I sent him down to the beach."

"I didn't see him," Stella said, even though she realized she had—when she'd been talking to Dave.

Her mind was clearer now. "What did he want?"

"Oh, honey. When a man like that comes around, don't make him chase you."

Stella's mouth felt dry. "Do you know him?"

"Not until I met him a little while ago," Amelia gushed into the phone. Stella was used to Amelia's antics—one good reason she never confessed anything about her dating life. "He's a good one, Stella. Don't let him get away."

She laughed. Amelia was too much sometimes. "I don't even know him. He bought something for his mom yesterday, and the day before he came in with his daughter. He's divorced."

"Oh," Amelia paused. "Never mind. It just means that he has a bit of experience. How old is his daughter?"

"Maybe six or seven."

"Perfect. Young enough to not have to worry about a rebellious stepdaughter."

"Amelia!" Stella said, laughing again. The woman had never married but seemed to have all kinds of advice on dating and relationships. "We haven't even been out on a date."

"Well, what's stopping you? He said you had his number."

"I do," Stella said, falling quiet for a moment. "You know how it is with mom. Things are really busy right now and—"

"Your mother would be the first to push you out the door," Amelia said. "Do you think that she wants you to wait on her so much?"

Stella swung her legs over the chair, her heart feeling heavy. "I couldn't bear the thought of anything happening to her."

"She's doing better than she has in a long time," Amelia said, her tone softening. "Look, dear. You've been wonderful to your mom, and you've done a fabulous job with the shop over the past year. But I agree with your mother—you need to go date a man."

"So my mom's in on this too?"

"Why do you think I'm here?" Amelia asked, chuckling. "I might be moving in."

Stella smiled and took a deep breath. What would her mom and Amelia think if they knew Andrew had been by the day before? It didn't matter, she wasn't going to tell them because she was never going to contact Andrew again.

"Just one date, Stella," Amelia insisted. "Call that man. What's there to be afraid of?"

Stella thought of the fortune from the night before. *Do the thing you fear and love is certain.* Except she wasn't looking for love. She wasn't looking for anything, but with Amelia, and now her mom, dead set on this, she might call Evan after all.

Eight

Evan nearly dropped the sauté pan he held in one hand when he realized it was Stella calling him. He turned down the burner and answered the phone.

"I guess you met Amelia," she said immediately.

"Yeah. She was filling in for you?" Evan said. He couldn't believe how nervous he felt at the sound of Stella's voice—like he was in middle school talking to a girl on the phone for the first time. He waved at one of the employees to take over the mushroom and onion sauce, then he walked out of the hotel kitchen into one of the huge storage rooms where he wouldn't have a dozen people listening to his side of the conversation.

A sigh came through the line. "You impressed her."

Evan furrowed his brows. The words didn't match the tone. "She seemed . . . enthusiastic."

Stella laughed, and Evan smiled at that.

"That's the perfect word to describe Amelia," she said. "Sorry if she was pushy or nosy or—"

"Look, Stella," Evan said, releasing a nervous breath.

"I'm glad you called, but if it was at Amelia's insistence, then I want you to know that you're off the hook."

"Oh, she insisted all right," Stella said. "But . . . I don't want to be off the hook unless you want me to be."

Evan moved the phone to his other ear. For some reason his ear had become very hot. Her teasing words had made him feel more bold, more sure of himself. "Are you flirting with me?"

"Maybe a little."

Evan heard the smile in her voice. "In that case, you're definitely *on* the hook."

She laughed.

He had her on the phone, and now he couldn't let her go without asking her out. "What are you doing about 10:30 tonight?"

"Sleeping," she said, amusement in her voice.

"Perfect. Then you aren't too busy for dinner."

"Nothing is open that late," Stella said. "Not even takeout."

"I have connections," Evan said. "But you'll have to meet me."

"Oh really? Where?"

"Come to the Seafood Grille at the Mariposa."

"10:30? Why so late?" she asked.

"I hate crowds," Evan said.

Stella laughed, and even after they hung up, Evan could still hear her laughter.

The hours passed both too slow and too fast. Tension increased in the hotel kitchen since the governor's family and entourage arrived at 7:30 p.m. Although Evan had been planning the meals for days, he wanted everything to go off without a hitch. He checked and double-checked everyone's work from dicing the grilled chicken for the chicken parmesan salad, to drizzling raspberry cream sauce over the chocolate cheesecake dessert.

He'd researched the family's favorite dishes, and then had put a twist on them. By 9:00 p.m. when the desserts were being served, one of the waiters came into the kitchen and told Evan that the governor wanted to meet him.

This is it, Evan thought. A recommendation from the governor or one of his staff would put the new resort on the map for Californians. He hoped the news was good, and if it wasn't, then his best wasn't good enough.

As Evan walked toward the two tables filled with the governor's family and others, the governor stood. "Mr. Rockham," he said, extending his hand.

Evan shook it, his eyes quickly scanning to see if the guests had been eating or merely picking at their food.

"The dinner was excellent," the governor said.

Relief shot through Evan. They chatted for a few minutes about the menu, the hotel, and then Evan asked about the upcoming wedding.

"You'll have to ask my wife about that," the governor said with a wink. "I'm here for the food."

Evan laughed. "We'll keep you happy then."

By the time Evan returned to the kitchen, he was elated. The governor had been much more personable than he expected, and the compliments seemed genuine. Cleanup had already begun, and Evan pitched in, working as quickly as possible. The sooner the staff left for the night, the sooner he could start cooking for Stella.

Nine

Stella regretted wearing heels about two seconds after getting out of her car. The new Mariposa Hotel was imposing and gorgeous, and it was definitely a place for fancy people, but Stella wasn't fancy. And by dressing up this way, she felt more than uncomfortable. She had no idea what Evan would be wearing, and what kind of message did she want to send him anyway?

But Amelia had insisted—had even rallied her mother to insist as well—which led to Stella pulling out a dark lavender dress that fit more snugly than Stella was used to. At least the straps were thick and Stella didn't have a lot of cleavage to show off anyway.

"Have you seen that place?" Amelia had asked. "It's a five-star resort—the women probably wear furs even though it's warm."

"Furs and diamonds," her mother had pitched in.

Stella felt totally betrayed. "I guess I'll have to add diamonds to my next vendor order."

Amelia had laughed. "You can borrow mine." She started to pull off her earrings.

"No," Stella had said. "Too much. I'll wear the dress. I'll wear the heels. I'll even put on some mascara or something. But not the diamonds."

Thankfully, Amelia put her earrings back on. "Don't come home early," she said, with a conspiratorial wink. "We won't be waiting up."

Stella had glanced over at her mom, and her mom smiled oh-so-innocently. "I feel like I've been set up." But she couldn't help smiling back at her mom.

And now, here she was, walking toward the glittering hotel.

"Hello, ma'am," the bell hop at the front entrance greeted her.

Stella nodded to him, hoping that she looked like any hotel patron. Once inside, she followed the signs for the Seafood Grille. As she walked along the marbled floor, she practically gaped at the huge framed landscape paintings and the massive display of fresh flowers on elegant hall tables.

She slowed as she neared the restaurant. The lights were dim, and no one was at the host's podium. She took a few steps into the restaurant, her heart sinking. Maybe she'd misunderstood the time.

"Stella." On the other side of the restaurant, Evan had come out of the kitchen doors. He wore a white chef's jacket.

"You're here," she said as she walked toward him. They met in the middle of the room. "And I'm way overdressed."

Evan smiled at her. "You look beautiful. Perfect, really, like you belong in this hotel."

Stella glanced around the restaurant, feeling a bit flushed at his compliment. "This place is closed."

"The kitchen isn't," Evan said, reaching for her hand. He led her around the tables toward the kitchen.

He's holding my hand, and I'm letting him. His hand was

warm and strong and somehow put her at ease even though she was in a deserted five-star restaurant.

Evan led her into the kitchen, his hand still capturing hers.

Stella pulled him to a stop, staring at the room. It was as large as the restaurant. Silver gleamed everywhere, from the overhead can-lights to the metal surfaces and artfully arranged pans. "This place is amazing."

Evan laughed, squeezed her hand, and let go. He motioned to a table on one side of the room that had been set with a tablecloth and plates and utensils. A couple of lit candles glowed as a centerpiece. Stella could almost hear Amelia gushing over it all.

"Have a seat, and I'll bring over the food," Evan said, holding out a chair for her.

Stella sat down and watched as he carried over a covered platter. "No waiters tonight?"

"I guess they were all too tired." Evan set down the platter and removed the lid.

It was some sort of chicken dish with creamy potatoes and seasoned vegetables. It looked delicious and smelled wonderful.

"Not quite what the governor ate, but I didn't think you'd want leftovers." He moved off and grabbed a couple of wine flutes along with a bottle of wine. Then he wrote something down in a ledger.

"Five-star restaurant leftovers are probably pretty great," Stella said.

Evan laughed, setting down the wine glasses and pouring them about half full.

"So . . . what did you feed him?" She took a sip of wine, watching Evan.

He sat across from her. "A little bit of each of their favorites."

Stella was mesmerized as he described the recipes. The way he talked about food was like an artist talking about blending the perfect color. "Did you always do the cooking when you were married?" she blurted out. She could have choked—just because she was wondering about it, didn't mean it was polite to ask. "Sorry about that. I didn't mean to ask such a personal question."

"It's all right," Evan said, his gaze amused. "As long as I can ask you a personal question as well."

Stella took another sip of wine. "Deal."

Evan started cutting his meat with a fork and knife—which appeared to be sterling silver. "Being a chef isn't the same thing as being a construction developer, and your house is the only one on the block that's never quite finished, or being a janitor and the last thing you want to do when you get home is clean. Cooking is something that I never get tired of."

"I guess if we all get hungry enough, we'll end up cooking."

"Or ordering takeout."

Stella flushed, but she didn't think he knew exactly how his comment sounded to her. Stella cut into her food and took the first bite. It was heavenly. "This is excellent. Really." She took another bite. "So do you have a fully equipped kitchen at your place?"

He grinned. "With a pink fairy-princess bedroom in my 'pad,' it's not the standard bachelor hang out." He ate a bite of his food, then said, "I'm pretty picky, so my kitchen is fairly well stocked. It's not like I'm cooking gourmet all of the time, but I like fresh ingredients and have my favorite recipes. My ex-wife, Michelle, is really picky. I had to stick to the basics with her." He took another bite. "Now, it's my turn to ask you a question."

Stella raised a brow.

"Has Andrew bothered you again?" he asked.

She couldn't have been more surprised by his question, but she realized that he was probably curious—after that kiss and all. Her neck heated up, and she took another sip of wine. "He's texted a couple of times and called once, but didn't leave a message."

"Did you guys date long?"

"A couple of years," Stella said. "Everyone liked him in the program, and he was a magnet with the women. I guess he was with me too."

Evan held her gaze as he said, "I'm not surprised he noticed you—you're hard to miss."

Ten

"Evan . . ." It had been a long time since she'd been complimented . . . and she didn't count Andrew. Stella stared at Evan for a moment, then smiled. "How is it possible you're divorced? I mean, you're sweet, good-looking, and you cook. You're like the dream man."

She nearly regretted her questions when he turned red. He gazed at his wine glass for a moment before answering. "I had no control in my marriage. And I'm not a controlling person, but what I mean is that I had no say. No voice. It was like I was put in a corner to observe while Michelle ran everything and made all of the decisions."

Now Stella did regret being so blunt with him. The haunted look in his eyes was back, darkening their sea-color. She was about to apologize when he continued.

"A strange thing happened to me when Katie was born," he said. "I'd always thought I loved my parents, my sister, even my wife. But Katie was something else. It was like she was a part of me, and everything I did was now for her."

Stella nodded. She could definitely see that when he'd been in the shop with his daughter.

Evan took a sip of his wine. "Maybe Michelle noticed that, and she didn't like it. Since I worked afternoons and evenings, I'd spend all morning with Katie while Michelle shopped or spent time with friends. Sometimes I felt like we were trading our kid back and forth."

He looked down at his plate of food with a shrug. "Despite Michelle's love for deep fried food, she was very picky in other areas. Katie was toilet trained by eighteen months. She was reading by the age of three with the help of a private tutor. Before she turned four, she was in a private preschool that only movie stars' kids attended."

"Wow," Stella said, trying to process it all in her mind. Was Michelle a trust fund baby or something? It didn't sound like she had a career. Then he told her about Michelle's insistence that Katie move to Japan for a year. Stella's mouth dropped open. She didn't want to bash his ex-wife out loud, but Stella was definitely trashing her in her mind.

"That's pretty much my marriage in a box," Evan finished. His gaze met hers tentatively. "Sorry to dump it all out there."

"That's fine. I guess I would have found out eventually."

"Eventually." His smile was back, which was much better than the previous storminess in his eyes. "I like the sound of that. It implies more of this."

Stella moved to take another sip of wine, then thought better of it. Evan's gaze was much too encompassing, and her body temperature was rising. "Can I have a glass of ice water?"

"No problem," he said, standing to fetch it.

"So you have joint custody of Katie?" Stella asked when he brought it back.

"Yeah." Evan sat down. "Although with the two-hour drive between us, I only get her about one weekend a month." He pushed the food around on his plate.

Stella was getting full too. "This food is amazing—really. Did you always want to be a chef?"

"Not specifically. I was a latchkey kid, and so I was on my own a lot. I guess I got tired of cold cereal and started experimenting." Evan rose and gathered the plates.

Stella stood too. "I should do that since you cooked."

"You're my guest," Evan said waving at her to sit back down. "I hope you like cheesecake."

Stella groaned. "I love it, but I'm stuffed."

Evan set the plates into a vast sink, then opened one of the massive refrigerators. A moment later he came back with two chilled plates of cheesecake drizzled with chocolate sauce, and topped with blackberries.

"Take one bite, and then you can take home the rest."

Stella stared at the yumminess. "I could never take this home."

"I have a to-go box."

She met his gaze. "Oh, it's not that . . ." She hesitated. "It's my mom. You know she's diabetic—but she doesn't have much self-control." Stella had never told another person this much about her mom. She wouldn't call her mom a food addict, but maybe someone who couldn't resist. If it was in the house, then she'd eat it, no matter what the risk.

Evan didn't look too concerned. "You can take the whole cheesecake home to her—it's sugar-free."

"Really? How is that possible?" The dessert looked much too good for that.

"Just taste it," he said with a grin.

Stella did. It was creamy, smooth, sweet, and the combination of the chocolate and raspberries perfect. She looked up at Evan. "I don't believe you."

He leaned back in his chair, his eyes steady on hers. "I have a whole slew of recipes for people with special dietary needs. The best thing about them is that you don't need to lose the flavor because some of the ingredients have to be altered."

"If my mom tasted this, she'd ask you to marry her," Stella said, thinking about the smuggled M&M's she'd found under the couch the week before. She had to do a thorough inspection every couple of days.

Evan laughed. "Is she as pretty as you?"

"Very funny," Stella said, her face burning up. She took a swallow of the ice water, then dug into the cheesecake. She didn't care if she was full. Each bite was divine.

"Will you continue to work at the shop if your mom gets better?" Evan asked.

Stella set her fork down. She really had to stop eating, or she'd never go back to takeout again. "She won't get better, at least not enough to do what she used to. And . . ." she started, a realization coming to her, "although I never expected to come back after college, I've enjoyed it—mostly."

"What would make it better?"

Stella found that she was staring at him, and she backtracked quickly. "Nothing, really. I mean, it's a quiet place if you're local. People are always coming and going, so there isn't really a point to establishing a relationship."

"Like dating someone?"

Embarrassment heated her cheeks. "That too." She gave him a sheepish smile.

"You're here tonight," he said.

She laughed, wishing she didn't feel so embarrassed. "True. Although it's practically the middle of the night."

"Practically . . ." He smiled.

"What about you?" she asked. "Is this a temporary job for you?"

"Being the head chef is a move up in my career, but I don't like being so far from my daughter. I'd love to stay for a while, but a few things depend on that."

"So you like your job that much?"

Evan's gaze held hers for a moment, then he nodded. "I got lucky."

But Stella didn't think he was talking about his job now. He rose and cleared the dessert plates.

Stella stood as well and carried the wine glasses and utensils to the sink where Evan stood rinsing everything off. "I'm serious about taking the cheesecake home," Evan said. "The rest is in a box. See what your mom thinks."

"I'd love to." Stella looked around for a dishwasher. "Do we load these somewhere?"

Evan turned off the water. "No, we'll leave them soaking in the sink. The kitchen will open around 5:00 a.m., and I'm not going to mess with Mr. Goodrich's method—he only allows things to be done in a certain order."

"I wish I had a Mr. Goodrich at my house."

Evan laughed. He dried off his hands, then pulled out the rest of the cheesecake from the refrigerator. He crossed to Stella, and reached for her hand. "Come on, I'll walk you to your car. We don't want to keep Amelia up too late."

"You're probably right." She followed him out, trying to ignore the way her stomach fluttered like crazy at his casual touch. They exited a side door that opened onto the parking lot.

Stella breathed in the cool, salty air. It had been a great evening. And that had everything to do with the man holding her hand right now. Yeah, he had some history, some heartbreak in his past, but that just made him all the more interesting to her. Maybe it wouldn't be so complicated to date him, especially since the more she was around him, the more she liked him.

"There's my car," Stella said, coming to a stop as they reached her VW.

"Vintage, huh?"

"Seemed to fit Seashell Beach, so I bought it when I moved home." She dug in her purse for her keys. When she found them, Evan held out his hand.

She gave him the keys, and he unlocked the back door

and set the cheesecake on the seat. Then he opened the driver's door for her.

"Thanks," she said. "I think you're pretty much perfect, Evan Rockham."

He laughed. "I'm not even close."

Stella realized he hadn't moved back and was standing very close to her, his left arm leaning on top of the door. He reached for her hand again, and Stella's breath hitched. This time his thumb caressed her palm, sending goosebumps up her arms.

She wondered if it would be too forward to kiss him on their first date. *Yes.* Except she'd already kissed him. He was quiet, not saying anything, just watching her. Even though the night was dark, she felt like she could see the color of his eyes. It wasn't only that his eyes were incredible, but everything about him was pretty awesome as well. "Do you cook for all of your dates?"

"No, only the ones I'm trying to impress." Evan leaned closer, and if Stella moved back, she'd be sitting in her car. So she stayed still, almost feeling the warmth from his body.

"Why would you want to impress me?"

"Because you're pretty amazing," he said in a soft voice. "You left a prestigious college to run a jewelry shop for your mom."

She loved the way his soft tone sent warm shivers through her body. "It's a great shop."

He smiled. "It is. And you chose your mom over your spoiled boyfriend."

"That wasn't as hard as it might sound." Standing here with Evan made her realize that she and Andrew were never a good match.

Evan's fingers threaded through hers "I love that you have Post-it reminders stuck to your walls," he said.

"Really?" Stella laughed. "It just proves that I can't remember anything unless it's written on a fluorescent square of paper and tacked right in front of me."

"It's much better than those electronic devices everyone else uses." Evan tugged her hand toward him, and she naturally moved closer. "And one more thing, I love that you called me today."

Stella knew he was going to kiss her. There wasn't any doubt. And if it had been two days earlier, she probably would have stepped away. But it wasn't two days earlier, and she had enjoyed looking into this man's sea-colored eyes and letting him tell her what he loved about her. So, she didn't move back.

His fingers released hers, and one hand brushed against her jaw, then moved behind her neck. Stella knew immediately that this kiss was going to be a lot different than their first kiss in the office.

Evan's lips touched hers, and he kissed her softly, tentatively, as if he was unsure of her reaction. Stella melted into the kiss, sliding her hands up his chest, then behind his neck. She pulled him closer, kissing him back, and his hands wrapped around her waist. Her body seemed to meld with his, her pulse hammering like mad.

The touch of his mouth warmed her through, and the kissing turned more intense. Evan moved her until her back was pressed against the car. She lowered her hands to his shoulders, feeling the strength there as she held onto him. Evan's kiss slowed, and she was able to catch her breath. When he lifted his head, she opened her eyes.

"Hey," he whispered.

"Hey," she whispered back. She smiled, still cocooned between his body and the car. Whatever was happening, she didn't feel lonely anymore.

Eleven

Evan rolled over in bed with a groan. His cell was ringing, and it felt like he'd barely fallen asleep after his date with Stella. A quick glance at the time told him it was almost 3:00 a.m. But his heart nearly stopped when he saw that Katie was calling.

He'd given her a basic cell phone to call only him. It was the best way to stay in touch with her about simple things like asking how school was going without going through Michelle first.

"Katie?" he answered.

"Daddy?" Her little voice coming through the line tugged at his heart.

"Is everything okay?" he asked, sitting up in bed and switching on his lamp.

"Mommy's not home, and I'm scared."

Panic shot through Evan. "Where did she go?"

"She went with R-Randy."

Evan knew about Randy—Michelle's latest fling. He had to admire a man who could put up with her. None of her boyfriends lasted very long. "You're there alone?" He tried to keep the panic out of his voice so he didn't scare Katie.

"Mrs. Gordman is here, but she's snoring on the couch."

Relief shot through Evan. Katie wasn't alone—she just wanted her mom. "Well, your mom is late, that's all. Go to sleep, and when you wake up, I'm sure she'll be home."

"She said she wouldn't be home for two days," Katie said, a pout in her voice.

"What?" If Michelle was gone for the weekend, why wouldn't she bring Katie to him?

"She said I would be bored, so I had to stay home," Katie said, then yawned.

Anger pulsed through Evan. Why wouldn't Michelle bring Katie to him or at least give him the option? Or even better, wait to spend the weekend with her boyfriend when it was Evan's turn with Katie? He hated divorce. But he'd hated being married to Michelle even more. It was times like this that he wished he'd tried to get full custody during the divorce proceedings. He decided he'd have to make a call his lawyer to modify the custody agreement so that he'd be the first choice babysitter.

"Look, sweetie," Evan said after taking a measured breath. "It's the middle of the night, and you'll be super tired tomorrow if you don't go back to sleep. How about I tell you a story?"

"About the green giant?"

Evan laughed quietly. "Sure. Now lie down and close your eyes."

Ten minutes later, he could hear Katie breathing softly and steadily. He didn't dare fall asleep for a while in case she woke up needing him again, so he kept the phone next to his pillow. He didn't expect to sleep. Thoughts of Stella returned with full force. They'd kissed and talked for another hour in the parking lot. It was like he could tell her anything. He'd never felt that comfortable with another person so quickly—

not even Michelle. He didn't know if he'd ever felt like he could totally be himself with Michelle. The more he analyzed their relationship and marriage, the more he realized it had always been all about her. It had just taken him years to see it.

Evan turned on his side, thinking about how Stella hadn't exactly been shy in returning his kisses. The thought shot heat through him. She was definitely interested in him—and wasn't afraid to show it. And knowing that she hadn't dated anyone since Andrew the year before told Evan that she wasn't a player. He thought of the way she fit against him, and how she'd run her fingers along his neck and shoulders, then told him to kiss her some more.

Being with Stella was not about the physical attraction though. He'd been watching and listening to her, wondering how she'd be around Katie. That was more important than being with a woman who liked him or made him feel good. Evan had to think about the long term because Katie was his priority.

Evan thought about his daughter at home without any parents around right now. Things were about to get even more sticky with Michelle. He sighed in frustration, deciding that maybe he should take Katie for the summer. But would that be any better? She'd have to hang out with a babysitter here in Seashell Beach. What was the difference between that and Mrs. Gordman?

Evan must have fallen asleep because when he opened his eyes next, his bedroom was flooded with light. He checked his cell phone and called Katie.

"You're not at school yet?" he asked.

"It's Saturday!" she said.

Evan laughed. "I know, silly. What are you going to do today?"

"I don't know. Mrs. Gordman says she's watching a program, then maybe we can go to the petting farm." Katie's voice lacked its usual enthusiasm.

"That sounds like fun," Evan said. "Can you feed the goats for me?"

"Okay," her voice became brighter. "Can you buy me a rabbit?"

"A rabbit? What do you want that for?" Katie always requested pets, but Michelle had never allowed any such things in their home. Maybe he'd check with the owner of the apartment building to see if there were any restrictions. Except he really didn't want a rabbit.

"They're so furry!"

"You're absolutely right," he said with a laugh. "We'll talk about it some more when you come to see me again." He said good-bye to her, grateful that she seemed in better spirits now. He hoped she'd have fun at the petting farm.

The next phone call was a bit harder. First he showered and dressed, then when he'd gone through half of a cup of coffee, he called Michelle.

She didn't answer. Of course. So, because he knew it would annoy her, he called her right back. Which was probably childish, but Michelle seemed to bring that out in him.

"Evan, I'm in the middle of something," she said by way of answering. "If it's urgent, text me."

"I just talked to Katie . . . In fact, she called me at 3:00 in the morning."

"Is something wrong?" Michelle asked, and Evan was mollified a bit when he heard the worry in her voice. He knew she loved their daughter as much as he did, but they had two completely different ways of showing it.

"She was scared, and she was missing you."

"Oh, Evan. She's a drama queen. You know that."

Evan knew that Katie wouldn't have to be a drama queen if her mom paid a little attention to her. Katie had to resort to extreme tactics to get anything from Michelle.

"I could have taken her while you went out of town," he said.

Michelle sighed. "Yeah, but I didn't have time to drive her up." A muffled giggle sounded as if Michelle was trying to cover up her laughter. It was obvious she was with Randy. Probably still in bed.

"I could have come to pick her up," Evan said, trying to keep the sharpness out of his voice. What he really wanted to say was that it seemed like Mrs. Gordman was the one raising their daughter instead of Michelle. Yeah, he got that she needed breaks and that she was dating and that one hundred percent of her life didn't need to be about a kid, but today he was feeling more protective of Katie.

"Well, you just had her, and I'm sure you would have grumbled about it if I called you," Michelle said, her voice sounding pouty.

Evan breathed out, trying to calm his growing frustration. "It might have taken some rearranging with work, but you know Katie comes first." He almost added "*for me.*" It turned out he didn't have to. Michelle was all too happy to take their discussion to the next level.

"Whatever, Evan. Stop pretending you're the perfect dad. Katie told me that the governor was coming to your hotel, and so maybe I was thinking of you first." She muffled her voice again, saying something to Randy. "But I really don't care what you think of my motivations. When I have my daughter at home, I'll make the decisions as to what does and does not go on."

Evan rubbed his temple with one hand, while gripping the phone with the other. It took all of his patience to keep his voice neutral. "I don't want to argue. I wanted to let you know that I can take her, even if I'm cooking for the President of the United States." He took a breath as Michelle scoffed. "And if you think if you're going to be really busy this summer, I'd be happy to keep her longer. Even the whole summer if you need me to."

Michelle was quiet, which surprised Evan. He thought she'd immediately say no, then later allow him to extend beyond the normal two weeks. He heard her murmur something to Randy, then he said something back.

"Okay, I'll think about it," Michelle said.

Evan straightened. This was unlike Michelle, but maybe it was Randy's influence. He wondered if he should or shouldn't be grateful for that. Randy was the reason now that Katie was spending the weekend with a babysitter. And this boyfriend was the latest in a long string over the past three years.

"Thanks," Evan said, grateful for this step forward.

When he hung up with Michelle, he started to feel more and more excited. If Katie spent the summer with him, maybe he could persuade Michelle to let her go to school in Seashell Beach. Surely there was a prestigious private one that even Michelle would approve of.

He took a sip of his coffee, feeling elated, but then he realized having Katie living him would complicate his life in other areas. He set down his cup. His budding relationship with Stella might come to a screeching halt if she realized dating Evan now included two.

Twelve

Stella fidgeted with a pearl ring display. Evan would be coming in any minute on his lunch break. It was 3:00 in the afternoon, but since Evan started work later in the day, he had an odd lunch time. She looked toward the door as someone walked past the shop. Not Evan. They'd texted a few times this morning, and every time he wrote, her heart jumped.

Maybe it was because she could still feel his arms around her and his kisses on her mouth. Evan had been right; Amelia had waited up for her, and then, this morning, they'd all had cheesecake for breakfast. It had been a long time since Stella had seen her mother able to eat something enjoyable that wouldn't shock her system. Stella wanted to kiss Evan again just for that.

Stella pulled out one of the pearl rings and slipped it on. She'd done the inset work for the pearls herself. The rings were one of the more popular items in the shop, and they also sold well online. She twisted the ring on her finger, wondering if it was possible to fall for a man so soon . . . this hard? Maybe it was the wine she'd had with dinner.

Maybe it was because being around Andrew had made her realize how much she missed being with a man. Or maybe Amelia's excitement had become her own excitement. Or maybe it was seeing her mom close her eyes in pleasure as she ate the cheesecake Evan had made for her.

The door jingled, and Stella looked up to see Evan walk in.

The second she saw him, she knew she wasn't falling for him for anything other than *she* wanted to be with him. Evan walked toward her with a half smile. Stella barely had time to slip the pearl ring off and put it back before Evan leaned down and kissed her cheek. It was only a kiss on the cheek, but it made her all too aware of him. She didn't know how it would be when she first encountered Evan after their date the night before. Now she knew. Sweet.

"Are you here to shop for some more jewelry?" she teased, putting a little space between them in case a customer came into the shop.

"No, I'm here to steal you away." He wasn't letting her move too far. "What are you hungry for?"

She was hungry for anything. "What? You didn't cook for me?"

Evan laughed. "I didn't want to be late."

"I thought we could order takeout," Stella said. "Then I won't have to put up the *closed* sign."

"Why are you putting up the *closed* sign?" Amelia asked, coming out of the office.

Stella turned. "I thought you were leaving today."

"Change of plans." Amelia grinned and sidled up to Evan, looking him up and down. "That cheesecake was divine."

"Thank you," Evan said, his face turning pink.

Stella wanted to laugh. "We were, uh, about to order takeout."

"If you two want to go get lunch, I'll mind the shop." She looked at Stella and wagged her eyebrows.

Stella wanted to laugh at Amelia's antics. But at that moment, she was really glad that Amelia had decided to stay

She and Evan left the shop, and Evan slipped his hands into his pockets. Stella felt disappointed that he didn't hold her hand, but it was probably better—they'd only been on one date after all. She thought of how Amelia had conveniently come into the shop so they could go to lunch . . . it was almost as if she was spying on them.

"What are you smiling at?" Evan asked, nudging her.

"Oh, just everything, I guess."

"Where do you want to go to lunch?"

Stella already knew. "Let's go to The Fortune Café—it's not as great as your cooking, of course. I ordered it the other night, and it was really good."

"Thanks," Evan said.

He seemed more quiet than he had the night before. Maybe he hadn't slept much like she hadn't.

Stella hadn't been inside the café before, but she knew it was next to the watch repair shop.

When they reached the door of the restaurant, Evan opened it for Stella. They stepped into the dim interior, and the scent of fragrant spices hit Stella. The place was nearly empty, and Stella assumed because it was between the lunch and dinner hour. A waitress walked toward them, the name *Emma* on her name tag. She wore the standard server's uniform—black pants, white button-down shirt, and a white apron. "Two?" she asked.

"Yes," Evan said. "Can we sit by the window?"

"Certainly," the woman replied. She led them to a table in the corner of the restaurant that overlooked Tangerine Street.

Stella sat down, impressed that the red tablecloths were real fabric.

"Have you eaten here before?" the waitress asked, taking out an order pad from her short apron. Emma was a really pretty woman with beautiful brown eyes, but Evan seemed more interested in the menu than the waitress. Always a good sign.

"I've ordered takeout," Stella said.

Emma's eyebrows lifted. "You did? How was it?"

Stella was surprised at the question. It seemed that the waitress was very interested.

"It was really good," Stella said.

"I'll let the cook know." The waitress glanced at Evan, then back to Stella. "Did you get a fortune?"

Stella was even more surprised now, especially since she remembered the fortune quite clearly. "I did. Isn't that standard with all orders?"

The waitress seemed to hesitate. Then she smiled. "Yes. I'm curious about that kind of stuff—Chinese fortunes, good luck charms. I always wonder if they ever come true."

Stella shrugged. "I still remember mine, but I guess time will tell if it does come true." She opened her menu, wondering why the waitress was prying so much.

"What's the cook's specialty?" Evan asked, and the waitress launched into a description of a few dishes.

They all sounded great to Stella.

Evan ordered a shrimp dish and Stella ordered her standby, cashew chicken.

He fell silent again after the waitress left. Stella hadn't expected this—she wasn't sure what she expected, but it wasn't a quiet Evan. He'd been sweet when greeting her, but it seemed that now he was pretty distracted.

She looked around the restaurant at the Asian décor and red tablecloths. "This place has a great ambiance."

Evan nodded, and Stella wondered if he'd really heard her.

She thought about the questions the waitress had asked her about the fortune cookie. Emma's questions were more than curious. *A bit strange.* Stella shook off the thought and asked Evan about his day at work. He briefly mentioned the governor's family, who had left after lunch.

He was too quiet—granted she'd only been on one date with him, but the Evan of today was a lot different than the man of last night. "Is everything all right?" she finally asked.

He lifted his eyes, as if he'd just realized she was talking to him. His intent gaze made her stomach flip, and memories of kissing him the night before came back full force.

"Sorry. I have a lot on my mind. Katie called at 3:00 a.m."

"Is she okay?" Stella asked.

"Yeah," Evan said, his tone subdued. "Her mom was out of town, and she was stressed about that."

Stella exhaled, relieved that maybe his silence wasn't about her. "Does she travel for her job or something?"

"No. Boyfriend."

Evan didn't need to elaborate. Stella knew by the tone of his voice how he felt about it. But a new worry had grown. Anytime the subject about his ex-wife came up, he seemed so melancholy. Was it possible that he regretted the divorce? That he was still in love with Michelle?

The waitress came back, carrying their food. Frankly, Stella was grateful for the distraction. This lunch date wasn't going quite like she'd envisioned.

They started eating, and Stella said, "Do you like it?" She figured that since he was a cook, he'd be a lot more discerning.

"It's really good," Evan said, sounding impressed, but he didn't elaborate.

Stella asked him a couple more things while they ate, but by the time the waitress came back to refill their drinks, she was ready to go. Whatever was going on with Evan seemed to be beyond her reach. She just didn't know him well enough to make it her business to pry.

And even though she felt that his silence wasn't really about her, how many times would this happen if they continued dating? Every time his daughter called or he had to deal with something concerning his ex-wife?

"We're out of fortune cookies," the waitress announced, walking up to their table. "Sorry." She slid the bill on the table. "I'll be your cashier as well."

"Thanks," Evan said, setting his credit card on top the bill.

Stella wanted to ask about the fortune cookies, but it was probably better to get back to the shop. Evan signed the credit card receipt when the waitress returned, and they left together.

By the time they stepped outside, Stella's eyes were smarting. *Really mature.* "Hey, Evan, I have a quick errand to run. Do you mind if we split up here?"

He looked faintly surprised, but only said, "Sure. I'll see you later."

She gave him a quick smile, then turned and walked in the opposite direction, just to put space between them. When she reached the street corner and stopped to wait for the crosswalk sign, she glanced toward The Fortune Café.

Evan was still standing in the same spot she'd left him. Watching her. *So now he notices me.* She couldn't read his expression from this distance. Strange, she decided. Really strange.

Thirteen

Evan had been trying to talk himself out of it all day—while he was at work, while he went to lunch with Stella, and on the drive back to the Mariposa. But by the time he left the hotel at 9:30 p.m., his mind was made up.

He was going to ask his ex-wife for full custody. But only after Katie spent the entire summer with him. Evan hoped that easing Katie into living with him full time, in addition to letting Michelle have a taste of more freedom, would work in his favor.

The only problem was he'd been on a great date the night before with a fabulous woman. And this would change everything. When he arrived at his condo, he paced the floors, thinking of how he could still have a dating life while his seven-year-old daughter lived with him. Stella had been great around Katie, she'd even remembered his daughter's name having only been around her once. But he knew firsthand how complicated relationships could be.

There were really only two options that he saw. Involve Stella in everything that included Katie, which Stella might not go for. Or cut things off with Stella entirely. He knew Katie would like Stella, and he could imagine his daughter becoming attached to her. But things were too new between them, and he had no way to predict the future.

He exhaled. He also couldn't let things slide with his daughter. Dialing Michelle's number, he closed his eyes, hoping that she'd thought about his offer. When she answered, he said, "You probably know why I'm calling."

"Yes." Her tone sounded patient for once. "I've talked to Katie about it, and she seems excited to spend the summer at your place."

Evan sank onto the couch, relief flooding through him, although he still didn't have Michelle's answer. "And what do you think?"

"Well, at first, I wasn't too excited about it. But after talking to Randy, he mentioned that I could travel with him on some business trips. So it might work out after all."

"Great," Evan said. "When's a good time to pick her up?" He hated to act too pushy, but he was going to take all the momentum he could get.

"Maybe Thursday? She has a birthday party at her friend's on Wednesday night."

"Okay, I'll plan on Thursday." When Evan hung up, the relief of Michelle's answer replaced any concerns or worries he might have had before.

He leaned back on the couch, thinking about what he'd just committed to, and how it was definitely going to change his life and everything in it. Dates like last night wouldn't happen unless he had a sitter . . . and even then he didn't know if he'd want to stay out so late.

Evan knew he liked Stella. And although he'd completely annoyed her at lunch today with his preoccupation over Katie, Stella hadn't gone crazy on him—which Michelle would have definitely done. He appreciated that, but he knew he needed to apologize and then explain some hard truths to her. Before he could talk himself out of it, he left the apartment and climbed in his truck. It was almost 10:00 p.m., but he hoped to catch Stella still in her shop.

When he pulled up alongside the curb next to the jewelry shop, he breathed a sigh of relief. The *closed* sign was showing, but a light was on somewhere in the back.

He walked up to the shop and peered through the glass door. The light was coming from the open office door. Did she leave it on every night light that? Evan scrolled through the contacts on his cell phone. He typed a text to her: *Can you talk for a minute? I'm at the front of your store.*

Seconds later, Stella came walking out of the office. Watching her, Evan hoped she'd be understanding, and he realized how much he was also hoping that she'd be really open to the change Evan's life was about to take.

She opened the door, her gaze curious.

"Hey," Evan said, stepping inside, and taking in her appearance. Her hair was in a ponytail, and her eyes looked tired, making him want to do something that would help her. "Working late?"

"Always." Stella shut the door and folded her arms, eyeing him with suspicion. He couldn't blame her.

"So . . ." he started. "Without dumping my whole sad story on you, Katie is coming for the summer—the whole summer. And at the end of it all, I'm going to ask for full custody."

Stella didn't say anything, and it was too dim in the shop to read her expression. He wished he knew what was going on in her mind.

"And I need to apologize to you." He scrubbed a hand through his hair. "I was a bit distracted during lunch, and I—"

Stella laughed, cutting off Evan. "Distracted? Look Evan, I don't need you to use your daughter as an excuse not to take me out again." She let out a sigh. "You came to my rescue with Andrew, and I really appreciate it. But I can also handle the bad news." She moved to the door and opened it. "I hope you have a nice summer with Katie, and really, last night was great. But I can see that you're not really ready to date again."

Evan stared at her. *He* wasn't ready? He'd come here to talk to her about *her* not being ready or willing to date a guy with a full-time kid. "Stella—"

"It's okay, really. I'll be fine. You'll be fine. Life will go on." Her voice trembled, but she refused to meet his gaze as she opened the door wider.

Evan stepped outside, feeling really too stunned to know what to say. He still hadn't moved away when she shut the door. Through the glass, he watched her walk back to her office. Stella hadn't gone crazy on him; she'd gone cold. And somehow that felt worse. The office light clicked off seconds later, and then there was nothing.

Fourteen

Stella couldn't bring herself to throw away the fortune printed on a slip of paper that had prompted her to call Evan, so she moved it to the bottom drawer of her desk and set it way in the back, next to the Post-it he'd written his number on. She had his number in her phone still, not that she planned on using it, ever.

Fortunes didn't come true. Love was definitely *not* certain. Not in the case of Andrew or of Evan. Stella looked around the shop with its customers milling about. Things were back to normal . . . before-Evan-normal. Amelia had even gone back home. Stella had finally told Amelia that she wouldn't be dating Evan anymore, and the woman's sigh on the phone reached across the thirty miles that separated them.

Stella had laughed at Amelia, reminding her it had only been one date, and the guy was too caught up in his status as a divorced man with a horrible ex-wife that he didn't have time to realize life could be good again.

Not that Stella's life was all that great, but she was okay. Her mom was doing as well as could be expected. The business was busier than ever, especially with the tourist season now in full swing. And she might even go to one of David's barbeques where she could reconnect with her former friends. She was still debating that.

When Evan had texted her an apology, she'd ignored it. Then he'd texted her again, apologizing *again*, in the form of: *I didn't intend the conversation to go that way, but after thinking about it, I believe you're right. I need to figure out myself before combining my past with the present.*

She finally wrote back: *I only wish the best for you.* The sooner Stella forgot about him, the better.

It was clear that he was not ready to include another woman in his life other than the two who were already in it. Stella's first fear had resurfaced ten-fold. Andrew had taught her that relationships were complicated enough without all the extra history.

Stella's phone rang, and she flinched, thinking it might be Evan. But of course it wasn't. She didn't recognize the number, but she answered it anyway in case it was a new vendor who happened to have her cell number instead of the shop number.

The recorded message made her blood run cold.

An emergency alert has been issued for Leslie Novak. An emergency alert has been issued for . . .

Stella rushed out of the shop into the office, and threw open the back door. She ran the short distance to the house, hoping that her mother had pressed her emergency responder by mistake.

The sound of sirens made her heart sink, although she told herself that it could have still been a mistake or maybe an electronic malfunction. Stella unlocked the door with trembling hands and shouted into the house, "Mom?"

Without waiting for a reply, she ran into the living room, frantically looking for her mother, hoping she'd be watching TV in her chair. The TV was on—but the chair was empty. "Mom!"

Stella checked the bedroom next, but her mom wasn't in there either. The sirens were growing louder, and panic set in full force. She moved into the hall, and saw that the bathroom light was on. Her heart nearly stopped . . . she could see the edge of her mom's slipper.

"Mom," she whispered, rushing to open the door. Her mother's body was blocking it, so Stella had to slip in sideways.

Her mom was on the bathroom floor, and blood seeped from a wound on her forehead. Stella knelt down, grabbed her mom's hand, and with her other hand, felt for the pulse in her neck. Her mother's pulse was throbbing, and Stella felt like crying with relief.

"Mom, wake up."

She's alive . . . but what happened?

A loud pounding came from the front door, and Stella called out, "Come in! We're in the bathroom."

When two paramedics appeared, taking over transporting her mother to the living room, then checking all of her vitals, only then did Stella realize she'd been crying. "She's diabetic," she told them as they worked.

Her mother moaned, and her eyes fluttered open, then shut again.

But to Stella, that was a good sign. "Is she going to be all right?" she asked in a shaky voice.

One of the men looked up. "We need to take her to the hospital."

Stella nodded, feeling numb. She followed the stretcher out of the house, and somehow got into her car and followed the ambulance. They didn't use their sirens or lights driving to the hospital, so Stella hoped that was a good thing.

By the time she parked and made it into the ER, she had collected her thoughts. She had to call someone to close the shop down. Amelia was too far away. Who knew what the customers thought when she ran out on them?

The nurse at the ER desk said that her mother was in the exam room, that she was awake, but they were going to run some tests.

"Do you know what happened?" the nurse at the front desk asked.

Stella's eyes filled with tears again as she explained to the nurse that she'd been a couple of minutes away, but it looked like her mom had passed out.

After writing down some notes, the nurse said, "Have a seat in the waiting room, and I'll come and get you when we know more."

Stella couldn't sit, couldn't join the couple of people there who stared at their phones with miserable expressions on their faces. She paced the lobby, went outside a couple times, then walked around the waiting room. The ER was a hub of activity, and Stella's stomach continued to knot tighter and tighter.

She texted Amelia, who responded that her car was in the shop, but to keep her posted. She could most likely come up the next day to help out with anything. But for now, the shop was abandoned.

Do the thing you fear...

Stella scrolled to Evan's number. He was the closest person she knew to the shop. It would take him only twenty minutes total to get there, close it up, then drive back to his job.

With a deep breath, she sent him a text.

She'd started pacing again, waiting for Evan's reply when her phone rang.

"Evan?" she answered.

"Is your mom okay?"

For some reason, hearing his concerned voice made her start to unravel. She took a steadying breath before replying. "I'm not exactly sure yet. They said she's awake, and they're doing tests."

"I'm really sorry," he said.

Stella nodded even though he couldn't see her. Tears burned in her eyes, and she blinked them back, taking slow breaths. She didn't need to break down now. The doctor could be coming out any moment with a report.

"I'm leaving the hotel now," Evan was saying, "and I'll close down the shop. Should I leave the back door unlocked?"

Stella tried to focus and think beyond the emotions swirling inside of her. "Yes, I have the keys with me, so you can turn off all the lights. Put out the *closed* sign, and lock both doors."

"Miss Novak?" a woman's voice said behind her.

She turned to see a nurse wearing scrubs. "Thanks, Evan, I need to go." Stella hung up, and her heart rate doubled as she waited for the nurse to speak.

"I'm Jennie," the nurse said. "Come with me; the doctor would like to meet with you."

"How is my mother doing?"

"She's alert and doing fine, but there are some things to discuss." The nurse pushed through a door, leading the way down a glossy hallway. "Dr. Anderson will go over everything with you."

Jennie led Stella into an empty exam room where a doctor stood, reading a chart. He looked up, his thick eyebrows drawing together as he saw Stella. "Miss Novak?"

"Yes," she said, clasping her hands together tightly.

"Your mother's nerve damage has grown worse. She says her legs gave out, and that's how she fell and hit her head." He looked down at his chart and flipped a page over. "The tests have indicated that the damage is irreversible, which you probably already know."

Stella nodded, trying to process the information.

He looked up at her, lowering the chart. "She'll need a wheelchair. It will prevent future falls, and to be frank, the damage will continue to progress."

Stella felt as if she'd swallowed a huge rock and it was sitting in her chest, pushing pain throughout her body. She'd read about all of the side effects of diabetes and studied them in depth after her mother's stroke the year before. But a wheelchair?

Tears burned behind her eyes, though she refused to let them fall.

"Jennie will set you up with what you need. Do you have any questions?"

Stella exhaled. She glanced over at the nurse, then back to the doctor. "Does my mom know yet?"

"We'll go in and talk to her together," Dr. Anderson said.

The walk to her mother's room was much too short, not giving Stella much time to pull her thoughts together. On one hand, Stella knew that her mother's health would continue to decline, but to actually see it happening tore at her heart.

"There you are," her mom said as Stella walked in with the doctor and nurse. A tech was adjusting the oxygen flow on the machine her mom was hooked up to. "I got stitches!"

Stella smiled. "Your first, ever." She crossed to her mom's bed and grasped her hand. There were about four to five stitches on her mother's temple, along with an ugly bruise.

"Looks like this will be serious," her mom said, eyeing Dr. Anderson.

Stella squeezed her mom's hand. "You're going to get more spoiled."

Dr. Anderson started talking about the nerve damage that had progressed, and Stella watched as her mom put on an incredibly brave face. Stella had never been more glad that she left her master's program and Andrew. Being here with her mom at this moment and holding her hand as the doctor told her how her life was about to change yet again was the most important thing to her.

Stella was exhausted by the time she left her mom resting in the hospital room. They'd moved her to the recovery wing and would keep her overnight for observation, then she'd be outfitted with a wheelchair in the morning.

Stella had forgotten about the shop when she walked into the waiting area and found Evan sitting in a chair. She almost did a double-take. "Evan?"

He looked up, his expression curious, his eyes searching hers. He stood as she crossed to him.

Stella wasn't sure exactly how it happened, but she was suddenly in his arms, and he was holding her. The tears came hot and fast, and thankfully Evan didn't say anything, didn't press for information.

After a few minutes, when Stella had felt like she could talk without breaking down again, she pulled away.

"Sorry about that."

Evan smiled. "Can you leave for a little while?"

Stella glanced toward the entrance. It was dark outside. "What time is it?"

"About nine," he said, grasping her hand. "Come on. I can bring you back later."

Stella nodded, then followed him outside and climbed into his truck. She closed her eyes as he walked around and got in on the driver's side. He said nothing as he started the engine. He reached for her hand.

She let him hold it, if nothing else, to not feel like she had to handle everything on her own. Keeping her eyes closed, she relaxed in the seat as the truck moved, turning corners, accelerating, decelerating.

When the truck stopped, she opened her eyes. A fluorescent sign flickered above them, and Evan had pulled up to a glowing menu.

"We're at a *drive-through*?"

Evan smiled. "What do you want?"

She looked past him and peered at the menu. "A chicken sandwich and a lemonade." She didn't really care what she ate, but she was starving.

Evan ordered for her, then added his own sandwich. As they pulled forward to pay, Stella said, "This must be painful for you. Fast food?"

He laughed. "I'm not that much of a food snob. But still, I'll try to keep any complaints to myself."

They were silent as Evan drove away from the restaurant, then turned into a parking lot that connected to Pismo Beach. He started unwrapping his sandwich, so Stella did the same.

After a couple of bites, Stella said, "She needs a wheelchair now."

Evan nodded, waiting for her to continue.

So she did. She told him everything the doctor had said. Then she told him how she'd found her mother on the bathroom floor, bleeding, and unconscious. She told him that Amelia should be coming up the next day, although she didn't know about the wheelchair part yet.

"Your mom is a lucky woman to have you," Evan said.

"I don't know about that," Stella said. "A better daughter would have known the signs of nerve damage before it ended in a serious fall. I mean, she hit her head pretty good."

Evan looked over at her. "My mom's not sick, but I understand how you feel. I mean, anything that ever happens to Katie, I feel like I should have done something more. Even now, it's tough not to be with her all of the time. And I keep blaming myself for it."

"Guilt."

"Yeah," he said.

"We make a great pair."

Evan smiled, and the numbness of Stella's day started to slip away.

"Want to go for a walk on the beach?" Evan asked.

Stella's eyes pricked with tears. This was a man she could fall in love with. Too bad his heart wasn't available. But a walk would still be nice. "I'd love to."

Fifteen

"You're a barefoot kind of girl?" Evan asked as Stella slipped her shoes off.

"Yep." Her tone sounded lighter than it had in the past hour.

He thought the sand might be a little cold, but then he decided, *Why not.* He slipped off the loafers he'd thrown on after his work shift. After closing up the jewelry shop, he'd gone back to the hotel until after the dinner rush. But he was having a hard time focusing, so he finally told the assistant chef that he had to leave.

And he was more than glad he did. Seeing Stella in the hospital had made him realize how selfish he was. Everyone in his family was healthy, his daughter was healthy, and knowing only a fraction of what Stella had been dealing with for a year made him feel like a jerk.

Stella was walking slightly ahead of him, so he could see her profile in the moonlight. He wondered what she'd do if he kissed her. Of course he'd have to explain himself a bit. And then he'd have to question why he was even considering it. So much for his one hundred percent devotion to being a dad.

Stella's feet moved slowly in the sand, and Evan realized the sand wasn't cold at all . . . just refreshing. Would he really be neglectful if he dated with Katie living with him? It was pretty normal for divorced people to start dating again. And of course Michelle hadn't waited at all, which made him want to not be a thing like her.

They walked closer to the waves, stepping onto the wet sand. There were plenty of lights shining behind them from the coastal shops, and people were walking on the boardwalk. But now they were far away enough that it felt like it was only them on the beach.

"Thanks for this," Stella said, glancing at him, then looking back over the ocean. She folded her arms. "I mean, it was nice enough of you to close up the shop for me, even though things were kind of tense the last time we talked."

"About that," Evan said, surprised at how fast his heart was beating. Maybe it was because his heart knew what he wanted to say before his brain did. "I know you're probably sick of me trying to apologize, but . . ."

Stella met his gaze, a half smile on her face. She was so unassuming . . . so calm.

"I'm tired of having a depressing story," he said.

She lifted an eyebrow. "You mean your divorce story?"

"Yeah, and when you asked me to close the shop for you, I realized I was happy to help you. And that I'd be happy to help you again, anytime, every day." He exhaled, not sure if he was even making sense. "I guess what I mean is that I want to be more than I am right now—more than the label of a divorced man with a kid who's always wrapped into his own box of problems."

Her eyes were still on him, and he wanted to take her hand, but wasn't sure if he should. "What kind of label are you thinking of?" she asked.

"Maybe something without a label . . . that's unique. That's just Evan . . . and Stella."

She looked away, staring at the ocean.

He wished he could read her mind. Even though he was telling her he wanted to date her, he still was unsure how it would work out with Katie in the mix, and the predictable stress that would always be there from his ex.

She turned back to him, and his stomach knotted. "I guess I can help you change that label," she said in a quiet voice.

Stella moved closer, and Evan was afraid to move, to breathe. Her hands slipped into his, sending warmth rushing through his body. And then, without comprehending exactly how it happened, he was kissing her, and she was kissing him back.

She fit into his embrace perfectly, and his worries about balancing everything began to fade. He was only present here, now, with Stella's arms around him, her lips on his.

"Stella," he whispered against her mouth.

"Yes?" she whispered back.

"I need to apologize in advance that I still might be an idiot in the future."

She laughed, moving her fingers along the back of his neck, sending goose bumps down his back. "I'll just have to remind you that your luck has changed."

"I don't think I'll need to be reminded of that," he said, brushing his lips against hers. Her hands moved down his chest, making his heart beat harder.

"Do you know why I called you?" she asked, her hands settling at his waist.

"Why?"

"Because I was afraid to."

He gazed at her, trying to figure out what she meant. She nestled against him, wrapping her arms around him. So maybe it wasn't bad news.

"I was following the advice of a fortune cookie. It told me to do that thing that I fear, and love would be certain."

He closed his eyes, inhaling her scent, everything that was Stella. "Do you believe that love can ever be certain?"

"Of course. Look at you and your daughter. Me and my mom." She lifted her head to look at him. "I'm always doing things that I fear."

"I meant . . . between us."

She held his gaze, and his pulse raced faster with each passing second. "I guess we'll have to find out."

He laughed, pulling her against him for another kiss. "I'm in."

Sixteen

Stella kept watching the front entrance for any sign of Evan and Katie. He was bringing her by this afternoon, and she was more nervous than she expected.

The last few days with Evan had been great. He'd helped her get her mom settled, charmed Amelia until Stella thought Amelia might outright propose to him, and he'd brought over a bunch of freezer meals that her mom could not compliment enough.

I think you have three women in love with you, Evan, Stella thought, her face heating at what she might have admitted to herself.

Falling in love with a man this quickly is impossible. Truly impossible. No matter what that fortune cookie said.

Two people walked up to the shop, and Stella froze. But it was a mother with a young girl. Not Evan and Katie. The woman peered in the windows at the displays, then moved on. It was just as well.

Stella crossed to straighten a collection of bracelets for the third time that day when the door jingled. Her eyes flew to the door to see who'd entered. Evan stepped in, holding his daughter's hand.

"Oh, it smells so good, Daddy! Like last time!"

He grinned, his gaze not on Katie, but on Stella.

"Can I help you?" she said above the pounding of her heart.

"I think you can," Evan said. Katie tugged away from him and scampered off to examine a row of flower rings.

He walked slowly to Stella, his sea-colored eyes on her. She wanted to melt on the spot, but instead remained upright. "Are you looking for anything in particular?" She struggled to keep her expression straight.

Evan stopped right in front of her, their bodies a few inches apart. "You."

Her eyes locked with his, and even though they weren't touching or kissing, she could feel him against her skin. "I can help you with that."

"Daddy?" Katie's voice cut in.

Stella looked down to see Katie standing there, watching them. Stella hadn't even noticed the little girl walking toward them.

"Katie, this is my friend, Stella," Evan said, grasping Stella's left hand.

"Hello, Katie, we met once before." Stella crouched down so she was eye-level and extended her right hand.

"I remember," Katie said, shaking her hand. "You're the pretty one I told my mom about."

Stella straightened, her face flushing. "You told your mom about me?" She glanced at Evan, but he didn't seem to know what Katie was talking about.

"When did you tell your mom about Stella?" Evan asked.

"When I gave her the necklace, silly Dad," Katie said.

"And what did you say?" Evan asked.

"That you were acting funny around a pretty lady—the lady that worked in the store. But I didn't know her name yet."

Stella bit back a laugh. Evan's face was bright red.

"I wasn't acting funny around her."

Katie nodded. "Yes, you were. Like you are now."

"How?" Evan asked, spreading his hands. "How am I acting funny?"

"You keep staring at her," Katie said in a matter-of-fact voice. "It's okay, Daddy, I think she's pretty too."

Stella laughed, and then Katie started laughing.

Evan looked from Katie to Stella, then back to his daughter. "I'm not staring at anyone," he protested.

Stella moved to Evan's side and laced her fingers through his.

Katie lifted her small shoulders. "Mommy says that men don't get some things."

"I think Katie's right." Stella grinned and nudged Evan.

"Oh, so now it's the two of you against me. You don't even know each other."

"But we're both girls," Katie said with a triumphant smile. She looked at Stella. "Does this mean you'll come with us on our picnic?"

Stella glanced at Evan. "Am I invited?"

His arm snaked around her waist. "You're always invited. And . . . there she is, on cue."

Amelia entered the shop, coming in through the back door of the office. "Hi, Evan." But her gaze was on Katie. "This must be Katie!" She held out a jeweled hand and shook the little girl's hand. "Nice to meet you, Miss Katie. I'm Amelia."

Stella looked from Amelia to Evan. "You planned this?"

He smiled and leaned down to kiss Amelia on the cheek.

"Go on, you three," Amelia said. "Have fun."

Katie latched onto Stella's hand and practically dragged her out of the shop. Evan's daughter sure was friendly—a kid with no reservations. Stella liked that.

"So where are we going?" Stella asked once they left the shop.

"To the beach!" Katie said. "My dad got us Chinese food . . . and a whole bag of fortune cookies. He said I could have three of them."

Stella looked over at Evan, who was holding Katie's other hand. "Three, huh? How many do I get?"

Evan winked. "As many as you want." He stopped at the truck and pulled out a blanket from the car and handed it over to Katie. To Stella he said, "Can you carry the umbrella?"

"Sure." Stella took the umbrella, then Evan grabbed the bags of food. He hefted a beach bag with towels and beach toys over his shoulder.

"I can carry more," Stella offered.

"I've got it," he said, and managed to have a free hand to hold onto Katie's. They crossed Tangerine Street together, then walked through the beach access alley. The place was crowded, but they found a spot a few yards from the wet sandbar.

Stella and Katie spread out the blanket, and Evan set up the lunch with a flourish. Stella laughed as he arranged the folded napkins and the plastic forks and knives just so.

"This is the fanciest picnic I've ever had," she teased.

He looked up and grinned. "You'll have to get used to it."

His eyes were more blue today than green as their gazes locked, and Stella's heart skittered. She watched him serve up the food for Katie, who ate about five bites, then complained she was full. Evan talked her into eating two more bites; the reward was one of the fortune cookies. Suddenly, Katie could eat more, and when she broke open her fortune, her eyebrows crinkled together. "What does this mean?" she asked, handing the paper slip to Stella.

Stella glanced at Evan, then read the fortune aloud: "Love surrounds you." She smiled at Katie. "It means you're a very lucky girl and have a lot of people who love you."

Katie nodded, her expression serious. "I do. I really do. Like Daddy. And my two grandmas and grandpas. And my mommy. I think my babysitter only likes me, though. But my Aunt Lisa says she loves me. "

Evan smiled and leaned over to kiss the top of Katie's head. "You are surrounded."

Tears burned in Stella's eyes, and she could only nod and smile as she blinked them back.

"*Now* can I play with the buckets?" Katie asked, turning her blue eyes to her dad.

"Sure," Evan said, sliding over the beach bag. "But stay where we can see you."

Katie flashed a smiled at Evan and Stella. She dug around for some plastic buckets and animal-shaped toys, then pulled out a small shovel as well.

Together, they watched Katie dig in the sand a few yards off. A couple of little kids joined her, and pretty soon Katie was orchestrating what looked to be an entire collection of castles.

"Do you want to read your fortune?" Evan asked, capturing her attention. He was leaning back on his elbows, his upper body in the shade of the umbrella, his legs stretched out in the sun.

"I think I like my last one. I don't want to tempt fate again." She settled onto her side, facing Evan.

He smiled. "All right. I'll open one, and you can eat the cookie."

"Don't you like them?"

"I've had better desserts."

"Of course you have," Stella said, watching as Evan pulled off the plastic from the small brown cookie.

He cracked it open and read the paper slip.

"Well?" Stella prompted.

He turned on his side, facing her, with an amused smile.

Stella reached for it, but he held it away, and instead leaned forward and kissed her, making the shade they were under suddenly hot. She let the kiss go on for a few seconds, then snatched the fortune from Evan.

"Hey."

She laughed and sat up, disentangling from him. She read the tiny script: *A kiss is like a thousand words.*

"Oh," she said.

Evan sat up, moving next to her. His arm slid around her shoulders, and she turned her head and smiled at him.

"I have more to say." He kissed her again, his lips lingering this time.

Stella let him linger. It might be a single kiss, but there were a thousand promises behind it.

Coming Soon . . .

Boardwalk Antiques Shop

A tangerine street ROMANCE
A NOVEL IN THREE PARTS

Julie Wright
Melanie Jacobson
Heather B. Moore

About Julie Wright

Julie Wright started her first book when she was fifteen. She's written over a dozen books since then, is a Whitney Award winner, and feels she's finally getting the hang of this writing gig. She enjoys speaking to writing groups, youth groups, and schools. She loves reading, eating, writing, hiking, playing on the beach with her kids, and snuggling with her husband to watch movies. Julie's favorite thing to do is watch her husband make dinner. She hates mayonnaise, but has a healthy respect for ice cream.

Visit her website: JulieWright.com

About Melanie Jacobson

Melanie Bennett Jacobson is an avid reader, amateur cook, and champion shopper. She consumes astonishing amounts of chocolate, chick flicks, and romance novels. After meeting her husband online, she is now living happily married in Southern California with her growing family and a series of doomed houseplants. Melanie is a former English teacher and a sometime blogger who loves to laugh and make others laugh. In her downtime (ha!), she writes romantic comedies and pines after beautiful shoes.

Visit her website: MelanieJacobson.net

About Heather B. Moore

Heather B. Moore is a *USA Today* bestselling author. She writes historical thrillers under the pen name H.B. Moore, her latest is *Finding Sheba*. Under Heather B. Moore she writes romance and women's fiction. She's the co-author of The Newport Ladies Book Club series. Other women's novels include *Heart of the Ocean, The Fortune Café*, the Aliso Creek Series, and the Amazon bestselling Timeless Romance Anthology Series.

Visit her website: hbmoore.com

Or blog: MyWritersLair.blogspot.com

If you enjoyed *The Fortune Café*

You'll also love *Prejudice Meets Pride*
from *USA Today* bestselling author Rachael Anderson

www.ingramcontent.com/pod-product-compliance
Lightning Source LLC
LaVergne TN
LVHW010155070526
838199LV00062B/4363